MEMORY

GRAND STREET
64

This issue of *GRAND STREET*
is dedicated to the memory of
JAMES LAUGHLIN, 1914–1997.

FRONT COVER Sophie Ristelhueber, from Fait, Kuwait, 1992. Cibachrome print, 39 3/8 x 51 3/16 in.

BACK COVER Willie Doherty, At the Border 5 (Isolated Incident), 1995. Cibachrome on aluminum, 40 x 72 in.

TITLE PAGE Walter Murch, Grey Melon, 1965. Mixed media on paper, 19 x 15 1/8 in.

TABLE OF CONTENTS Willie Doherty, The Bridge (diptych), 1992. Two black-and-white photographs, each 48 x 72 in.

An excerpt from "Not About Nightingales," by Tennessee Williams, appears here by permission of The University of the South, Sewanee, Tennessee. Copyright © 1998 by The University of the South.

"Funerals" and "Illness" by James Laughlin. Copyright © 1998 by the Estate of James Laughlin; used by permission of New Directions Publishing Corp.

Excerpt from Blindness by José Saramago copyright © 1998 Editorial Caminho, Lisbon, 1995. English translation copyright © by Giovanni Pontiero, 1997. To be published by Harcourt Brace & Company.

Grand Street (ISSN 0734-5496; ISBN 1-885490-15-1) is published quarterly by Grand Street Press(a project of the New York Foundation for the Arts, Inc., a not-for-profit corporation), 131 Varick Street, Room 906, New York, NY 10013. Tel: (212) 807-6548, Fax: (212) 807-6544. Contributions and gifts to Grand Street Press are tax-deductible to the extent allowed by law. This publication is made possible, in part, by a grant from the New York State Council on the Arts.

Volume Sixteen, Number Four (Grand Street 64—Spring 1998). Copyright © 1998 by the New York Foundation for the Arts, Inc., Grand Street Press. All rights reserved. Reproduction, whether in whole or in part, without permission is strictly prohibited. Second-class postage paid at New York, NY, and additional mailing offices. Postmaster: Please send address changes to Grand Street Subscription Service, Dept. GRS, P.O. Box 3000, Denville, NJ 07834. Subscriptions are $40 a year (four issues). Foreign subscriptions (including Canada) are $55 a year, payable in U.S. funds. Single-copy price is $12.95 ($18 in Canada). For subscription inquiries, please call (800) 807-6548.

Grand Street is printed by Hull Printing in Meriden, CT. It is distributed to the trade by D.A.P./Distributed Art Publishers, 155 Avenue of the Americas, New York, NY 10013, Tel: (212) 627-1999, Fax: (212) 627-9484, and to newsstands only by Bernhard DeBoer, Inc., 113 E. Centre Street, Nutley, NJ 07110, Total Circulation, 80 Frederick Street, Hackensack, NJ, 07601, Ingram Periodicals, 1226 Heil Quaker Blvd., La Vergne, TN 37086, and Ubiquity Distributors, 607 Degraw Street, Brooklyn, NY 11217. Grand Street is distributed in Australia and New Zealand by Peribo Pty, Ltd., 58 Beaumont Road, Mount Kuring-Gai, NSW 2080, Australia, Tel: (2) 457-0011, and in the United Kingdom by Central Books, 99 Wallis Road, London E9 5LN, Tel: (181) 986-4854.

GRAND STREET

EDITOR
Jean Stein

MANAGING EDITOR
Pablo Conrad

ART EDITOR
Walter Hopps

POETRY EDITOR
William Corbett

DESIGN
J. Abbott Miller, Paul Carlos, Scott Devendorf
DESIGN/WRITING/RESEARCH, NEW YORK

ASSISTANT EDITOR
Julie A. Tate

ASSISTANT ART EDITOR
Anne Doran

ADMINISTRATIVE ASSISTANT
Lisa Brodus

INTERNS
Topher Brown, Yoon Sook Cha, Risa Chase, Rachel Kushner, Elizabeth Ozaist

ADVISORY EDITORS
Hilton Als, Edward W. Said

CONTRIBUTING EDITORS
Dominique Bourgois, Colin de Land, Mike Davis, Raymond Foye,
Kennedy Fraser, Jonathan Galassi, Stephen Graham, Dennis Hopper,
Hudson, Jane Kramer, Charles Merewether, Michael Naumann,
Erik Rieselbach, Robin Robertson, Deborah Treisman, Fiona Shaw,
Robert Storr, Michi Strausfeld, Katrina vanden Heuvel, Wendy vanden Heuvel,
John Waters, Drenka Willen

FOUNDING CONTRIBUTING EDITOR
Andrew Kopkind (1935–1994)

PUBLISHERS
Jean Stein & Torsten Wiesel

Letter to Thalia: Whiffit

SUZAN-LORI PARKS

because it helps me remember things, writing them down does

or so I thought until I really thought

about it. walking down 6th avenue arms loaded with groceries
wondering where I'm going and I cant remember then remembering
I have a list, I'd made a list just this morning outlining my steps and
my list is in a pocket but which one? My hands straining against the
bag-plastic, my arms pulling down, keeping a little bend in the elbow
so the arm wont fall off into the street what with all these purchases:
four boxes of soy sausage, soy milks, an assortment of hair care products
and walking with such purpose even though I cant remember where
I am going but I did write it down, I *did*, so I wouldnt *forget*....

 Writing, until just today, seemed like something to remember by. All my writing
until now has put the bones back together through words on the page. The page could
remember the dismembered "venus" and "the last black man;" the page could even
be a remembering place for an "america play's" Foundling Father. The plays working
like archaeological digs and the bones, previously those bones which "could not be
found," were resurrected onto the page, hauled out of forgetting to inhabit the stage.
On the page the bones *were* found and gathered into some sort of shape; the
characters inhabited by actors, breath of life running through them again, skin on
those bones again, character inhabiting a *plot* walking around and talking—

7

maybe as they *used* to (theater as an incubator to recreate history) or maybe not—who knows for sure—the fact of memory takes a front seat to accuracy.

who remembers jesus? the apostles do and gospell him down.

Up until today thats how I experienced writing—as Memory's Mother. Until there I am walking down 6th avenue turning a corner onto 13th that corner where the schoolbuses are always parked walking right into another truth of it: that writing down does not always help me remember—that writing sometimes helps me *forget*.

*   *   *

I have heard that *smell* is the sense of memory. And I have a confession to make which I may have made to you already but I feel the thrill of this confession having made it to a new beau just last night at the Public. (Bonnie was so sweet, we stopped by out of the blue and she gave us a tour). Later we sat in a corner, he cradles my hands in his palms and he smells my wrists and murmurs something—the kind of murmur one picks up, repeats, plays back without even thinking. I take his hands up mimicking him, remembering him in gesture, playing at smelling and then confessing:

ME: I cant smell, you know.

BEAU: Never have?

ME: I cant remember.

BEAU: You been to the doctor about it?

ME: Theres a nerve up in yr forehead. Thats all I know. Smelling is connected to memory.

BEAU: Whats my name?

laughter.

I approximate smelling with certain facial expressions, akin to those I make at a party when I meet someone I should remember but dont. Nose bridge scrunches into folds eyes crow eyebrows come together everything gathering together where the smell nerve is said to be as the memory hides, divided and undetectable, on the 2 separate sides of my brain and this scrunching will whole it again and by wholling remember it, but the smell passes mysteriously along with the familiar face.

It's a different kind of feeling, writing as something to forget you by. Writing this letter to you. I forget something, myself maybe. Maybe I am remembering myself to you.

> *2 people in a diner talk about the gulf war. "Who was president back then?" "Clinton or Bush?" and then a long silence.*

if memory could be a sense of awareness instead of baggage, a pristine passport instead of a heavy old suitcase filled with unfashionable dirty clothes that are all too small around the midriff.

I'm working on a new play. The setting is the future, post WW4, post a particularly devastating Plague of Amnesia. A running joke:

MAN: *of course you remember the Plague of Amnesia.*

WOMAN: *the what?*

MAN: *sounds like you haddit, sister.*

Every time I sit down to write a new piece I cannot remember how I went about writing the last one, that is, I cannot remember how to write, how to make it happen, how to make the words come and all that. And I was all set, before today, to write down a meticulous list of instructions detailing how I write things—I'd write all this down and put the list away and then, next time I sat down, *hopeless*, infront of the page,

9

not knowing how to *do it*, I would whip out my instructions and, remembering myself, remind myself how to write. Such was my little scheme. Until today. Until I realize that writing has as much to do with forgetting as it has with remembering. All those books on my bookshelves suddenly look different. Perhaps theyre not just pages of precious memories, perhaps some of them are full of things writers were longing to *Forget.*

> *when I count to 3 you will wake*
> *you will have no memory of what you have said*
> *you will not be troubled by the memory of what you have seen*
> *1: there is an open door*
> *2: you cross the threshold; the path, miles long, you cross in an instant*
> *3: you are awake*

Hurrying along the street, a patch of sun, more like a sliver really, orange-yellow. The sun reminding me of something—that summer in west Texas when we cracked eggs on the sidewalk and tried frying? albino Africans? schoolbuses and taxi cabs sing: "they paved paradise and they" and I suddenly remember where I'm going: on my way to buy orange roses.

Sense of Autobiography

PABLO NERUDA

Sixteen years ago I was born, in a town,
dusty, white, and distant, that I no longer know,
and since that is a bit trivial and naive,
let's go back, my wandering friend, to my younger days.

I believe in few things in life. It has not brought me
anything like the things I have brought to it.
Proud, emotional, I made fun of what hurt me,
and suffering was to my spirit as two is to three.

Nothing else. I remember, when I was ten,
I drew up a plan for myself, against the setbacks
that lay in wait for me on the way ahead:

to have loved a woman and to have written a book.
I've failed. My book is still in manuscript,
and I've loved not one woman, but five or six. . .

The Little Schoolteacher

The little schoolteacher, blond as a wheatfield,
so blond that at first they thought she was English,
is just as forlorn as ever, so full of sorrow
          she seems
to have grown sick with grieving since she came.

Some call her Celia, others Marta;
she answers always in utter indifference.

It is so long now since she last had a letter
that it seems that nobody anywhere misses her.

The little ones in her class adore her although
she seems to become more mournful by the day —
sad when she speaks to them of faraway stars,
sad even when she asks them eight times three.

And yesterday, spelling for them a name in dictation,
some mist from the past seemed to rise to her eyes
and she stood behind her desk not saying a word. . .
Then, feeling the weight of her never-ending sadness,
the children in her class —poor little darlings
who have no idea what they're doing!—all burst into tears.

Sense of Smell

Fragrance
of lilies. . .

Oh, the sweet twilights of my far-off childhood
that flowed as over a bed of tranquil waters.

And later a handkerchief fluttering in the distance.
A star twinkling in a sky of silk. . .

Nothing more. Feet worn from long wandering
and a pain that shudders, rises, and grows sharper. . .

And there, far-off, church bells, mass, novenas,
and yearnings, virgins with such soft eyes. . .

Fragrance
of lilies. . .

Translated from the Spanish by Alastair Reid

Note on Pablo Neruda

These three poems were written in 1920, when Neruda was sixteen, in Temuco, in the south of Chile. Neruda's earliest poems, more than 300 of them, filled three notebooks. Not long ago, a photocopy of the notebooks came to light, and the poems were published in 1996 as *Cuadernos de Temuco*. Although a good number of the poems are explorations or exercises, some of them even written to accompany early love letters (his and those of his friends), a few of them would reappear, in different versions, in Neruda's first book, *Crepusculario* (1923), like the poem "Sense of Smell," originally called "Nostalgia." Overall, the writings in Neruda's Temuco notebooks show an early and precocious fecundity of language, a fecundity that never left him. The preface quotes a characteristically wry remark of Neruda's, made toward the end of his life: "When I die, they will publish even my shoes."

Alastair Reid

FOUR STORIES

MURADHAN AND SELVIHAN OR THE TALE OF THE CRYSTAL KIOSK

A WOMAN CALLED HEDDA GABLER

A BLOODY MURDER OF LOVE IN BOYACIKÖY

3

ç c

We are gods of evil. Demanding and bruised.

Any moment in life, we can assume any role. Coward, frightened, traitor, violent, savage, sacrificing. We are therefore intense, complicated, and treacherous, unhappy, pitiless in the extreme. Because we are alone. Absolutely alone. Because we don't know how to love. Nor how to be loved. Because no one taught us life. We found things by groping in the dark. Always late. And already having forgotten much. Underground, we tried to produce life, a web of relationships. To produce life underground! When others can't do it properly overground. . .

We wash ourselves in a dark room. Left behind are blurry photographs. Ah, the dark room where we wash our urges.

—three shadows in the dark room,
people who can't form twosomes,
trying threesomes—

In these baths, we wash our urges, our drives (all people are like the negatives of photographs), always left behind are blurry photographs.

(Here, family men, bank directors, respectable retirees, civil servants, famous doctors, dentists, lawyers, gray-haired or bald, big-bellied important men struggle under the young apprentices from industrial districts or the bullies of Tophane, trying to balance the unequaled world with their butts. They have left their respectability in the dressing rooms upstairs, together with their clothes. For this reason they can coil their large, knotty, gold-ringed fingers around their fat, hairy butts and seek men while scratching themselves. Or they can believe they have revived their youth by wrapping their shriveled lips thirstily around the dark, hairy reed of a young porter from the Yem harbor.

In the evening, holding the newspaper and their quotidian life under their arm, they can ring the doorbell with a smiling face and answer the "Who is it?" coming from inside with an easy "It's me."

Nothing has happened.

Life goes on.)

Always left behind are blurry photographs.

We don't recognize ourselves. Because we have struggled with ourselves, our sexuality for long years and fallen tired, now we don't know. We know nothing. Not even why we make love, or whether lovemaking gives us pleasure. We feel an intense desire to annihilate. An intense urge to negate, to curse, to pollute. (Or an intense love)

Only the dead are holy.

I feel an intense desire to annihilate.

Hate permeates all my emotions.

This marble slab comforts me. I feel an infinite desire to destroy (perhaps everyone does). As I get closer to myself, I destroy myself. Even I am not a safe retreat for myself. Walls in ruins on all four sides, evil eyes scattered in all four corners.

I sink to the bottom, eternally. I course down an endless fall.

Endless fall. (Where do I hold on?)

Hate permeates all my emotions.

I have the indifference of men who have known all forms of savagery in wars. As if I have attained the secret of humanity. As if I have seen all that the creature called human is capable of doing. I have also reached a point beyond sexuality. (Because our entire life was about sexuality. Forever in the shadow of our curse.) For now, here is covered with fog, nothing will remain by morning.

Morning, ah, morning.

i am still falling. sounds of water come from all the fountains. in the dark room there are people who pillage one another. i constantly fall somewhere

17

inside me (now we are all an abyss) the dome turns to the tune of a waltz, i turn, the altar turns, i am offered as a sacrifice. Chants reach my ear. Soon the sound of church bells. . . In my day-to-day ordinary life I have lived through a visible fall. (Wasn't this what I wanted?) Yes, a fall. Where do I hold on? (Even while falling) This is the divine miracle of degeneration, until eternity. Or an addiction to falling. Deep, holy waters are at the bottom of eternity. There, I want to reach there at once.

At once.

⋆　　⋆　　⋆

A BLOODY MURDER OF LOVE IN BOYACIKÖY

Does it hold a place in the history of the streets descending to the sea? It's unknown. Yet, the streets besieged by the roving seas come and meet at this one stop.

The Boyacıköy Stop.

The Boyacıköy Stop is where sorrow dwells. It's autumn throughout the seasons. Descending, there is a telephone booth to the left. Its paint is peeled; it has a worn-out look. If you didn't know the history of telephone booths, you'd think this one was a century old. It resembles the old Greek taverns, the small makeshift fish restaurants along the shores. (Come, the sea's coy maid, come, the songs) It's like abandoned farms, deserted wooden huts. Like abandoned lives. As though you couldn't call anywhere from there, it is only for those who yearn to speak. For calls without hope, calls for sorrowful news, deaths, suicide, separation, unrequited love, and the like. . . Those destitutes of the telephone, those who try to overcome the solitude of night on the telephone can be telephoned from there. Those in search of land mines among numbers on the hopeless lines of address books, those who hold onto nights by taking refuge in calls cut unanswered, in a voice, in a breath, all those can be telephoned from there.

Behind it, a foggy sea beats restlessly about. A suicide-dark sorrow lingers over it in smoky folds. No one learns the other's tongue on that telephone.

One speaks, feeling the cold, hands hidden in pockets, with a shivering voice. Calls about postponed rendezvous, exhausted meetings, salvaging marriages, come-back-to-me calls. Nothing changes. Smoke over the sea lingers.

There is an old two-story house behind the booth. It bears the look of desertion in its face worn out by the southwest wind. Rain keeps beating at its windows (wet streaks on the glass). Its youth passed too soon. On the lower floor, vacant shops, on the upper floor, a small restaurant that has not changed its decor or menu for years. Every building, every street, every detail seems to have positioned itself according to the sea. It stands face-to-face with the sea.

Descending, a pharmacy on the right, a bell on its door—inside, a man as old as the sea, white-haired, wearing round glasses, smiles behind the medicine boxes—next to it, a barber shop with a single seat, and on the corner, a soldier, his eyes forever fixed on the sea, waiting. He stares at the sea, he can't take his eyes away. As if he guards not the corner but the sea. And he looks like he is from Kars, or Erzurum. He hasn't seen the sea until his military service. And as if he thinks he will never be able to leave the sea. Who knows, perhaps he is sick with a fisherman's bleak love. He'll settle it with the sea.

All these stand against the sea, with the silence of a photograph, and wait.

On their descent to the Boyacıköy Stop, so many side streets from Reshitpasha, form the outskirts of Emirgan (and all are small, cobblestoned, full of houses with stone thresholds, knockers on their doors, and plants gushing from their caged windows, streets climbing up, climbing down) reach and join this long street leading to the sea and resembling more than anything else the scaly backs of fish. Just the way the small streams flow to a mighty river in their yearning for the sea.

And the street takes these smaller streets by the hand, takes the small—tired, shuttered, stodgy—shops along the sidewalks by the hand, and descends to the sea every day.

Throughout the seven hills, this street is among Istanbul's oldest, descending to the sea.

People walk the side streets to go to work in the morning, or one place or another in the afternoon. At times they forget the sea or put it out of their mind. But when they turn from the side streets to this one, they understand that the sea exists. It's right there. Ahead of them. Their heartbeat quickens. Their steps become faster. The sea suddenly accosts them like Byzantine brigand (Were there such brigands in Byzantium? Or have they been ushered into the allusion from somewhere else?)

$\star \quad \star \quad \star$

A WOMAN CALLED HEDDA GABLER

A woman came, crossing the Republic Boulevard.

A man who smoked a pipe at the same time as he had a platinum bracelet on his wrist with his name on it, at the same time as he wore on his pinkie a golden ring, thick as a digit, with a diamond on its white center, at the same time as he herded all his goats on his beard, at the same time as he had nervous tics, at the same time as he marketed his goods in a hurry, at the same time as he tried to be friends with anyone he met for business's sake, at the same time as he had a wife, a mistress, stocks and bonds, at the same time as he ingratiated himself to a printer to sell him machines, a man who frequently showed his yellow teeth while making jokes that he alone laughed at, who was very sure of his place in the world and society, this man who had a very distinguished personality, she wanted to insult him with a fury, to curse a mouthful at him and spit on his face.

At the same time, all the businessmen's values represented in his person (his very distinguished person), all his manners deemed proper by the times, all the ignorance of such men who knew English and French and German but not Turkish, their wives, mistresses, and all the entertainment spots they went with them, the disgusting decors of those places, the latest model cars they drove, the thick treads of their tires, and their fat wallets, all the papers they signed, the books, the checks, at the same time the two telephones they constantly checked, the secretaries attending to those telephones, the secretaries with glasses, those without, their ultimate hope of marrying their bosses, she wanted to curse a mouthful at all of them, punch them, spit at them.

Yet, as always, without doing any of this, pasting instead a smile on her face that meant something between a fake, ingratiating "Have a good day, sir," and a slight aloofness (which was very difficult for her), she shook his sweaty hand (which was very difficult for her), left the man and came.

After that, while walking down the broad avenue, looking at the shop windows for a long time, she ran into/came eye to eye with/got to know hundreds of young murderers—or planned to do all this but could do none—and left the side of one, let's say

you know, one who was both a stutterer and talkative and made you think for a long time how he managed to be so, who possessed a slow, placid mind but was an impeccable blond beauty, who, with his youth, beauty, and vigor, demolished the unhappiness of sad and old homosexuals, bisexuals circling around that horseman's monument, who met them inside the cruel circle they endlessly walked, and who went with them, for a small fee, to the baths, cinemas, parks, the quiet, desolate parts in new construction sites, behind wooden screens, and once there, acted very shyly, one who dropped out of school in seventh grade like all dropout kids, who went to the movies every night because his mother and father fought every night, who had younger siblings he didn't love, he couldn't bring himself to love, who lived in one of the outskirt slums that clung to the city like a parasite, on a street with houses built overnight, stacked against each other, but who was himself as beautiful as a Greek sculpture or an Assyrian relief, who wore corduroy pants with thin ribs, who had difficulty when speaking, listening and trying to understand, but not when making love, whose eyes often disappeared between his long abundant lashes, whose dreamy face put romances to shame, the young man with steppe-yellow hair and whose name was Faruk, she left the side of this young man and came.

The young man who had worked in industrial plants but now worked nowhere, who roamed around with the money he made off of faggots, who kicked but never got kicked, who would do his military service next year, who didn't know what he'd do after that, had even a fainter idea of what he'd do later, and no idea at all of what would happen much later, because he was a dropout, because he was never loved, because he was never wanted, because he had no job, the young man who, in his young life, had never slept with a woman, this boy who took advantage of the crowded bus and pressed himself into her back, she had asked this boy nothing at first, said nothing at first, and then took him to the coal cellar of an apartment and gave herself to him, forgetting, yearning to forget, the businessman and his values, the dinners, all the nights spent with him, and all the days, and all the telephone conversations, all the sight-seeing episodes in the car, and all the hairdressers of his wives, and all their manicurists—who shared the same longings—all the videos, the stereos, all his drinks, all the liquor trays and carts, and his bohemian crystals, and his foreign-brand cigarettes, his pipes, his pipe tobacco and his pouches, the printer's machines, their import or marketing, yearning to forget all of it and for this reason being able to forget none, she made love breathlessly in this coal cellar, tearing at this young body, his copper-glow blondness, his virility, his spear-like body. The truth she experienced, this affair without past or future and therefore absolute, she deemed it her life's only truth and sensed that she would live nothing but this from now on, and in parting, she put his fee in his pocket—which he didn't ask for—his allowance—which the boy might not have wanted—the rose-colored thousand notes, enough of them to match the extent of her dreams, left the side of this boy and came.

Afterward, she paid an obligatory visit to the woman—the obligation had made her forget the closeness of the distance of her relationship to the woman—who bore the truthfulness of an old photograph and therefore always reminded her of a faded shade of brown, who had cats, pots and consoles and tulles and translucent peignoirs and pom-pom slippers and opal dinner sets and silvers—in plastic—and brilliant diamonds—in plastic—and heart—in plastic—and who always spoke of old mansions—sold—summer kiosks—burned—palaces—in plastic—phaetons, German lace and servants, tutors, bailiffs, maids, who existed only because she spoke about them and couldn't live without them, who, while trying to live, turned plastic, who wound unerringly all the clocks that chimed throughout the salons (all the clocks on the tables, walls, stands, those that weren't on tables, walls, stands), and who, when she couldn't speak, convinced herself she was alive by listening to the ticking of the clocks, and who, for some reason, cooked for herself more food than she could eat, who tossed the leftovers—in plastic—in the trash and preserved herself by preserving an old table, an old custom, an old kitchen, who hasn't left her house since then, who couldn't, who forgot the street, the avenue, the city, the country, the history and the shelves on which all were lined, the dust on the shelves, who forgot more and more and came to embody forgetfulness, fading, amidst those tulles, those cats, those cornices, she brought to this last woman a single gladiola in a sheer box—no longer being manufactured—and came.

With everything she brought she came.

With everything she carried she came.

With everything she lived until then she came.

With all she didn't live (in bits and pieces) she came.

Her name was Hedda Gabler.

Very tired, very sad, full of remembrance, having experienced much and traversed the beloved hell of all this, bearing all, shouldering all, wearing their exhaustion, she walked, her winged skirt sweeping the ground of the windy street in "Windy Street," she walked through all the streets, all the avenues, all the pavements, all forms of existence, all the monuments—in plastic—and came.

Hedda Gabler, one evening, just when the sky was turning dark, as she turned dark, as her dreams, her hopes, her future, her yearnings turned dark,

and not just all she lived, but all she imagined as well, their weight and grief, the lasting uncertainty of how else she could protect her womanliness, her sexuality, her humanity inside the Lie & Mistake, her heedlessness, the million times she asked herself how she could heed herself, all the questions and all the answers—in plastic—after having walked through all this, one evening, Hedda Gabler came to the Republic Star Restaurant in Ulus.

She came back with a pitch-black pistol in her hand.

She was looking for a partner for her death.

She didn't want a loveless death.

Besides, love as black as a pistol could not be eternal; she knew.

Into this old Ankara restaurant that still had glowing white tablecloths, porcelain plates, chairs as dark as tree barks, a coatroom with its attendant in a gray uniform, she came, having walked through all the histories, all the congresses, all the reforms and all the revolutions,

That evening, just when the sky was turning dark, Hedda Gabler came to the Republic Star Restaurant in all her magnificence.

To the chandeliers, to their republic lamps, to the fruit bowls, to the porcelain vases, to the black uniformed waiters, she came.

To Uncle Apulos she came.

To Uncle Apulos's son Aleko she came.

Hedda Gabler didn't want eternal love.

$\star \quad \star \quad \star$

MURADHAN AND SELVIHAN
OR
THE TALE OF THE CRYSTAL KIOSK

The Crystal Kiosk sat on that mountain top.

And what a mountain it was. Not just any old mountain. You know, there are mountains that embrace other mountains, as if dancing in a ring, standing side by side, barring passage. And still other mountains press their feet against other hills, other mountains,

and they rise and rise.

This was none like these.

It stood alone in the middle of a vast, desolate steppe. Its might was its solitude. Alone and mighty, it rose without embracing any mountain or hill, without leaning or pressing against any. Dignified, grave, self-confident, it rose slowly, with calm. As if in no hurry, as if it would stand there till the day of doom, as if even the flood couldn't touch it. . . It had no sharp cliffs, sudden and violent, that opened chasms in its midst. It rose slowly along its smooth hills and fitting slopes. In this manner, its awesome greatness assumed modesty.

Gazing at it, human beings thought that they could climb it easily, that they would make it to the top one day. The mountain was hope's safe.

It was grandiose, free of anger. Once upon a time, it had lived an angry, furious youth and spewed fires at its foot. Now youth had grown cold, petrified, turned into the ever-widening rings of small, fine-needled lacy hills. Everything had come to pass. Its fury had subsided. What used to be called wrath was no more than a youthful temper.

Its beauty was calm. Pure white clouds circled the pure white snow on its peak. The snow was the clouds' elusive threshold. The snow's color illuminated the clouds, the clouds' the snow. (When the sun came between them, the pure whiteness would dissipate, turning into a haze of vaporous colors.)

The mountain experienced all four seasons at once. (Human beings always dreamt of going there one day. They passed the time with dreams of the ascent, and many died before attaining this forever-deferred dream. Without ever climbing the mountain. . . Everything remained unfulfilled, the hope, the fancy, the journey.)

And at times they returned from half-finished journeys. Defeated, having discovered the mountain's truth. (It could not be climbed) Having learned an important lesson for the remainder of their life. A wisdom they would not have been able to attain unless by daring the task, by attempting the journey. (The mountain and human beings had tested each other.)

From then on, their lives could no longer include the hope of climbing that mountain.

What you call mountain is an orb of fire, wrestling the sun, you'd think. Its flames the color of war. In early spring, fiery purple flowers swarm its surface. Down the slopes, all of nature is overshadowed, as if sheltered under a bird's wing. One side of the mountain is immersed in light, the other side in the clouds' shadow. The fog takes over the mountain, in ring after ring. One rising inside another, denser, narrowing rings reach the mountain's peak, climb layers upon layers, spiraling. In the end, a cloud of fog rests on the peak, hangs like a gentle tulle under the eternal veil of snow.

A never-lifting tulle.

The mountain is the native land of the flower.

Not only the flower, but the water, the springs, the myriad healing plants.

Leaving the mountain's heart, the brooks carry life to the river. They flow along the valleys, like thin silvery ropes. Without hurting or frightening anything, as if intent on remaining unnoticed. If you reached the springs replenishing the brooks, you'd be seized with wonderment. Dip your hand, it freezes, put a flower in the water, it stays fresh round the seasons. Delicate icy lace surrounds the mouth of each spring. Water embroidery, water filigree, laces of ice.

Gazelles descend to the foot of the mountain. Every time they pause, it's a sight. Magical.

These lakes are called winter lakes in the summer; you'd think they were clouds fallen on the grass. Every bird flying over a lake comes face-to-face with itself, descends, its wing touches the water. Motes of silver get caught in its plumes; ascending again, it draws a thin silvery flash in the sky.

In winter, ice sheets over the lakes. Silver has frozen. Fog descends. You'd think it was steam rising off of silver. The leaves get covered with clouds of snow, the evergreens and pineneedles shawl themselves in tulle.

The birds' custom begins with the morning.

The sky awakens with the flutter of wings.

The nine lakes of mountains hold mirrors to the sky. The gazelles descending to the lakes fall in love with themselves.

On their return to the forest, they bear an absence in their hearts. An absence that would never leave them. Some aspect of their face and heart has stayed behind on the lake's icy surface. They search the forest in vain. They have lost a part of their face. The lakes make the gazelle a wanderer. The ice clouds the eyes of all gazelles—like fog, like mist. From then on, they would seek their hunter everywhere they looked.

In the summer, the ice thaws; yet the gazelles have long departed.

Love is a hallucination.

Green shows the seven provinces its seven thousand shades, proves it is the color of paradise. Flowers no one knows, no one has seen—native only to this mountain—cover the sides of the path without pretense, as if standing in salute.

And the path

is a snake that has shed its skin and becomes like the white marble. Giving ear to an Indian flute, it meanders coquettishly, with a thousand airs, climbs up the mountain and reaches the gates of the Crystal Kiosk.

there, it spreads as waves of white foam, becomes a waterfall on the stairs with long fine-chiseled stones.

the path ends at the stairs, the last surge of foam. the snake spent.

where the foam dies out, a night-blue crystal gate.

night blue.

The path is too awesome to welcome just any traveler. As if it would throw off its back the visitor it didn't like or deemed unfit for itself. As if it would stretch itself like the snake and shake the wanderer off. More than a path, it resembles a river coursing upward. As if it's cut in the stone. As if flowing endlessly. As if frozen during the ascent.

Written on the mountain's forehead, the long path is like a promised journey.

It is such a destiny that only those marked with it are allowed passage.

It is like an ivy with myriad roots spun around the mountain. Its marble is veiny. Tempered in a thousand ovens, laid out painstakingly. The sound of hoofbeats leaves long echoes, announces the approaching traveler to the Crystal Kiosk.

Beauty speaks in a thousand tongues.

The mountain is a long fairy tale written in a thousand tongues.

One look and you'd think the kiosk was made of glass.

You'd think they carved it with the avalanches broken off the snowy peak. Look at its walls and you'd make out its chambers. Is it a fancy? a vision? it's uncertain. As if spirited away from a dream.

in sunlight, the kiosk seems ablaze,

at crimson dusk, it turns forest green,

you'd think it's a mighty plane tree in the forest, grafted from seven roots, sprawling itself out in seven thousand arms, its palm extending to the forest, to the heart of the forest, a beneficent and bountiful plane tree.

in the black of the night, it is the moon's teardrop. So when the mountain cold turned to frost, it froze like that,

when the moon calms down, so it does.

at sunrise, it is the sun's twin. the charmed mirror in which the sun sees itself.

it stands witness to the sun's secret.

They say that thousands of workers toiled to build this kiosk; now no one knows their names. That awesome teardrop, it is said, is crystal cut from their labor's sweat.

with autumn comes the rain, the walls don't hold the water, as if the rain doesn't touch them—still there is a sense of relief, a feeling of being cleansed—

the kiosk has tall, sharp towers (the moon hides behind them) tall towers scattered to four corners (the moon plays puss-in-the-corner among them) round, magical towers. (They hide echoes, secrets.) Long candles (pale, flickering) move about the arched windows. From one window to another, they move solitarily, as if wandering. The hands holding them are invisible.

Judas trees bleed the color of blood in the evenings; in the candles' trembling light, the lost scents of Judas trees. . .

All the villages, all the villagers are in love with the

mountain,

with this kiosk.

This kiosk is the farthest light, the most radiant.

So many clans, so many villages, so many tribes brighten their poverty by gazing endlessly at the kiosk. They migrate, see the kiosk once, and leave along their trajectory a bundle of fairy tales about the kiosk. The crystal kiosk is the fairy tale of night, day

the four seasons

the poor

the rich.

Time flows, even the Crystal Kiosk disappears.

let's say the moon has stopped crying

let's say the mirror cracks in the middle, turns to salt, unable to bear its own charm let's say the plane tree collapses, rots and turns to soil

The Crystal Kiosk flows down the mountain (streams into the river, meets the sea, let's say) flows across the history (mixes in wars, in settlements, let's say)

its fairy tale remains.

and that tale, a thousand people hear, one understands.

The Crystal Kiosk remains to no one. (Poetry withers, legend is exhausted in those mountains. No poet climbs the mountains anymore.) Yet it leaves us a saying, a word. It leaves so that we can pass the word on to those who come after us, so we leave a story. Each story is in charge of its own moral, bound with it. (Each poet bears the seal of his own word)

to reach the path of the fairy tale,

life must be spent on the paths of truth.

Each morning, all the people of surrounding villages and clans used to wake up gazing at the kiosk.

The Crystal Kiosk was the morning star showing the day its way. The kiosk's chisel work used to blend in the mountain's panorama, in the gazelle's love,

and in those mornings, human beings used to think that they could, that they must, go to the mountain.

And that one say they would. . .

Translated from the Turkish by Aron R. Aji

Proverbs

TOMAŽ ŠALAMUN

Who lives in the error that color is culture
and fish is nature will get sober.
The trees are hair on the skin planted by us.

In front of the eyes it is bright, behind the eyes it is dark.
Turning the head is total utopia.

Your hands will be burned to let you be without hands.
You will be charged for switching rails and killing people.

The bird gets scared,
the worm gets scared,
the brain covers up.

Mountains, all their life on the spot,
crush the distance.

Space is only for one color: white.

There are no bonds for the seventh day.

Who has the same name as the other
and who has the same name as you
misses electricity.
Every mythological status is bread.
To the earth, which is hollow
and surrounded by walls of carpets of grass,
we will cut the artery, so the air will rush out.
Let giants eat the sandwich.

Translated from the Slovenian by the author and Phillis Levin

meltdown

peter nagy

Meltdown

I am for richness of meaning rather than clarity of meaning. . . . In an inclusive rather than an exclusive kind of architecture there is room for the fragment, for the contradiction, for improvisation, and for the tensions these produce.

Robert Venturi
from *Complexity and Contradiction in Architecture*

Venturi's rationalization to support the extreme Ur-modern architecture he celebrates in his groundbreaking book of 1962 seems to me to work as a manifesto for life in the 1990s. Replace the word "architecture" with any number of possibilities—art, life, politics, nation, cuisine, religion, sexuality—and one sees just how prophetic his formal analyses of the time were. In no place is this more evident than India, a country built upon and virtually defined by complexity and contradiction.

I have put together a portfolio of images of Indian art and architecture to illustrate not only what magnetically drew me to the country initially, but also the anchor that holds me firmly there. This is a very small sampling of the rich creations that arose from the usually violent cultural clashes throughout the history of the subcontinent. First is the Gandharan art from what is now the border area between Pakistan and Afghanistan: a synthesis of

Buddhist imagery and Greco-Roman modeling, evidence of Alexander's turnaround point. From the Himalayan kingdom of Ladakh come the details of the frescoes at Alchi: figures from Tibetan Buddhism stylized by Muslim painters from Kashmir, schooled in the techniques of Persian miniatures. The northern Rajasthan desert area of Shekhawati is known for its mural paintings on the outsides of buildings; shown here are examples of colonial influences on that tradition resulting in hybrids of a Deco or *Mitteleuropa* bent. Another example of the European influence is in the work of the painter Raja Ravi Varma, a prince from Travancore in south India. Not only the first Indian to paint with oils on canvas on a large scale but also the first to foreground realistic portraiture solely for its own ends, Varma's images influenced both the representation of Hindu gods in popular lithographs and the beginnings of the Hindi cinema. And finally details of Le Corbusier's Millowners Association Building in Ahmedabad, where the father of the International Style created an exquisite shell suited to the very harsh climate—architecture that time and India herself have turned into a well-seasoned curry.

Peter Nagy

PAGE 33:
Bodhisattva, Gandhara, 2nd century, C.E.

PAGE 33 (INSET):
Head of the Buddha, Gandhara, 2nd century C.E.

PAGE 34 & 35:
Fresco details from the Sumtsek at Alchi, Ladakh, 12th century, C.E.

PAGES 36 & 37:
Details of interior wall paintings (PAGE 36) and architectural details (PAGE 37) from the area of Shekhawati, northern Rajasthan, c. 1900.

PAGE 38:
Raja Ravi Varma, *Princess with a Musician*, c. 1900.

PAGE 38 (INSET): Raja Ravi Varma, *Nala and Damayanti*, c. 1900.

PAGES 39 & 40:
Le Corbusier, the Millowners Association Building, Ahmedabad, Gujarat, 1957.

41

NINA BERBEROVA

It was autumn when I arrived in the city. A powerful, insistent wind raced through the streets. I could sense but not see an ocean on three sides of me (the city was on a cape)—over there, in the harbor, among the docks, along with the cruisers and giant freighters. From there the ocean hurled its rain and hurricanes down upon the city. Shredded skies, heavy morning fogs that lay on the roofs, and people, so many people.

I was staying in a hotel downtown. It was as if I still couldn't get up the nerve to go further uptown, as if I might still be on the verge of going back to where I'd come from. The man on duty had only one arm and wore a great big medal that swung against his chest. It was a medal for saving lives. But whose? I kept wanting to ask him. I had so much to do and worry about right away, though, that I never did get around to asking. What lives? If they were ordinary lives, like mine, then just how did he go about it? But there was never a quiet moment for this question. I was looking for a job. I was looking for a refuge. Money was in short supply and time was flying. The unfamiliar mirage all around me seemed to share nothing whatever in common with my entire life and destiny to date.

There are attics and basements for men like me. I decided to find myself a room first. I walked up and down the side streets of downtown for a long time before I saw a paper sign: Room for Rent.

"Why don't you take a whole building?" the janitor told me, and he led me to the four-story building next door. It was propped up by heavy boards leaning against the facade. "You could live here in peace until summer, but they're razing it then."

I declined, primarily because there wasn't a pane of glass in any of the windows. You could see the cheerful but dirty wallpaper of the second-floor ceiling through the hole in the first, but that could have been patched easily. As I was walking out, I recalled a scrap of a poem:

I'd like to go
Where they hammer nails with violins
And feed the evening fires with flutes, —

Which is to say, for a moment, I felt like a violin or a flute. It's a good thing no one could tell that I'd started feeling sorry for myself.

The other room, which I found at dusk, was all done up in cretonne— huge green flowers and pink leaves. It covered the two beds. The short woman, her arms crossed high across her breast as if she were about to burst into song, pointed to one of the two beds and said, "That's where I sleep."

Before she said this she gave me a touching and actually rather humble look.

I bowed and walked out.

Green flowers and pink leaves, the street-level windows, and rain that fell suddenly, straight down, and very hard, not with a dancing, ingratiating slant but rather with a confident sound: I'll strike everything, crush everything. That was what the evening was like for me. "But you cannot, you simply cannot let it get you down," I told myself. "You're a violin, or a flute, or a drum, that fate has been beating on for twenty years. Despair is prohibited. Spitting on the floor is prohibited. What could that stranger ever tell you? Jumping out the window will lead to no good, too. *Pericoloso sporgersi.*"

The next morning I headed uptown.

On the tenth, fifteenth, twentieth floors of huge buildings, right under the roof, they sometimes rent out garret rooms. Cheap. Life goes on downstairs: elevators go up, dogs bark, telephones ring, perfume wafts; people living in warm, spacious apartments play games. But under the roof a corridor runs all the way around the building and looks out at four streets, the numbered doors follow closely one after the other: 283, 284, 285, and then, out of the blue, 16, 17, and again, in the almost quiet of the clouds, 77, 78, 79, a landing, a turn, the service elevator descending with someone's trunks, a trash receptacle as big as the Tsar Bell in the Kremlin but without a piece knocked off, a light burning, the corridor ahead a couple of hundred yards long. A fire extinguisher, a hose, a trap door to the roof. If you opened it at night, in would rush the starry gloom, the chill of coming nights and days, and that same autumn wind, that same nearby ocean that rings the city, droning, and the rumble of the streets somewhere below, an incessant, fiery rumble.

I paid for a week in advance and moved in that evening. I locked the door. I wasn't locking myself in; I was trying to lock the world out. And then another world, many times greater than the first, welled up inside of me, here, within these four walls. This world had an ocean, too, a city, a sky, an endless stream of people walking past me, rain, and wind. Besides these, though, it also had the memory of a journey: the sun, the Italian town where you and I stayed not so long ago, the fragrant shore where toy boats strung with lanterns sailed by in the evening, and the pink stream that hung over a volcano as old as the universe. At first you thought the potted palms in the hotel garden were artificial, but one morning a flower bloomed with a light pop.

All of this was mine, needed and beloved by me alone, alive only inside me. I was trying to lock out what belonged to everyone. You could hear its hum and rumble from far away, but you didn't have to listen to it. I washed up, had a bite of cheese, bread, and apple, and lay down on the narrow, hard, but clean bed. Suddenly, reflected light began streaming through the uncurtained window—onto me and everything around me.

The red needle of a distant skyscraper was reflected in the sink, and a blue flame fell on the face of my watch. Something orange played with the door lock, and the ceiling suddenly looked as if it had been sliced by a long ray. Something flickered in the corner. I didn't guess right away that these were the buttons on my jacket, which I had dropped on the chair. It was as if an airplane had sailed over me from wall to wall, nearly grazing me with its propeller. A precise raspberry circle ran across the ceiling (a fire truck racing somewhere with its distant clanging). God knows how many times it had already been reflected before flitting in my eyes. A lilac spark lay on my chest for a few moments before shifting to the glass and staying there. At the time it felt as if, despite the fact that I had settled on the eighteenth floor, the entire city was running down my shoulders, face, and arms, as if the street were passing not somewhere below but here, across and through me, and blinking in my eyes with dozens of reflected lights.

I woke up after noon and saw that the room needed painting. I got dressed, went out into the corridor, locked the door, which bore the number 199, and rang for the elevator. It was the service elevator, which was the only one I was allowed to use. A man in a gray livery jacket and frayed trousers greeted me politely. I asked him whether I could go up and down myself without bothering him. He said that was quite impossible, but that if I liked I could use the other two elevators at the end of the corridor, where the trash bins were.

"What a large building," I said as we flew down. "There must be twenty entrances."

"Twenty-four entrances," he said, "forty-two elevators, and 3,656 tenants."

"Exactly 3,656?" I exclaimed. This figure reminded me of the flowering palm.

"Exactly," he replied.

Before buying paint and a brush, I spent rather a long time walking around the street. I had arrived a week before and already was starting to understand a lot and guess even more. The diversity of faces that flashed by astonished me. There was no majority in this city; all the people were unusual. This was what distinguished it from the cities I had seen before. What was even more amazing was that I could not forget for a second that all these millions of women and men—or else their fathers, or their grandfathers—had taken the same journey as I had. So there was this absence of a majority and an equality of pasts, and one more circumstance that surprised me in an odd way. But I'll get back to that later.

I bought paint and a brush, returned to my room, and began painting the gray door a pale green. Immediately, I started to sing. The paint went on evenly and smelled of drying oil. I painted and sang, trying not to splatter the floor or myself. I began to get the feeling that I could live here, that in this room—as one of 3,656 tenants in this building—I was in the right place, and that after the first night spent here something had insinuated itself into me, filled me, laid down with me in bed, and was now pulsing through my veins.

I painted and sang—and thought, meanwhile, about how, if you were with me, you would be standing next to me and saying, Isn't there an apron

46

you can put on? You'll smear yourself and ruin your only trousers! And suddenly, as if in revenge for that thought, I let a fairly long drip that reminded me of the shape of a willow leaf fall on my knee.

I rubbed for a long time, but the spot wouldn't go away. I stopped singing and scratched distractedly at the material, which had worn thin over long years of wear. The spot doubled in size. Now it was huge, dry, and white. And suddenly I remembered seeing painters working by the stairs at the end of the corridor when I was going out in the afternoon for paint. And painters, according to my lights, ought to have turpentine.

"Maybe here the painters have something even better than turpentine," I told myself, as I wiped off the brush and smoothed my hair. By the way, about turpentine. The fact that my first childhood memory is connected with it has left me with a special, though rather unusual, feeling for turpentine all my life.

I was not yet three. One evening I came down with a cold. My mother (quite young and ever cheerful) ran out to the pharmacy and gave me a sweet, tasty medicine. I had to take it every four hours, for my cough. In the night I woke up and saw my mother standing over me, smiling, rosy with sleep, wearing a long white gown trimmed in lace and offering me a spoonful. I swallowed the sweet, tasty stuff, holding it for a second in my mouth preliminarily. Suddenly I saw the vision with the empty spoon in her hand disappear, melt away. She'd fainted. My mother was lying on the floor, unconscious, having realized she had given me not my medicine but the turpentine she had rubbed me down with before bed.

They wouldn't let me fall asleep. The doctor loomed over me like a tall tower and interrogated me. Did it burn? Hurt? They had me drink hot milk. "It was very tasty," I said. "Give me more." If I were not afraid of being misunderstood, I would say that this memory of the swallowed turpentine lent a certain cast to my entire life.

Hastily putting myself in order and buttoning my top button, I went out, locked the door, and went to the left, toward the exit: 198, 197—all the doors were identical. At about 155 the corridor took a turn, and there were 12, 13, 14. And indeed, on the broad landing, where huge, dry mops were stood up on end, two painters, one black and one white, were stroking the wall with broad brushes, and the paint was coming out nice and even , without

47

any bubbles.

"Pardon me," I said. "Could I have a little turpentine? You see I. . .by accident. . ."

I showed them the spot.

The black man and the white man both looked at me and at the spot and turned away, each continuing to stroke his own corner deftly and evenly.

"Turpentine, please," I repeated.

The black man tugged at his nose.

"Here's the thing, sir," he said, but as if he weren't addressing me. "There's a man living in room 274 who has what you need. At least that's what we've heard. But we don't have any turpentine. Am I telling the truth or what?"

The white man let out a sound that expressed sympathy.

"There's a man living there who definitely has what you need sometimes. Or so we've heard," the black man continued, "and that's why I am telling you. Go to his room and knock on the door as hard as you can. You'll find your turpentine there, if what they told us is true. Am I telling the truth or what?"

Once again the white man emitted a sympathetic grunt, and it seemed to me that all this might very well be the truth. I thanked him and continued on. Soon the corridor made another turn; it doubtless ran all the way around the building.

How many times I turned with it I don't remember anymore. I was looking for door 274. Once I thought I'd found it: there was 271, 272, 273, but then it started back with single-digit numbers. I figured at some point I'd reach my own room this way, but when? And what awaited me in the meantime?

The ceiling lights were switched on. From time to time I heard sounds coming from behind doors, first here, then there: water flowing, someone arguing, a sewing machine running, hammering. A child beginning to cry. According to my calculations, at least a quarter of an hour had passed and I was still walking and walking—and then suddenly I came to an impasse, or rather, a staircase that spiraled downward. I took a look, leaning over the railing. And I was drawn down.

What I saw astonished me. It was a covered street complete with stores, offices, lamps, mail boxes, shoeshine men. The only thing it didn't have was automobiles, and the shuffling of feet over the stone slabs reminded me of that little Italian town. But that's beside the point. Now that I'm used to it all, I know that sometimes, in the huge buildings of this city, on one of its upper floors, they set up something like a street. I certainly see nothing strange in the fact that, for the convenience of the people living in the building, a post office has been opened below me, that a tobacconist, a hairdresser, a shoemaker, a pharmacist, and a baker have opened their own establishments. That first time, though, it all seemed to me like a fantastic dream, and for a moment I doubted that I myself had rented a room on the eighteenth rather than the second floor. The ceiling, however, told me that I was not outside but inside the building. A little girl was standing in front of a bookshop window scratching the top of her head. A fat man sprawled out in a chair watched his shoes being shined. The sounds of song came from a radio store and the smell of pastries from the little blue sweets shop.

I didn't walk down that street. I ran. Shops alternated with offices. I noticed a sign for a dentist. There were homes and land for sale, prairies, riverbanks, and lake shores. Here was a domestic employment bureau. Round lamps hung on iron rings, a mailman dashed by, two women jabbering and laughing looked straight at me. And suddenly I came to a spiral staircase. Whether it was the same one or a different one I couldn't tell, but I ran up it.

I ran up and recognized a familiar series of doors, which I walked by quickly, checking the numbers.

After about twenty minutes I began noticing that I was getting close to the door I was looking for. Now the numbers were going backward: 277, 276, 275. At last! Door 274, no different from the other doors, right in front of me. Except that it was ajar.

Knocking cautiously on the doorjamb, I took a deep breath. No answer was forthcoming. I knocked once more and quietly walked in. The room, twice as big as mine, was piled high with furniture. There was even one armchair on top of the cupboard, which was open wide and spilling bits of old material, evidently upholstery fabric. Pictures were hung all the way to the ceiling. One showed a ship in full sail over a stormy sea. Old picture frames were stacked in a corner. A marble bust of some Roman stood amid the rubble. The entire right-hand wall was taken up by a broad, old sofa upholstered in a Scottish plaid, and on it, calmly, in a comfortable pose, as if he were expecting someone, sat the master of this room, a man nearly sixty. He was smiling. His face was pleasant—once it had been handsome, but the features were flabby now, the eyes bloated. They were big, dark, somewhat sad, but good eyes, intelligent eyes, under heavy lids, in a soft and good face. His hair was in disarray and longer than men ordinarily wear it. He had on an old—very old—loose jacket and shoes on his feet. Once again I looked him in the eye and bowed slightly.

"Pardon me," I said, almost not feeling shy although at that moment my arrival seemed rather odd even to me. "The painters told me—they're working over there—about turpentine. . . . You must be an artist, right? I have this spot here, and I'd like. . ."

Still smiling calmly and cozily, he took a bottle off a shelf. "People live so amazingly," I thought, "and everyone in his own way. Especially during the day. At night, all kinds of lights must find their way here, too."

The man moistened a clean rag with turpentine, squatted with a slight crackling of bones, and wiped my knee. The familiar smell tickled my nostrils. The doctor had towered over me. His glasses had gleamed in the dark sky and his beard had raced by like a cloud. "That's very odd," he said angrily, and for the umpteenth time he shrugged. And my mother, who had put on some kind of skirt, was holding on to the wall to keep from falling a second time. I never saw her so serious again afterward. "It's absolutely incomprehensible. The child must be made of pig iron!" I was sitting on the bed and looking at them avidly in hopes of a second spoonful. "My little puss, my chick, my sweetkins! Throw up! My darling!" my mother pleaded. I shook my head. I didn't even understand her murmurings, why she was begging me so in such humiliating fashion.

The man straightened up with more slight crackling. The spot was gone.

"What did the painters tell you?"

"They told me to knock as hard as I could!"

"What fools!"

"But your door was ajar."

"That was their idea of a joke. I never close it. Whenever someone needs to, they come in."

"What about at night?"

50

"I shut the door at night."

"What does your window look out on? May I take a look?"

While I was picking my way over to the window, he said:

"Except that I'm not an artist. I'm a framer and upholsterer."

I looked out the window and saw roofs and skyscrapers that were already familiar to me. In the dusk of the gathering night, lights glowed, advertisements flashed, the red needle, my nocturnal raspberry friend, reached into the high and cloudless sky directly in front me. Above it an airplane with a blue star on its tail flew by, and some word blinked and pulsed well beyond the bridge.

"Take a look through my binoculars," the man said, handing me the heavy old instrument by its strap. "A marvelous view! Over there, between those two smokestacks, sometimes you can see the sea, and a little more to your right you can see the zoo."

I brought the binoculars up to my eyes, twirled one little wheel and then the other. And suddenly a block away, in a lit window that hung in front of me in the sky, I saw a room and two little boys in it. They were standing at the table, and each one had a knife in his hand. Each had just cut his own arm and was trying to drip blood on the piece of paper that lay in front of them. One of them was wearing a feathered headdress and the other a Mexican mask pushed back on his forehead. I looked higher up. A woman was attempting to open the closed drawer of a high narrow bookcase, trying to find the right key. She was in a dreadful hurry, and in the left-hand corner of the room I couldn't hear it but I could see very distinctly a record playing. The record was spinning.

In a neighboring window a carcass was lying on the sofa, and a dog was circling it mournfully. The sad, elegant, pedigree borzoi shuddered and looked out the window, so that our eyes actually seemed to meet for a moment.

"What kind of binoculars are these?" I said, swallowing my built-up saliva. "What on earth is this?"

The man smiled at me trustingly and gently.

"This is nothing! There are even better. Once I held in my hands a gadget they say a German saw Petersburg through in '42, and then, a year later, the pyramid of Cheops."

I looked again. The boys had signed their names in blood, the dog was looking at me as if it were made of stone, and the record was turning. A floor lower a drawing class was in session, and lower still two couples were dancing in the semi-dark. More to the left, where the facade of that distant building ended, through the gap, the harbor lights twinkled on a white steamer that had sailed out to sea. The dark blue water was flooded with violent reflections, black smoke hung perfectly still, and beyond it you could just make out a flat island with a tall radio tower. (Was that the green eye that had spent last night on my shoulder?) The flat island turned muddy, and beyond it was the real and boundless ocean.

I bent over a little, and there, far far away, under the stripped trees of some park I didn't know, where white, round streetlamps shone with hundreds of lights, in the autumn gloom, I saw wild beasts behind their cages. I saw a guard signal to a tiger to go through a small low door, which it did, and the door dropped. On a sand-sprinkled clearing, a pensive, two-humped camel laid his shaggy little head on the back of another.

A large heavy hand dropped onto my shoulder. I remembered where I was. "Now he's going to ask me to leave," I thought.

"This is a very entertaining activity," said the man, and at close range I now saw his tired, dark brown eyes and his thin but broad eyebrows tinged with gray. "You can look and look until your eyes go funny. I don't do it anymore. Maybe sometimes at night, when I can't get to sleep, if someone has an uncurtained window."

Could he have seen me yesterday from this window? I thought at that moment. Is that possible? Of course not. That's impossible. We can't see what's going on in our own building.

"Won't you have a seat?"

There was now a chair behind me, a lamp had been turned on, and a glass had appeared in front of me. Our conversation flowed as if we had known each other for a long time, a little bit about everything: beauty and the greatness of this big city, where to look for work, how to use the telephone booth by the elevator, and where to buy bread and milk. A few precious words about insignificant matters, and a quiet voice and a big hand pouring me wine, and the attentive expression with which he listened to me. I felt good. I felt untroubled and warm. I told him I was happy to have met him, that he had amazing, unusual, mind-boggling binoculars, that if you really tried, I was sure, even from here, you could see the pyramid of Cheops through them.

And once again I walked over to the window.

The dog was gone. So were the boys. The ship had gone around the island and had probably been sailing at full speed for a while. Certain windows, though, windows that hadn't been there before, were now lit up here and there. I began looking. A ceiling light was burning in a narrow room. There was a table and a chair. And some kind of bucket. A man was sleeping on the bed. There was something familiar about him. No, it just seemed that way.

A woman opened the door slowly and walked in. She stopped, looked, and walked over to the sleeping man. The bucket was full of light green paint and on top of it I had set down my brush. You came up to me and put your hand on my chest, your skinny, ever-cool hand, and a moment later you took it away and lowered your eyes to me. You were wearing the same dress you were wearing the day I left. It was too long for you, but there was no time to deal with alterations or to mend it at the collar, where it was coming apart at the seam. A lock of your hair fell on my forehead, you kissed me, you began to cry. You were with me. You were telling me something. It was probably about "us." You were always talking about "us." Not "you," my happiness with "you," but "us." It's not when people switch to the familiar form of "you," it's when they switch to "we." "You" can be taken away in parting to the end of the earth, but not "we." It breaks down the moment they part.

"Finish your wine," said the man whose guest I still was. "I'm sure you'll find a job in your field very soon, and in general I can see you are an educated man. You know how to behave in society."

"Forgive me," I said, hastily making my way to the exit. "I've overstayed my welcome, and I came without being introduced and with a request right away. I don't know how to thank you."

"There, you see?" He smiled. "Didn't I say you were a polite, educated man? Stop by any time. You're always welcome. I light the fire on Saturdays and my girlfriend comes over. I'll tell her to bring a lady friend for you. She's a young girl and works as a cashier. We feed the fire with that old harp lying in the corner. I've already sawed it in two."

I stepped out into the corridor. My door turned out to be almost next to his. It was locked, of course, just as I had left it. And inside, of course, there

53

was no light on—when I went out it was still light and I'd had no reason to turn it on.

Now I can say something about that observation I made when I went out that afternoon for paint. I realized then that every person brings whatever he can to this big city. One brings the shadow of Elsinor's prince, another the long shadow of the Spanish knight, a third the profile of the immortal Dublin seminarian, a fourth some dream, or thought, or melody, the noonday heat of some treasure, the memory of a snow-drifted grave, the divine grandeur of a mathematical formula, or the strum of guitar strings. All this has dissolved on this cape and formed the life I plan to take part in too from now on. With you, who is not here with me but who is alive in this air I breathe.

—1952

Translated from the Russian by Marian Schwartz

TONY SMITH

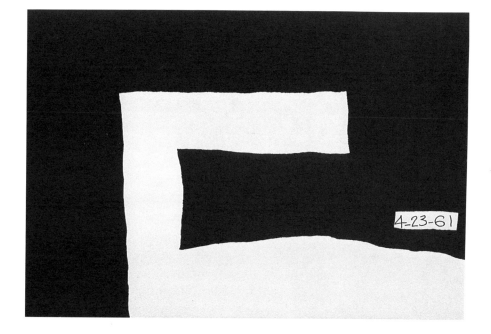

4-23-61

PAGE 55:
Untitled, 1961.

BELOW:
Untitled, 1961.

PAGE 57:
Untitled, 1934.

4-26-61

BELOW:
Will Jackson Pollock
Affect Our Cars?,
c. 1949–50.

PAGE 59:
Louisenberg #5,
1953–54.

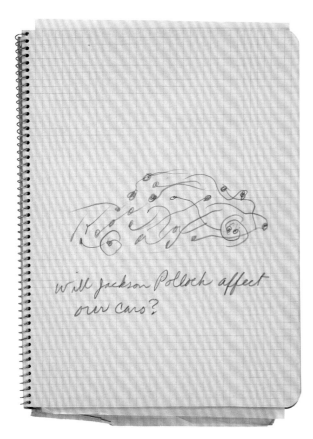

58

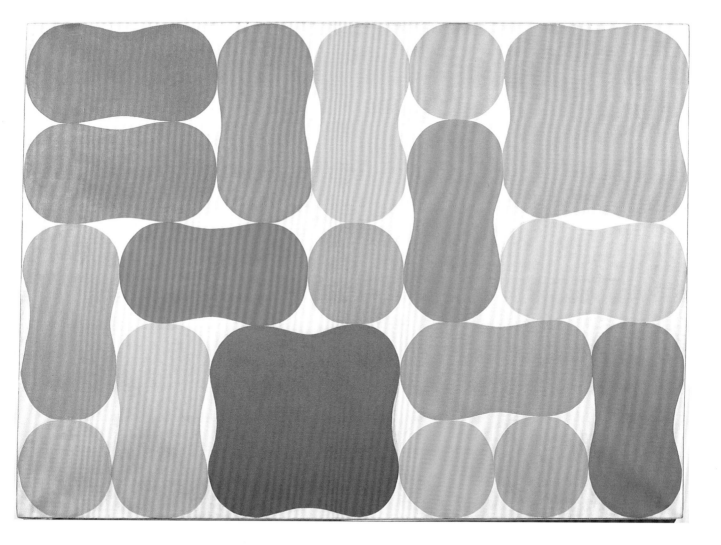

PAGE 60:
Untitled, 1962.

BELOW:
Untitled, 1962–63.

61

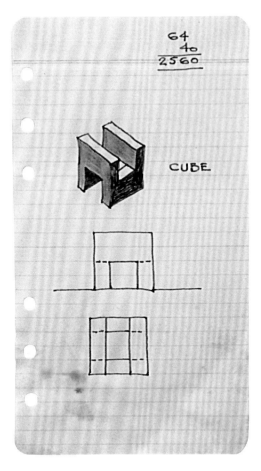

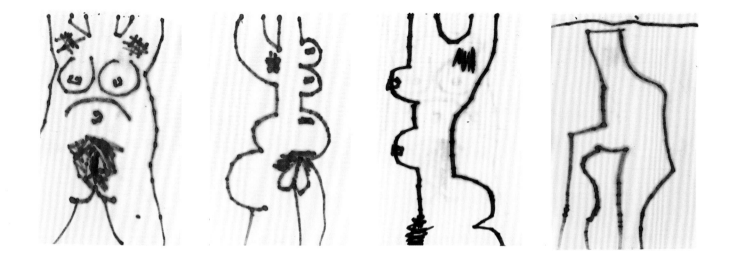

(The History of Cities) — The Crooked (shall

Even those who enter by the wrong gate, who take the

Dec. 28, 1967 "One Gate"

32'-35" "One Gate" SQ. O.A. 38

wrong path, will find their way.

What do you do when there is only one gate? S.P.F.!

Plastically this may seem too open, but, the majesty of the scale will give it cohesion. Earlier scheme is too oppressive

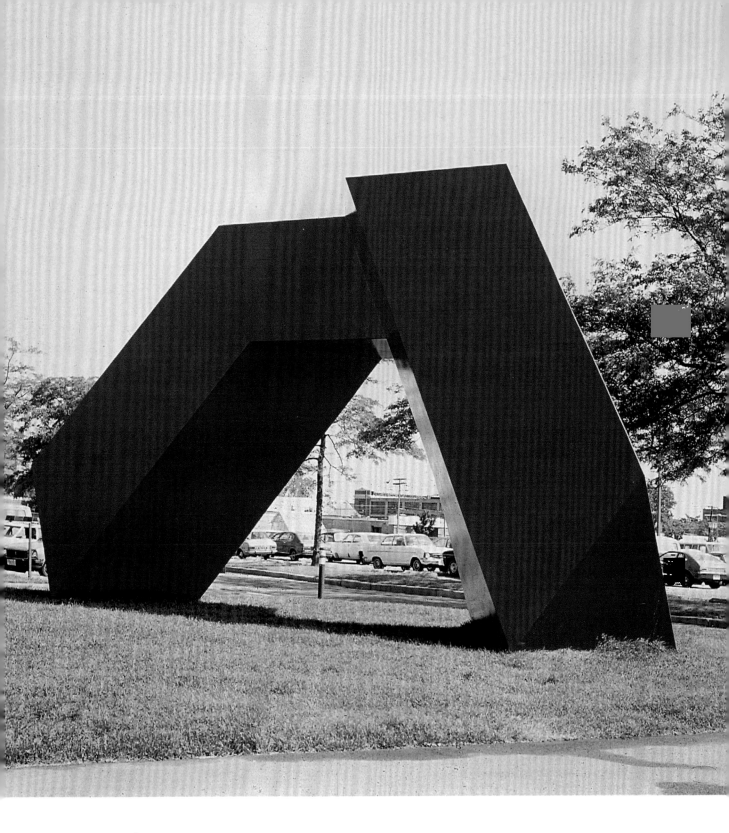

PAGE 64:
For Marjorie, 1961.

BELOW:
For J.C., 1969.

Tony Smith

"The pure products of America go crazy," William Carlos Williams, the Paterson, New Jersey doctor/poet warns readers in one of his prismatic odes to the everyday. His was a post-Whitman view of America's democratic vistas, with the ominous shadows fleshed out. Tony Smith, a prodigal son of neighboring South Orange, New Jersey, responded to Whitman's call for a native art of heroic aims and proportions, but he shared Williams's darker vision, as well. He had reason. Madness in a bottle claimed his close friend Jackson Pollock, while corrosive early fame—and more booze—ate away at the creative powers of another, Tennessee Williams. That Smith should have named two of his most important early sculptures *Eleven Are Up* and *The Snake is Out*, both slang expressions for chronic drunkenness, effectively places him at the bar beside them. An equally "pure product of America," he too flirted with disaster in the hard-living style of his generation.

But Smith never fully succumbed to the obsessions that bedeviled him and his contemporaries. It was not just that he instinctually pulled back from the brink his friends went over, but that he had been pacing himself all along. In fact, Smith did not come into his own until the 1960s, after most of his comrades had passed from the scene. Late-bloomer and aesthetic jack-of-all-trades, he successively mastered each of his chosen disciplines—painting, architecture, and sculpture—without ever pursuing professional status in any of them. His standards and methods were rigorously his own. As were his motives.

Intense, conflicted feeling, spiritual dilemmas, and mystic longings kept his mind in constant turmoil. For much of his life, rapturous theorizing consumed the energy these tensions spun off; a secretive ruminator and manifesto writer, Smith was also a wild, lyrical talker and, in the way of some autodidacts, a natural teacher. Like his alternately encyclopedic, incantatory, and aphoristic texts, Smith's drawings—which sometimes serve as manuscript illuminations—range from visual equations and thumbnail constructions to symbolist diagrams, transformational erotica, and aesthetic whimsy. (In the last category Smith's idea of a Pollock-style automobile is a match for his friend Ad Reinhardt's art cartoons.)

As an architect, Smith built few buildings, and fewer still remain intact. Nevertheless, inspired by Frank Lloyd Wright, his mentor, and Le Corbusier, his idol, he dreamed up cities. As a painter, he also worked small but thought big—which explains why his canvases, usually at the low end of easel-scale, evoke a grandeur out of proportion to their actual size. It was only as a sculptor that Smith was able to take his own full measure. Even then, there were qualifications. "I don't make sculpture. I speculate in form," he told a friend, and most of those speculations shaped up as tiny cardboard maquettes which he passed on to assistants or professional sheet-metal workers to enlarge. (A skilled but reluctant craftsman, Smith called upon his students and family—including daughters Kiki and Seton, now well-known contemporary artists in their own right—to fold and tape these models, as well other protégés, like Richard Tuttle, to make large wooden mock-ups he exhibited when industrial fabrication was too expensive.)

That Smith knew exactly how these fragile paper boxes would translate into imposing steel objects is plain from the results. Fixated since his youth by the

66

Bryant Park installation, New York City, 1967.

idea that America had yet to produce monuments equal to those of ancient civilizations or to its own vast and varied dimensions, Smith responded with four-square blocks, listing polyhedra, angular knots, ground-hugging arches and towering volumetric puzzles that in their variously obdurate, eccentric, and exalted permutations express this country's uneasy greatness. The big painterly gesture of Pollock thus found its unexpected equivalent in Smith's space-dominating, space-framing sculptures, just as the welter of masculine emotion typical of Williams's melodramas is contained in Smith's restless but firmly rooted "presences" as the artist liked to call them.

"The heart has its reasons of which reason knows nothing," wrote the mathematical genius and pitiless Catholic philosopher, Blaise Pascal. He too is somewhere in the crowd, behind Williams, Whitman, and the rest. And Smith, Pascal's co-religionist and soul-torn innovator in a tradition of rationalist modernism, echoed back, "Geometry has its reasons that reason cannot know." His work is the manifold proof.

Robert Storr

67

MARC COHEN

Evensong

Being alone is the next best thing
to being with her   Fleet skeletons of music
dance on fallen leaves   Silver birches
bathe in pools of afternoon sun
Amid the confusion
of spring dispersals
a misguided bird cracks
the shell of a crooked day

The music stops
Darkness coats the ugly day
sheds light
on the only way
to break the solitude

lay down beside her again

BLINDNESS

The arrival of so many blind people appeared to have brought at least one advantage, or, rather, two advantages, the first of these being of a psychological nature, as it were, for there is a vast difference between waiting for new inmates to turn up at any minute, and realizing that the building is completely full at last, that from now on it will be possible to establish and maintain stable and lasting relations with one's neighbors, without the disturbances there have been up until now, because of the constant interruptions and interventions by the new arrivals that obliged us to be forever reconstituting the channels of communication. The second advantage, of a practical, direct, and substantial nature, was that the authorities outside, both civilian and military, had understood that it was one thing to provide food for two or three dozen people, more or less tolerant, more or less prepared, because of their small number, to resign themselves to occasional mistakes or delays in the delivery of food, and quite another to be faced with the sudden and complex responsibility of feeding two hundred and forty human beings of every type, background, and temperament. Two hundred and forty, take note, and that is just a manner of speaking, for there are at least twenty blind internees who have not managed to find a bed and are sleeping on the floor. In any case, it has to be recognized that thirty persons being fed on rations meant for ten is not the same as distributing to two hundred and sixty, food intended for two hundred and forty. The difference is almost imperceptible. Now then, it was the conscious assumption of this increased responsibility, and perhaps, a hypothesis not to be disregarded, the fear that further disturbances might break out, that determined a change of procedure on the part of the authorities, in the sense of giving orders that the food should be delivered on time and in the right quantity. Obviously, after the struggle, in every respect lamentable, that we had to witness, accommodating so many blind internees was not going to be easy or free of conflict, we need only remember those poor contaminated creatures who before could still see and now see nothing, of the separated couples and their lost children, of the discomfort of those who had been trampled and knocked down, some of them twice or three times, of those who are going around in search of their cherished possessions without finding them, one would have to be completely insensitive to forget, as if it were nothing, the misfortunes of these poor people. However, it cannot be denied that the announcement that lunch was about to be delivered was like a consoling balm for everyone. And if it is undeniable that, given the lack of adequate organization for this operation or of any authority capable of imposing the necessary discipline, the collection of such large quantities of food and its distribution to feed so many mouths led to further misunderstandings, we must concede that the atmosphere changed considerably for the better, when throughout the ancient asylum there was nothing to be heard except the noise of two hundred and sixty mouths masticating. Who is going to clean up this mess afterward is a question so far unanswered, only in the late afternoon will the voice on the loudspeaker repeat the rules of orderly conduct that must be observed for the good of all, and then it will become clear with what degree of respect the new arrivals treat these rules. It is no small thing that the inmates of the second ward in the right wing have decided, at long last, to bury their dead, at least we shall be rid of that particular stench, the smell of the living, however fetid, will be easier to get used to.

As for the first ward, perhaps because it was the oldest and therefore the most established in the process and pursuit of adaptation to the state of blindness, a quarter of an hour after its inmates had finished eating, there was not so much as a scrap of dirty paper on the floor, a forgotten plate or dripping receptacle. Everything had been gathered up, the smaller objects placed inside the larger ones, the dirtiest of them placed inside those that were less dirty, as any rationalized regulation of hygiene would demand, as attentive to the greatest efficiency possible in gathering up leftovers and litter, as to the economy of effort needed to carry out this task. The state of mind that perforce will have to determine social conduct of this nature cannot be improvised nor does it come about spontaneously. In the case under scrutiny, the pedagogical approach of the blind woman at the far end of the ward seems to have had a decisive influence, that woman married to the ophthalmologist, who has never tired of telling us, If we cannot live entirely like human beings, at least let us do everything in our power not to live entirely like animals, words she repeated so often that the rest of the ward ended up by transforming her advice into a maxim, a dictum, into a doctrine, a rule of life, words which deep down were so simple and elementary, probably it was just that state of mind, propitious to any understanding of needs and circumstances, that contributed, even if only in a minor way to the warm welcome the old man with the black eye patch found there when he peered through the door and asked those inside, Any chance of a bed here. By a happy coincidence, clearly indicative of future consequences, there was a bed, the only one, and it is anyone's guess how it survived, as it were, the invasion, in that bed the car thief had suffered unspeakable pain, perhaps that is why it had retained an aura of suffering that kept people at a distance. These are the workings of destiny, arcane mysteries, and this coincidence was not the first, far from it, we need only observe that all the eye patients who happened to be in the doctor's office when the first blind man appeared there have ended up in this ward, and even then it was thought that the situation would go no further, In a low voice, as always, so that no one would suspect the secret of her presence there, the doctor's wife whispered into her husband's ear, Perhaps he was also one of your patients, he is an elderly man, bald, with white hair, and he has a black patch over one eye, I remember you telling me about him, Which eye, the left, It must be him. The doctor advanced to the passageway and said, slightly raising his voice, I'd like to touch the person who has just joined us, I would ask him to make his way in this direction and I shall make my way toward him. They bumped into each other midway, fingers touching fingers, like two ants that recognize each other from the maneuvering of their antennae, but this won't be the case here, the doctor asked his permission, ran his hands over the old man's face, and quickly found the patch. There is no doubt, here is the one person who was missing here, the patient with the black patch, he exclaimed, What do you mean, who are you, asked the old man, I am, or rather I was your ophthalmologist, do you remember, we were agreeing on a date for your cataract operation, How did you recognize me, Above all, by your voice, the voice is the sight of the person who cannot see, Yes, the voice, I'm also beginning to recognize yours, who would have thought it, doctor, now there's no need for an operation, If there is a cure for this, we will both need it, I remember you telling me, doctor, that after my operation I would no longer recognize the world in which I was living, we now know how right you were, When did you turn blind, Last night, And they've brought you here already, The panic out there is such that it won't be long before they start killing people off the moment they know they have gone blind, Here they have already eliminated ten, said a man's voice, I found them, the old man with the black eye patch simply said, They were from the other ward, we buried our dead at once, added the same voice, as if concluding a report. The girl with dark glasses had approached, Do you remember me, I was wearing dark glasses, I remember you well, despite my cataract, I remember that you were very pretty, the girl smiled, Thank you, she said, and went back to her place. From there, she called out, The little boy is here too, I want my mummy, the boy's voice could be heard saying, as if worn out from some remote and useless weeping. And I was the first to go blind, said the first blind man, and I'm here with my wife, And I'm the girl from the waiting room, said the girl from the waiting room. The doctor's wife said, It only remains for me to introduce myself, and she said who she was. Then the old man, as if to repay the welcome, announced, I have a radio, A radio, exclaimed the girl with dark glasses as she clapped her hands, music, how nice, Yes, but it's a small radio, with batteries, and batteries do not last forever, the old man reminded her, Don't tell me we shall be cooped up here forever, said the first blind man, Forever, no, forever is always far too long a time, We'll be able to listen to the news, the doctor observed, And a little music, insisted the girl with dark glasses, Not everyone likes the same music, but we're all certainly interested in knowing what things are like outside, it would be better to save the radio for that, I agree, said the old man with the black eye patch. He took the tiny radio from his jacket pocket and switched it on. He began searching for the different stations, but his hand was still too unsteady to tune into one wavelength, and to begin with all that could be heard were intermittent noises, fragments of music and words, at last his hand grew steadier, the music became recognizable, Leave it there for a bit, pleaded the girl with dark glasses, the words got clearer, That isn't the news, said the doctor's wife, and then, as if an idea had suddenly struck her, What time is it, she asked, but she knew that no one there could tell her. The tuning knob continued to extract noises from the tiny box, then it settled down, it was a song, a song of no significance, but the blind internees slowly began gathering round, without pushing, they stopped the moment they felt a presence before them and there they remained, listening, their eyes wide open tuned in the direction of the voice that was singing, some were crying, as probably only the blind can cry, the tears simply flowing as from a fountain. The song came to an end, the announcer said, At the third stroke it will be four o'clock. One of the blind women asked, laughing, Four in the afternoon or four in the morning, and it was as if her laughter hurt her. Furtively, the doctor's wife adjusted her watch and wound it up, it was four in the afternoon, although, to tell the truth, a watch is unconcerned, it goes from one to twelve, the rest are just ideas in the human mind. What's that faint sound, asked the girl with dark glasses, it sounded like, It was me, I heard them say on the radio that it was four o'clock and I wound up my watch, it was one of those automatic movements we so often make, anticipated the doctor's wife. Then she thought that it had not been worth putting herself at risk like that, all she had to do was to glance at the wrist-watches of the blind who had arrived that day, one of them must have a watch in working order. The old man with the black eye patch had one, as she noticed just that moment, and the time on his watch was correct. Then the doctor asked, Tell us what the situation is like out there. The old man with the black eye patch said, Of course, but I'd better sit, I'm dead on my feet. Three or four to a bed, keeping each other company on this occasion, the blind internees settled down as best they could, they fell silent, and then the old man with the black eye patch told them what he knew, what he had seen with his own eyes when he could still see, what he had overheard during the few days that elapsed between the start of the epidemic and his own blindness.

In the first twenty-four hours, he said, if the rumor going round was true, there were hundreds of cases, all alike, all showing the same symptoms, all instantaneous, the disconcerting absence of lesions, the resplendent whiteness of their field of vision, no pain either before or after. On the second day there was talk of some reduction in the number of new cases, it went from hundreds to dozens and this led the Government to announce at once that it was reasonable to suppose that the situation would soon be under control. . . . The Government therefore ruled out the originally formulated hypothesis that the country was being swept by an epidemic without precedent, provoked by some morbid as yet unidentified agent that took effect instantaneously and was marked by a complete absence of any previous signs of incubation or latency. Instead, they said, that in accordance with the latest scientific opinion and the consequent and updated administrative interpretation, they were dealing with an accidental and unfortunate temporary concurrence of circumstances, also as yet unverified, in whose pathogenic development it was possible, the Government's communiqué emphasized, starting from the analysis of the available data, to detect the proximity of a clear curve of resolution and signs that it was on the wane. A television commentator came up with an apt metaphor when he compared the epidemic, or whatever it might be, to an arrow shot into the air, which upon reaching its highest point, pauses for a moment as if suspended, and then begins to trace its obligatory descending curve, which, God willing, and with this invocation the commentator returned to the triviality of human discourse and to the so-called epidemic, gravity tending to increase the speed of it, until this nightmare tormenting us finally disappears, these were words that appeared constantly in the media, and always concluded by formulating the pious wish that the unfortunate people who had become blind might soon recover their sight, promising them, meanwhile, the solidarity of society as a whole, both official and private. In some remote past, similar arguments and metaphors had been translated by the intrepid optimism of the common people into sayings such as, Nothing lasts forever, be it good or bad, the excellent maxims of one who has had time to learn from the ups and downs of life and fortune, and which, transported into the land of the blind, should be read as follows, Yesterday we could see, today we can't, tomorrow we shall see again, with a slight interrogatory note on the third and final line of the phrase, as if prudence, at the last moment, has decided, just in case, to add a touch of a doubt to the hopeful conclusion.

Sadly, the futility of such hopes soon became manifest, the Government's expectations and the predictions of the scientific community simply sank without trace. Blindness was spreading, not like a sudden tide flooding everything and carrying all before it, but like an insidious infiltration of a thousand and one turbulent rivulets that, having slowly drenched the earth, suddenly submerge it completely. Faced with this social catastrophe, already on the point of taking the bit between their teeth, the authorities hastily organized medical conferences, especially those bringing together ophthalmologists and neurologists. Because of the time it would inevitably take to organize, a congress that some had called for was never convened, but in compensation there were colloquia, seminars, round-table discussions, some open to the public, others held behind closed doors. The overall effect of the patent futility of the debates and the occurrence of certain cases of sudden blindness during the sessions, with the speaker calling out, I'm blind, I'm blind, prompted almost all the newspapers, the radio and television, to lose interest in such initiatives, apart from the discreet and, in every sense, laudable behavior of certain organs of communication that, living off sensational stories of every kind, off the fortunes and misfortunes of others, were not prepared to miss an opportunity to report live, with all the drama the situation warranted, the sudden blindness, for example, of a professor of ophthalmology.

The proof of the progressive deterioration of morale in general was provided by the Government itself, its strategy changing twice within the space of some six days. To begin with, the Government was confident that it was possible to circumscribe the disease by confining the blind and the contaminated within specific areas, such as the asylum in which we find ourselves. Then the inexorable rise in the number of cases of blindness led some influential members of the Government, fearful that the official initiative would not suffice for the task in hand, and that it might result in heavy political costs, to defend the idea that it was up to families to keep their blind indoors, never allowing them to go out on the street, so as not to worsen the already difficult traffic situation or to offend the sensibility of persons who still had their eyesight and who, indifferent to more or less reassuring opinions, believed that the white disease was spreading by visual contact, like the evil eye. Indeed, it was not appropriate to expect any other reaction from someone who, preoccupied with his thoughts, be they sad, indifferent, or happy, if such thoughts still exist, suddenly saw the change in expression of a person heading in his direction, his face revealing all the signs of total horror, and then that inevitable cry, I'm blind, I'm blind. No one's nerves could withstand it. The worst thing is that whole families, especially the smaller ones, rapidly became families of blind people, leaving no one who could guide and look after them, nor protect sighted neighbors from them, and it was clear that these blind people, however caring a father, mother or child they might be, could not take care of each other, otherwise they would meet the same fate as the blind people in the painting, walking together, falling together, and dying together.

Faced with this situation, the Government had no alternative but to go rapidly into reverse gear, broadening the criteria it had established about the places and spaces that could be requisitioned, resulting in the immediate and improvised utilization of abandoned factories, disused churches, sports pavilions, and empty warehouses. For the last two days there has been talk of setting up army tents, added the old man with the black eye patch. At the beginning, the very beginning, several charitable organizations were still offering volunteers to assist the blind, to make their beds, clean out the lavatories, wash their clothes, prepare their food, the minimum of care without which life soon becomes unbearable, even for those who can see. These dear people went blind immediately but at least the generosity of their gesture would go down in history. Did any of them come here, asked the old man with the black eye patch, No, replied the doctor's wife, no one has come, Perhaps it was a rumor, And what about the city and the traffic, asked the first blind man, remembering his own car and that of the taxi driver who had driven him to the doctor's office and had helped him to dig the grave, Traffic is in a state of chaos, replied the old man with the black eye patch, and gave details of specific cases of accidents. When, for the first time, a bus driver was suddenly struck by blindness as he was driving his vehicle on a public road, despite the casualties and injuries resulting from the disaster, people did not pay much attention for the same reason, that is to say, out of force of habit, and the director of public relations of the transportion company felt able to declare, without further ado, that the disaster had been caused by human error, regrettable no doubt, but, all things considered, as unforeseeable as a heart attack in the case of someone who had never suffered from a heart complaint. Our employees, explained the director, as well as the mechanical and electrical parts of our buses, are periodically subjected to rigorous checks, as can be seen, showing a direct and clear relation of cause and effect, in the extremely low percentage of accidents in which, generally speaking, our company's vehicles have been involved. This labored explanation appeared in the newspapers, but people had more on their minds than worrying about a simple bus accident, after all, it would have been no worse if its brakes had failed. Moreover, two days later, this was precisely the cause of another accident, but the world being what it is, where truth often has to masquerade as falsehood to achieve its ends, the rumor went round that the driver had gone blind. There was no way of convincing the public of what had in fact happened, and the outcome was soon evident, from one moment to the next people stopped using buses, they said they would rather go blind themselves than die because others had gone blind. A third accident, soon afterward and for the same reason, involving a vehicle that was carrying no passengers, gave rise to comment such as the following, couched in a knowingly popular tone, That could have been me. Nor could they imagine, those who spoke like this, how right they were. When two pilots both went blind at once a commercial plane crashed and burst into flames the moment it hit the ground, killing all the passengers and crew, notwithstanding that in this case, the mechanical and electrical equipment were in perfect working order, as the black box, the only survivor, would later reveal. A tragedy of these dimensions was not the same as an ordinary bus accident, the result being that those who still had any illusions soon lost them, from then on engine noises were no longer heard and no wheel, large or small, fast or slow, was ever to turn again. Those people who were previously in the habit of complaining about the ever-increasing traffic problems, pedestrians who, at first sight, appeared not to know where they were going because the cars, stationary or moving, were constantly impeding their progress, drivers who having gone round the block countless times before finally finding a place to park their car, became pedestrians and started protesting for the same reason, after having first voiced their own complaints, all of them must now be content, except for the obvious fact that, since there was no one left who dared to drive a vehicle, not even to get from *a* to *b*, the cars, trucks, motorbikes, even the bicycles, were scattered chaotically throughout the entire city, abandoned wherever fear had gained the upper hand over any sense of propriety, as evidenced by the grotesque sight of a tow truck with a car suspended from the front axle, probably the first man to turn blind had been the truck driver. The situation was bad for everyone, but for those stricken with blindness it was catastrophic, since, according to the current expression, they could not see where they were putting their feet. It was pitiful to watch them bumping into the abandoned cars, one after the other, bruising their shins, some fell, pleading, Is there anyone who can help me to my feet, but there were also those who, naturally brutish or made so by despair, cursed and fought off any helping hand that came to their assistance, Leave me alone, your turn will come soon enough, then the compassionate person would take fright and make a quick escape, disappear into that dense white mist, suddenly conscious of the risk to which their kindness had exposed them, perhaps to go blind only a few steps further on.

That's how things are out there, the old man with the black eye patch concluded his account, and I don't know everything, I can only speak of what I was able to see with my own eyes, here he broke off, paused and corrected himself, Not with my eyes, because I only had one, now not even that, well, I still have it but it's no use to me, I've never asked you why you didn't have a glass eye instead of wearing that patch, And why should I have wanted to, tell me that, asked the old man with the black eye patch, It's normal because it looks better, besides it's much more hygienic, it can be removed, washed and replaced like dentures, Yes sir, but tell me what it would be like today if all those who now find themselves blind had lost, I say physically lost, both their eyes, what good would it do them now to be walking around with two glass eyes, You're right, no good at all, With all of us ending up blind, as appears to be happening, who's interested in aesthetics, and as for hygiene, tell me, doctor, what kind of hygiene could you hope for in this place, Perhaps only in a world of the blind will things be what they truly are, said the doctor, And what about people, asked the girl with dark glasses, People, too, no one will be there to see them, An idea has just occured to me, said the old man with the black eye patch, let's play a game to pass the time, How can we play a game if we cannot see what we are playing, asked the wife of the first blind man, Well, not a game exactly, each of us must say what we saw at the moment we went blind, That could be embarassing, someone pointed out, Those who do not wish to take part in the game can remain silent, the important thing is that no one should try to invent anything, Give us an example, said the doctor, Certainly, replied the old man with the black eye patch, I went blind when I was looking at my blind eye, What do you mean, It's very simple, I felt as if the inside of the empty orbit was inflamed and I removed the patch to satisfy my curiosity and just at that moment I went blind, It sounds like an allegory, said an unknown voice, the eye that refuses to acknowledge its own absence, As for me, said the doctor, I was at home consulting some reference books on ophthalmology, precisely because of what is happening, the last thing I saw were my hands resting on a book, My final image was different, said the doctor's wife, the inside of an ambulance as I was helping my husband to get in, I've already explained to the doctor what happened to me, said the first blind man, I had stopped at the lights, the signal was red, there were people crossing the street from one side to the other, at that very moment I turned blind, then that fellow who died the other day took me home, obviously I couldn't see his face, As for me, said the wife of the first blind man, the last thing I can remember seeing was my handkerchief, I was sitting at home and crying my heart out, I raised the handkerchief to my eyes and went blind that very moment, In my case, said the girl from the doctor's office, I had just got into the elevator, I stretched out my hand to press the button and suddenly stopped seeing, you can imagine my distress, trapped in there and all alone, I didn't know whether I would go up or down, and I couldn't find the button to open the door, My situation, said the pharmacist's assistant, was simpler, I heard that people were going blind, then I began to wonder what it would be like if I too were to go blind, I closed my eyes to try it and when I opened them I was blind, Sounds like another allegory, interrupted the uknown voice, if you want to be blind, then blind you will be. They remained silent. The other blind internees had gone back to their beds, no easy task, for while it is true that they knew their respective numbers, only by starting to count from one end of the ward, from one upwards or from twenty downwards, could they be certain of arriving where they wanted to be.

When the murmur of their counting, as monotonous as a litany, died away, the girl with dark glasses related what had happened to her, I was in a hotel room with a man lying on top of me, at that point she fell silent, she felt too ashamed to say what she was doing there, that she had seen everything white, but the old man with the black eye patch asked, And you saw everything white, Yes, she replied, Perhaps your blindness is different from ours, said the old man with the black eye patch. The only person still to speak was the chambermaid, I was making a bed, a certain person had gone blind there, I held the white sheet up before me and spread it out, tucked it in at the sides as one does, and I was smoothing it out with both hands, suddenly I could no longer see, I remember how I was smoothing the sheet out, very slowly, it was the bottom sheet, she added, as if this had some special significance. . . .

Then the old man with the black eye patch asked, How many blind persons are needed to make a blindness, No one could provide the answer. The girl with dark glasses asked him to switch on the radio, there might be some news. They gave the news later, meanwhile they listened to a little music. At a certain point some blind internees appeared in the doorway of the ward, one of them said, What a pity no one thought of bringing a guitar. The news was not very encouraging, a rumor was going around that the formation of a government of unity and national salvation was imminent.

When, at the beginning, the blind internees in this ward could still be counted on ten fingers, when an exchange of two or three words was enough to convert strangers into companions in misfortune, and with another three or four words they could forgive each other all their faults, some of them really quite serious, and if a complete pardon was not forthcoming, it was simply a question of being patient and waiting for a few days, then it became all too clear how many absurd afflictions the poor wretches had to suffer, each time their bodies demanded to be urgently relieved or as we say, to satisfy their needs. Despite this, and although knowing that perfect manners are somewhat rare and that even the most discreet and modest natures have their weak points, it has to be conceded that the first blind people to be brought here under quarantine, were capable, more or less conscientiously, of bearing with dignity the cross imposed by the eminently scatological nature of the human species. Now, with all the beds occupied, all two hundred and forty, not counting the blind inmates who have to sleep on the floor, no imagination, however fertile and creative in making comparisons, images and metaphors, could aptly describe the filth here. It is not just the state to which the lavatories were soon reduced, fetid caverns such as the gutters in hell full of condemned souls must be, but also the lack of respect shown by some of the inmates or the sudden urgency of others that turned the corridors and other passageways into latrines, at first only occasionally but now as a matter of habit. The careless or impatient thought, It doesn't matter, no one can see me, and they went no further. When it became impossible in any sense, to reach the lavatories, the blind internees began using the yard as a place to relieve themselves and clear their bowels. Those who were delicate by nature or upbringing spent the whole day restraining themselves, they put up with it as best they could until nightfall, they presumed it would be night when most people were asleep in the wards, then off they would go, clutching their stomachs or squeezing their legs together, in search of a foot or two of clean ground, if there was any amidst that endless carpet of trampled excrement, and, to make matters worse, in danger of getting lost in the infinite space of the yard, where there were no guiding signs other than the few trees whose trunks had managed to survive the mania for exploration of the former inmates, and also the slight mounds, now almost flattened, that barely covered the dead. Once a day, always in the late afternoon, like an alarm clock set to go off at the same hour, the voice over the loudspeaker would repeat the familiar instructions and prohibitions, insist on the advantages of making regular use of cleansing products, reminded the inmates that there was a telephone in each ward in order to request the necessary supplies whenever they ran out, but what was really needed there was a powerful jet from a hose to wash away all that shit, then an army of plumbers to repair the sewer lines and get them working again, then water, lots of water, to wash the waste down the pipes where it belongs, then, we beseech you, eyes, a pair of eyes, a hand capable of leading and guiding us, a voice that will say to me, This way. These blind internees, unless we come to their assistance, will soon turn into animals, worse still, into blind animals. . . . The person saying it, though in other words, late at

82

night, is the doctor's wife lying beside her husband, their heads under the same blanket, A solution has to be found for this awful mess, I can't stand it and I can't go on pretending that I can't see, Think of the consequences, they will almost certainly try to turn you into their slave, a general drudge, you will be at the beck and call of everyone, they will expect you to feed them, wash them, put them to bed and get them up in the morning and have you take them from here to there, blow their noses and dry their tears, they will call out for you when you are asleep, insult you if you keep them waiting, How can you of all people expect me to go on looking at these miseries, to have them permanently before my eyes, and not lift a finger to help, You're already doing more than enough, What use am I, when my main concern is that no one should find out that I can see, Some will hate you for seeing, don't think that blindness has made us better people, It hasn't made us any worse, We're on our way though, just look at what happens when it's time to share out the food, Precisely, someone who can see could supervise the distribution of food to all those who are here, share it out with impartiality, with common sense, there would be no more complaints, these constant arguments that are driving me mad would cease, you have no idea what it is like to watch two blind people fighting, Fighting has always been, more or less, a form of blindness, This is different, do what you think best, but don't forget what we are here, blind, simply blind, blind people with no fine speeches or commiserations, the charitable, picturesque world of the little blind orphans is finished, we are now in the harsh, cruel, implacable kingdom of the blind, If only you could see what I am obliged to see, you would want to be blind, I believe you, but there's no need, because I'm already blind, Forgive me, my love, if you only knew, I know, I know, I've spent my life looking into people's eyes, it is the only part of the body where a soul might still exist and if those eyes are lost, Tomorrow I'm going to tell them I can see, Let's hope you won't live to regret it, Tomorrow I'll tell them, she paused then added, Unless by then I, too, have finally entered their world.

But it was not to be just yet. When she woke up next morning, very early as usual, her eyes could see as clearly as before. All the blind internees, in the ward were asleep. She wondered how she should tell them, whether she should gather them all together and announce the news, perhaps it might be preferable to do it in a discreet manner, without ostentation, to say, for example, as if not wishing to treat the matter too seriously, Just imagine, who would have thought that I would keep my sight amongst so many who have turned blind, or whether, perhaps more wisely, pretend that she really had been blind and had suddenly regained her sight, it might even be a way of giving the others some hope. If she can see again, they would say to each other, perhaps we will, too, on the other hand, they might tell her, If that's the case, then get out, be off with you, whereupon she would reply that she could not leave the place without her husband, and since the army would not release any blind person from quarantine, there was nothing for it but to allow her to stay. Some of the blind internees were stirring in their beds and, as every morning, they were relieving themselves of wind, but this did not make the atmosphere any more nauseating, saturation point must already have been reached. It was not just the fetid smell that came from the lavatories in gusts that made you want to throw up, it was also the accumulated body odor of two hundred and fifty people, whose bodies were steeped in their own sweat, who were neither able nor knew how to wash themselves, who wore clothes that got filthier by the day, who slept in beds where they had frequently defecated. What use would soaps, bleach, detergents be, abandoned somewhere around the place, if many of the showers were blocked or had become detached from the pipes, if the drains overflowed with the dirty water that spread outside the washrooms, soaking the floorboards in the corridors, infiltrating the cracks in the flagstones. What madness is this to think of interfering, the doctor's wife began to reflect, even if they were not to demand that I should be at their service, and nothing is less certain, I myself would not be able to stand it without setting about washing and cleaning for as long as I had the strength, this is not a job for one person. Her courage which before had seemed so resolute, began to crumble, to gradually desert her when confronted with the abject reality that invaded her nostrils and offended her eyes, now that the moment had come to pass from words to actions. I'm a coward, she murmured in exasperation, it would have been better to be blind than go around like some fainthearted missionary. Three blind internees had got up, one of them was the pharmacist's assistant, they were about to take up their positions in the hallway to collect the allocation of food intended for the first ward. It could

84

not be claimed, given their lack of eyesight, that the distribution was made by eye, one container more, one container less, on the contrary, it was pitiful to see how they got muddled over the counting and had to start all over again, someone with a more suspicious nature wanted to know exactly what the others were carrying, arguments always broke out in the end, the odd shove, a slap for the blind women, as was inevitable. In the ward everyone was now awake, ready to receive their ration, with experience they had devised a fairly easy system of distribution, they began by carrying all the food to the far end of the ward, where the doctor and his wife had their beds as well as the girl with dark glasses and the boy who was calling for his mummy, and that is where the inmates went to fetch their food, two at a time, starting from the beds nearest the entrance, number one on the right, number one on the left, number two on the right, number two on the left, and so on and so forth, without any ill-tempered exchanges or jostling, it took longer, it is true, but keeping the peace made the waiting worthwhile. The first, that is to say, those who had the food right there within arm's reach, were the last to serve themselves, except for the boy with the squint, of course, who always finished eating before the girl with dark glasses received her portion, so that part of what should have been hers invariably finished up in the boy's stomach. All the blind internees had their heads turned toward the door, hoping to hear footsteps of their fellow-inmates, the faltering, unmistakable sound of someone carrying something, but this was not the noise that could suddenly be heard but rather that of people running swiftly, were such a feat possible for people who could not see where they were putting their feet. Yet how else could you describe it when they appeared panting for breath at the door. What could have happened out there to send them running in here, and there were the three of them trying to get through the door at the same time to give the unexpected news, They wouldn't allow us to bring the food, said one of them, and the other two repeated his words, They wouldn't allow us, Who, the soldiers, asked some voice or other, No, the blind internees, What blind internees, we're all blind here, We don't know who they are, said the pharmacist's assistant, but I think they must belong to the group that all arrived together, the last group to arrive, And what's this about not allowing you to bring the food, asked the doctor, so far there has never been any problem, They say all that's over, from now on anyone who wants to eat will have to pay. Protests came from all sides of the ward, It cannot be, They've taken away our food, The thieves, A disgrace, the blind against the blind, I never thought I'd live to see anything like this, Let's go and complain to the sergeant. Someone more resolute proposed that they should all go together to demand what was rightfully theirs, It won't be easy, said the pharmacist's assistant, there are lots of them, I had the clear impression they form a large group, and the worst is that they are armed, What do you mean by armed, At the very least they have cudgels, this arm of mine still hurts from the blow I received, said one of the others, Let's try and settle this peacefully, said the doctor, I'll go with you to speak to these people, there must be some misunderstanding, Of course, doctor, you have my support, said the pharmacist's assistant, but from the way they're behaving, I very much doubt that you will be able to persuade them, Be that as it may, we have to go there, we cannot leave things like this, I'm coming with you, said the doctor's wife. The tiny group left the ward except for the one who was complaining about his arm, he felt that he had done his duty and stayed behind to relate to the others his hazardous adventure, their food rations two paces away, and a human wall to defend them, With cudgels, he insisted.

Advancing together, like a platoon, they forced their way through the blind inmates from the other wards. When they reached the hallway, the doctor's wife realized at once that no diplomatic conversation would be possible, and probably never likely to be. In the middle of the hallway, surrounding the containers of food, a circle of blind inmates armed with sticks and metal rods from the beds, pointing outwards like bayonets or lances, confronted the desperation of the blind inmates who were surrounding them and making awkward attempts to force their way through the line of defense, some with the hope of finding an opening, a gap someone had been careless enough not to close properly, they warded off the blows with raised arms, others crawled along on all fours until they bumped into the legs of their adversaries who repelled them with a blow to their backs or a vigorous kick. Hitting out blindly, as the saying goes. These scenes were accompanied by indignant protests, furious cries, We demand our food, We have a right to eat, Rogues, This is outrageous, Incredible though it may seem, there was one ingenuous or distracted soul who said, Call the police, perhaps there were some policemen amongst them, blindness, as everyone knows, has no regard for professions or occupations, but a policeman struck blind is not the same as a blind policeman, and as for the two we knew, they are dead and, after a great deal of effort, buried. Driven by the foolish hope that some authority would restore to the mental asylum its former tranquillity, impose justice, bring back some peace of mind, a blind woman made her way as best she could to the main entrance and called out for all to hear, Help us, these rogues are trying to steal our food. The soldiers pretended not to hear, the orders the sergeant had received from a captain who had passed through on an official visit could not have been clearer, If they end up killing each other, so much the better, there will be fewer of them. The blind woman ranted and raved as mad women did in bygone days, she herself almost demented, but from sheer desperation. In the end, realizing that her pleas were futile, she fell silent, went back inside to sob her heart out and, oblivious of where she was going, she received a blow on the head that sent her to the floor. The doctor's wife wanted to run and help her up, but there was such confusion that she could not move as much as two paces. The blind internees who had come to demand their food, were already beginning to withdraw in disarray, their sense of direction completely lost, they tripped over each other, fell, got up, fell again, some did not even make any attempt, gave up, remained lying prostrate on the ground, exhausted, miserable, racked with pain, their faces pressed against the tiled floor. Then the doctor's wife, terrified, saw one of the blind hoodlums take a gun from his pocket and raise it brusquely into the air. The blast caused a large piece of stucco to come crashing down from the ceiling on to their unprotected heads, increasing the panic. The hoodlum shouted, Be quiet everyone and keep your mouths shut, if anyone dares to raise their voice, I'll shoot straight out, no matter who gets hit, then there will be no more complaints. The blind internees did not move. The fellow with the gun continued, Let it be known and there is no turning back, that from today onwards we shall take charge of the food, you've all been warned, and let no one take it into their head to go out there to look for it, we shall put guards at the entrance, and anyone who tries to go against these orders will suffer the consequences, the food will now be sold, anyone who wants to eat must pay. How are we to pay, asked the doctor's wife, I said no one was to speak, bellowed the armed hoodlum, waving his weapon before him.

Someone has to speak, we must know how we're to proceed, where are we going to fetch the food, do we all go together, or one at a time, This woman is up to something, commented one of the group, if you were to shoot her, there would be one mouth less to feed, If I could see her, she'd already have a bullet in her belly. Then addressing everyone, Go back to your wards immediately, this very minute, once we've carried the food inside, we'll decide what is to be done, And what about payment, rejoined the doctor's wife, how much shall we be expected to pay for a coffee with milk and a biscuit, She's really asking for it, that one, said the same voice, Leave her to me, said the other fellow, and changing tone, Each ward will nominate two people to be in charge of collecting people's valuables, all their valuables of whatever kind, money, jewels, rings, bracelets, earrings, watches, everything they possess, and they will take the lot to the third ward on the left, where we are accommodated, and if you want some friendly advice, don't get any ideas about trying to cheat us, we know that there are those amongst you who will hide some of your valuables, but I warn you to think again, unless we feel that you have handed in enough, you will simply not get any food and be left to chew your banknotes and munch on your diamonds. A blind man from the second ward on the right asked, And what are we to do, do we hand over everything at once, or do we pay according to what we eat, It would seem I haven't explained things clearly enough, said the fellow with the gun, laughing, first you pay, then you eat and, as for the rest, to pay according to what you've eaten would make keeping accounts extremely complicated, best to hand over everything at once and then we shall see how much food you deserve, but let me warn you again, don't try to conceal anything for it will cost you dear, and lest anyone accuse us of not proceeding honestly, note that after handing over whatever you possess we shall carry out an inspection, woe betide you if we find so much as a penny, and now I want everybody out of here as quickly as possible. He raised his arm and fired another shot. Some more stucco crashed to the ground. And as for you, said the hoodlum with the gun, I won't forget your voice, Nor I your face, replied the doctor's wife.

No one appeared to notice the absurdity of a blind woman saying that she won't forget a face she could not see. The blind internees had already withdrawn as quickly as they could, in seach of the doors, and those from the first ward were soon informing their fellow-inmates of the situation, From what we've heard, I don't believe that for the moment we can do anything other than obey, said the doctor, there must be quite a number of them, and worst of all, they have weapons. We can arm ourselves too, said the pharmacist's assistant, Yes, some sticks cut from the trees if there are any branches left within arm's reach, some metal rods removed from our beds that we shall scarcely have strength to wield, while they have at least one firearm at their disposal, I refuse to hand over my belongings to these sons of a blind bitch, someone remarked, Nor I, joined in another, That's it, either we all hand over everything, or nobody gives anything, said the doctor, We have no alternative, said his wife, besides, the regime in here, must be the same as the one they imposed outside, anyone who doesn't want to pay can suit himself, that's his priviledge, but he'll get nothing to eat and he cannot expect to be fed at the expense of the rest of us, We shall all give up what we've got and hand over everything, said the doctor, And what about those who have nothing to give, asked the pharmacist's assistant, They will eat whatever the others decide to give them, as the saying rightly goes, from each according to his abilities, to each according to his needs. There was a pause, and the old man with the black eye patch asked, Well then, who are we going to ask to be in charge, I suggest the doctor, said the girl with the dark glasses. It was not necessary to proceed to a vote, the entire ward was in agreement. There have to be two of us, the doctor remined them, is anyone willing to offer, he asked, I'm willing, if no one else comes forward, said the first blind man, Very well, let us start collecting, we need a sack, a bag, a small suitcase, any of these things will do, I can get rid of this, said the doctor's wife, and began at once to empty a bag in which she had gathered cosmetics and other odds and ends at a time when she could never have imagined the conditions in which she was now obliged to live. Amongst the bottles, boxes, and tubes from another world, there was a pair of long, finely pointed scissors. She could not remember having put them there, but there they were. The doctor's wife raised her head. The blind internees were waiting, her husband had gone up to the bed of the first blind man, he was talking to him, the girl with the dark glasses was saying to the boy with the squint that the food would be arriving soon, on the floor, tucked behind the bedside table, was a bloodstained sanitary towel, as if the girl with dark glasses were anxious, with maidenly and pointless modesty, to hide it from the eyes of those who could not see. The doctor's wife looked at the scissors, she tried to think why she should be staring at them in this way, in what way, like this, but she could think of no reason, frankly what reason could she hope to find in a simple pair of long scissors, lying in her open hands, with its two nickel-plated blades, the tips sharp and gleaming, Do you have it there, her husband asked her, Yes, here it is, she replied, and held out the arm holding the empty bag while she put the other arm behind her back to conceal the scissors, What's the matter, asked the doctor, Nothing, replied his wife, who could just as easily have answered, Nothing you can see, my voice must have sounded strange, that's all, nothing else. Accompanied by the first blind man, the doctor moved toward her, took the bag in his hesitant hands and said, Start getting your things ready, we're about to begin collecting. His wife unclasped her watch, did the same for her husband, removed her earrings, a tiny ring set with rubies, the gold chain she wore round her neck, her wedding ring, that of her husband, both of them easy to remove, Our fingers have got thinner, she thought, she began putting everything into the bag, then the money they had brought from home, a fair amount of notes varying in value, some coins, That's everything, she said, Are you sure, said the doctor, take a careful look, That's everything we have of any value. The girl with dark glasses had already gathered together her belongings, they were not so very different, she had two bracelets instead of one, but no wedding ring. The doctor's wife waited until her husband and the first blind man had turned their backs and for the girl with dark glasses to bend down to the boy with the squint, Think of me as your mummy, she was saying, I'll pay for us both, and then she withdrew to the wall at the far end. There, as all along the other walls, there were large nails sticking out that must have been used by the mad to hang treasures and other baubles. She chose the highest nail she could reach, and hung the scissors there. Then she sat down on her bed. Slowly, her husband and the first blind man were heading in the direction of the door, they would stop to collect possessions on both sides from those who had something to offer, some protested that they were being robbed shamefully, and that was the honest truth, others divested themselves of their possessions with a kind of indifference, as if thinking that, all things considered, there is nothing in this world that belongs to us in an absolute sense, another all too transparent truth. When they reached the door of the ward, having finished their collection, the doctor asked, Have we handed over everything, a number of resigned voices answered yes, some chose to say nothing and in the fullness of time we shall know whether this was in order to avoid telling a lie. The doctor's wife looked up at the scissors. She was surprised to find them so far up, hanging from one of the nails, as if she herself had not put them there, then she reflected that it had been an excellent idea to bring them, now she could trim her husband's beard, make him look more presentable, since as we know, living in these conditions, it is impossible for a man to shave as normal. When she looked again in the direction of the door, the two men had already disappeared into the shadows of the corridor and were making their way to the third ward on the left, where they had been instructed to go and pay for their food. Today's food, tomorrow's as well, and perhaps for the rest of the week, And then, the question had no answer, everything we possessed will have gone in payment. . . .

Ahead there was the sound of footsteps and voices, they must be emissaries from the other wards who were complying with the same orders, What a situation we're in, doctor, said the first blind man. . . . It has been impossible ever since we came into this place, yet we go on putting up with it, You're an optimist, doctor, No, I'm not an optimist, but I cannot imagine anything worse than our present existence, Well, I'm not entirely convinced that there are limits to misfortune and evil, You may be right, said the doctor, and then, as if he were talking to himself, Something has to happen here, a conclusion that contains a certain contradiction, either there is something worse than this, after all, or, from now on, things are going to get better, although all the indications suggest otherwise. Having steadily made their way and having turned several corners, they were approaching the third ward. Neither the doctor nor the first blind man had ever ventured here, but the construction of the two wings, logically enough, had strictly adhered to a symmetrical pattern, anyone familiar with the wing on the right would have no difficulty in getting their bearings in the wing on the left, and vice-versa, you had only to turn to the left on the one side while on the other you had to turn right. They could hear voices, they must be of those ahead of them, We'll have to wait, said the doctor in a low voice, Why, Those inside will want to know precisely what these inmates are carrying, for them it is not all that important, since they have already eaten they're in no hurry, It must be almost time for lunch, Even if they could see, it would do this group no good to know it, they no longer even have watches. A quarter of an hour later, give or take a minute, the barter was over. Two men passed in front of the doctor and the first blind man, from their conversation it was apparent that they were carrying food, Careful, don't drop anything, said one of them, and the other was muttering, What I don't know is whether there will be enough for everyone. We'll have to tighten our belts. Sliding his hand along the wall, with the first blind man right behind him, the doctor advanced until his hands came into contact with the door jamb, We're from the first ward on the right, he shouted. He made as if to take a step forward, but his leg came up against an obstacle. He realized it was a bed standing crosswise, placed there to serve as a trading counter, They're organized, he thought to himself, this has not suddenly been improvised, he heard voices, footsteps, How many of them are there, his wife had mentioned ten, but it was not inconceivable that there might be many more, certainly not all of them were there when they went to get the food. The fellow with the gun was their leader, it was his jeering voice that was saying, Now, let's see what riches the first ward on the right has brought us, and then, in a much lower tone, addressing someone who must have been standing nearby, Take note. The doctor remained puzzled, what could this mean, the fellow had said, Take note, so there must be someone here who can write, someone who is not blind, so that makes two, We must be careful, he thought, tomorrow this rascal might be standing right next to us and we wouldn't even know it, this thought of the doctor's was scarcely any different from what the first blind man was thinking, With a gun and a spy, we're sunk, we shall never be able to raise our heads again. The blind man inside, the leader of thieves, had already opened the bag, with practiced hands he was lifting out, stroking, and identifying the objects and money, clearly he could make out by touch what was gold and what was not, by touch he could also tell the value of the notes and coins, easy when one is experienced, it was only after some minutes that the doctor began to hear the unmistakable sound of punching paper, which he immediately identified, there nearby was someone writing the braille alphabet, also known as anaglyptography, the sound could be heard, at once quiet and clear, of the pointer as it punched the thick paper and hit the metallic plate underneath. So there was a normal blind person among these blind delinquents, a blind person just like all those people who were once referred to as being blind, the poor fellow had obviously been roped in with all the rest, but this was not the moment to pry and start asking, are you one of the recent blind men or have you been blind for some years, tell us how you came to lose your sight. They were certainly lucky, not only had they won a clerk in the raffle, they could also use him as guide, a blind person with experience as a blind person is something else, he's worth his weight in gold. The inventory went on, now and then the thug with the gun consulted the accountant, What do you think of this, and he would interrupt his bookkeeping to give an opinion, A cheap imitation, he would say, in which case the fellow with the gun would comment, If there is a lot of this, they won't get any food, or Good stuff, and then the commentary would be, There's nothing like dealing with honest people. In the end, three containers of food were lifted onto the bed, Take this, said the armed leader. The doctor counted them, Three are not enough, we used to receive four when the food was only for us, at the same moment he felt the cold barrel of the gun against his neck, for a blind man his aim was not bad, I'll have a container removed every time you complain, now beat it, take these and thank the Lord that you've still got something to eat. The doctor murmured, Very well, grabbed two of the containers while the first blind man took charge of the third one and, much slower now, because they were laden, they retraced the route that had brought them to the ward. When they arrived in the hallway, where there did not appear to be anyone around, the doctor said, I'll never again have such an opportunity, What do you mean, asked the first blind man, He put the gun to my neck, I could have grabbed it from him, That would be risky, Not as risky as it seems, I knew where the gun was resting, he had no way of knowing where my hands were, even so, at that moment I'm convinced that he was the blinder of the two of us, what a pity I didn't think of it, or did think of it but lacked the courage, And then what, asked the first blind man, What do you mean, Let's assume you had managed to grab his weapon, I don't believe you would have been capable of using it, If I were certain it would resolve the situation, yes I would, But you're not certain, No, in fact I'm not, Then better that they should keep their arms, at least so long as they do not use them against us. To threaten someone with a gun is the same as attacking them, If you had taken his gun, the real war would have started, and in all likelihood we would never have got out of that place alive, You're right, said the doctor, I'll pretend I had thought all that through, You mustn't forget, doctor, what you told me a little while ago, What did I say, That something has to happen, It has happened and I didn't make the most of it, It has to be something else, not that.

When they entered the ward and had to present the meager amount of food they had brought to put on the table, some thought they were to blame for not having protested and demanded more, that's why they had been nominated as the representatives of the group. Then the doctor explained what had happened, he told them about the blind clerk, about the insulting behavior of the blind man with the gun, also about the gun itself. The malcontents lowered their voices, ended up by agreeing that undoubtedly the ward's interests were in the right hands. The food was finally distributed, there were those who could not resist reminding the impatient that little is better than nothing, besides, by now it must be almost time for lunch, The worst thing would be if we got to be like that famous horse that died when it had already got out of the habit of eating, someone remarked. The others gave a wan smile and one said, It wouldn't be so bad if it's true that when the horse dies, it doesn't know it's going to die.

Translated from the Portuguese by Giovanni Pontiero

PHILIP NIKOLAYEV **A Visceral Yes**

Think of all the things a noncom can do to a private.
But that still leaves room for purity.
I took a test of English as a fourteenth language.
Charity begins at home,
that's the subject of my poem!
Wild cows work my engine.
Wild daydreams arise,
surprisingly ablaze with Paris.
You wanna find yourself a moister oyster?
Yes, what's up, priceless!
Nutcracker my ass.
I wish I were a wooden peg.
I wish I were a wooden peg
in the Woodberry Poetry Room.

{ MONOLITH *of* TIME }

WALTER MURCH

PAGE 96:
Brooklyn (Architectural Fragment),
1964.

PAGE 97:
Study with Melon, Onion, and Rock,
1961.

BELOW:
Stone Capital, 1965.

PAGE 99:
Car Lock, 1962.

LEFT:
Clock Study, 1962.

RIGHT:
Clock, 1965.

Walter Murch

According to Daniel Robbins, who organized Walter Murch's first retrospective, titles for Murch's pictures were generally assigned by his dealer, Betty Parsons, or by his friend, the artist Barnett Newman, the mentor behind the scenes at Parson's gallery during the forties. I would like to think that the title, *Monolith of Time*—given to a work that dates from 1941, the year of Murch's first show with Parsons at the Wakefield Gallery—might have come from Newman, although one can't be sure. With Newman's customary brilliance and flair for the portentous, the title captures the essential thematic where the work of two affiliated but very different artists just might intersect, both of whom ponder time's vastness and history's unwinding, monumental endurance, the resistance of physical matter.

The works on paper selected for this portfolio were all made twenty to twenty-five years after *Monolith of Time*, during the last decade of Murch's life, from 1957 to 1967. They distill his visionary practice of the still life genre to which he dedicated himself almost exclusively. Consider the fragment in *Stone Capital* from 1965: shadows hover on the composition's surface like a veil shimmering over an elephantine relic, while the center of the drum crumbles like a loaf of fresh bread. Or *Study with Melon, Onion, and Rock* from 1961, where the shadows move in like an undertow, dredging up the forms as much as modeling them—especially that of the rock on the right—and then depositing them like sediment rubbed into the ground. In *Clock*, from 1965, light becomes particle-bound, like antimatter that pulverizes the clock, atomizing time.

The ground layer in these works is wondrous. Murch was known to prepare sheets of paper for drawings by submerging them in water, exposing them out of doors, even walking over them in his studio, embedding natural history into the work before he made a mark. This weathering of the support has its counterpart in his feel for surfaces. "I bought a door lock on Amsterdam Avenue for 75¢," he recalled in a speech. "I took it and opening it —it was like opening a tomb. I had the same excitement. Inside there were bits of shiny brass, grease and dust, in simply incredible shapes. I painted this, and I hope I got some of this excitement in the work itself."*

Not the lock, but the thrill of opening it, and the vagabond beauty of the phenomena it revealed—the glance of light reflected on a patch of brass, distorted by a drop of grease, absorbed in a mote of dust. And probably not the *Car Lock* from 1962 reproduced here, which in its intricacy is more like a mortuary complex than a tomb. The nuts-and-bolts gizmo clearly fascinates Murch, as does the lovely carving of the curled acanthus leaves on the stonework *Brooklyn (Architectural Fragment)* from 1964. These manufactured things excite him, almost but not quite as much as the mottled atmospheric envelope of wash and pigment that he will mobilize to fuse them pictorially, to imply their undoing in time.

The divided secular status of the still life required that material display, the subject, be morally imbued with intimations of mortality and decay, or—by bestowing dignity on ordinary objects—made immanent, graced with spiritual power. In modernism's terms, the subject of a still life arguably laid itself bare, acting out nothing more than a composition, nothing less than a metaphor for art. Murch's work is ecumenical enough to take in these traditions, speak their language, and transfigure both, the classic and the modern. This seems especially so with respect to the later works on paper, where the object is transported, delivered for our contemplation to a painterly visual field, still luminous with Murch's excitement.

Neil Printz

---

* Walter Murch, quoted by Judy Collischan Van Wagner in *Walter Murch: Paintings and Drawings*, Hillwood Art Gallery, Long Island University, New York, 1986, p.13.

The Truth is a Seven-Headed Animal

She was a shadow lost in a flooded world. We still don't know her name or where she lives. Some say the poor woman's from a hole in the wall in the ragged Colinas district; others have seen her roaming the alleys of the Céu neighborhood, and God only knows whether she's a daughter of the city or the jungle. They say she tried to check into Santa Casa Hospital, but the security guard shooed her away and she was caught in a fierce downpour in the middle of Praça São Sebastião. The church was closed, the square deserted, house fronts silent. Somehow it all seemed linked to the dread that comes with the December rainy season here in Manaus. She must have felt the first contractions as she wandered the square outside our majestic Opera House. We can imagine her eyes searching for someone to help her, but there was not a living soul in sight. Rather than struggling with the stairs, she dragged herself up the nearest ramp to the entrance, somehow managed to pull open the massive wooden doors, and crawled inside.

The Opera House was empty. Now and again a sudden flash of light would scratch the window and a rumble boom down from the sky like a warning. Hauling herself along, the woman plunged into a shadowy place where nothing—except her damp body and wet hair—recalled the wet tumult outside. She found herself in the Opera House auditorium, where a sloping aisle led her down near the stage. She lay down on the velvety red between the rows, waiting for the propitious moment to give birth.

Maybe it was the thunder's crack that broke the silence reigning over the refuge—no one knows for certain what set the chandeliers that dangled from the high dome to swaying. We do know, however, that the disturbance registered in a small attic room where, stretched in a hammock, the self-proclaimed watchman of the Opera House lay drifting far from the world.

Álvaro Celestino de Matos—a taciturn 87-year-old with the accent of an immigrant from the Minho region of Portugal—woke with a start. There it was again—the strange noise he'd imagined he'd been dreaming: the voice of a singer from a distant night in childhood. He floated for a while in that shifting place where sleep and dream mysteriously merge, unsure whether what he heard was a product of the storm or of a certain Thursday in 1910: the famous day—still crystal in memory—when as a boy he had waxed and waxed the stage, lovingly preparing it to receive the precious feet of Angiolina Zanuchi, Soprano.

Nothing, or almost nothing, had changed about his modest room since that day: conspicuous on the wall beside the window was a photograph of the singer descending the gangplank of the Queen Elizabeth. But it was impossible to look at the photograph without also taking in the view out the window: a single church spire with a belfry and a bell as regular as the rain— until nightfall, when the silhouette of the church faded and a lunar disk appeared in the center of the window. These two images—the picture of the soprano and the profile of the Church of São Sebastião—were unalterably linked in both vision and memory. For how many years had he been gazing at them before sleep—sixty, seventy? He would drift off with those two images in his head, and on waking the first thing he'd do was to light the kerosene lamp, so that a flame lit up Angiolina's face beside the moon-flooded landscape.

Yesterday, when Seu Álvaro opened his eyes, the view from his window looked like an aquarium full of brownish water, and the contours of the singer's face had disappeared; only the broadside of the ship emerged from the murk of his attic room. The watchman wasn't sure in this lingering night whether the sound he heard was a human voice or the chords of a piano, but it no longer belonged to sleep or dream. It seemed to come from a long way off, probably from inside the Opera House, down below.

For a man approaching his nineties, the distance from the attic to the ground floor was practically an abyss. This did not discourage him. He decided to brave the journey armed with his Winchester, which had intimidated countless men and brought down countless animals in times past. Now, almost the same height as his stooped frame, the rifle served as a cane.

The descent was slow and arduous, but it wasn't fatigue that set him to shaking the moment he stepped onto the carpeted ground floor. Seu Álvaro realized that this sudden trembling had nothing to do with age; instinct told him that something ominous was about to happen this rainy morning. Was the half-open entryway door a sign of an intruder? He glanced out at the monument. Of the four bronze boats, only one was visible, seemingly adrift in the center of the square, and the wings of a submerged angel looked like an anchor floating free in space. Pushing the door fully open with the butt of the gun, the watchman noticed a red stain that trailed along the floor and disappeared into the auditorium. Choosing another route, he turned down one of the side corridors: a winding wall of doors that gave onto the main floor boxes. He had decided to slip into the seventh box and was already turning the doorknob when he heard the sound again—odder now, more threatening. And so he stood and waited a few seconds, and this moment of hesitation—the anxiety of an old man?—caused him to change his mind. Turning away from the door, a strange sensation led him to the backstage area. There he found a safe haven on the stage, with the painted canvas curtain separating him from the concert hall itself.

Wary but not unsteady—his past, his profession, and perhaps his rifle all helping to keep him calm—the watchman felt his way along the closest wall and found, among the spider webs, a wooden handle. He yanked it upwards. A thread of light shot toward him through a hole in the curtain, which glowed with sudden brightness from the other side. The watchman could well envision the shapes and colors of the immense paintings now visible in the hall: herons and storks surrounded by white lilies and other aquatic flowers, and a water nymph reclining on a shell that floated atop the "Meeting of the Waters" of the Rio Negro and the Rio Amazonas. Seu Álvaro moved up to the curtain, bringing his right eye directly to the hole, and shivered when he realized that the ring of light coincided with the water nymph's outlined navel. Steadying himself on his rifle, he scanned the hall, searching for the source of the noise that had awoken him. It was disheartening, somehow, to find the hall deserted, chandeliers and upholstery dusty, plaster busts of Bach and Shubert—in past times honored by famous pianists—lusterless.

Today the hall looked utterly abandoned, the boxes empty. . .until that one wide-open eye detected a shadow—perhaps a body?—down front near the stage. For the first time the watchman was a little afraid. He put on his glasses, bringing the hall into a clearer focus: more of his old friends, busts of Carlos Gomes, Racine, and Molière. And, there in a front row seat, the glistening body of a dark-haired woman.

The watchman lurched back from the curtain and stood there, imagining the painting on the other side: the water nymph lying on her shell, almost naked, a white and luxuriant body accented by the light. Then he touched his right hand to the curtain and gently caressed the nymph's belly; the roughness of the canvas on his skin jolted him into remembering that it really was a painting. He lined his eye up with the hole in the curtain again: the woman had crossed her legs. Her hair hung down over her breasts. From this distance he couldn't make out the expression on her face, but the eyes seemed large, almond-shaped maybe. Her posture, demeanor? That body was simply a body. Not more than twenty years old, he thought to himself, as the woman leaned back in her chair, cradling a baby in her arms. She enfolded the infant tenderly, and, when she opened her mouth, he expected a voice or a song; but it was merely a yawn. Then the woman began licking the baby's face, her lips and tongue gleaming in the light from the chandelier. As if in a dream, the hall suddenly went black, just like that. The watchman closed his eyes and struck the floor several times impatiently with his rifle. As the noise echoed through the theater, he guffawed once, then smiled at himself. Giving in fully to laughter, he didn't notice the loss of his gun until he staggered and fell to his knees. Two men dressed in white dragged him downstage through the gloom and deposited him in the middle of some old scenery: a small room with wooden walls and a single window that framed a church spire and belfry in a sky bright with tin foil stars, with a cardboard moon hung in the air like a mobile. One of the nurses flicked a light on and lunged at Seu Álvaro when he tried to climb into the hammock that was part of the old set. He was breathing heavily, his eyes never wavering from a certain spot on the curtain, as if to drill through to the front row seat just on the other side.

Night had fallen by the time they arrived at the Estrada de Flores Mental Hospital. We found him lying on a straw mattress. His hands were shaking badly, but on his wrinkled face he wore an enigmatic smile. Raspy-voiced and somber, he related what had happened yesterday morning in the Opera House. Dr. S.L., the psychiatrist on duty, stated that Senhor de Mato's declaration was consistent with that of a man who had for some time been suffering the swamp of senility. Before hospitalization, his nomad's life had followed the course of the seasons: in summer, dawn would find him in one of the bronze boats of the monument in the Praça São Sebastião, where he spent hours contemplating the statue of a woman. During the rainy season, he took refuge in the abandoned scenery of the Opera House, where he'd been found on several occasions, either singing or staring at one of the seats in the front of the hall.

One particular element in the former watchman's story caught our attention. In one of his pockets, the doctor found a very old photograph of a woman and a boy holding hands. The woman's fleshy body under her tight skirt, two plumpish arms, a fan clasped in her left hand—all of this is clearly visible in the picture. But the upper section of the photograph is blotchy, worn, making the woman's face unrecognizable. Could she be Angiolina, the alleged heartthrob of the watchman in his adolescence? Our archives confirm that "the divine Milanese soprano," as she was proclaimed by the citizenry, did in fact make a visit to Manaus on a December night in the year 1910.

Another hypothesis, suggested by Dr. S.L., proposes that the woman in the photograph is a local Amazonian pianist known to have given several recitals during the time Seu Álvaro worked as a watchman at the Opera House. Who could forget the story of how she later drowned not far from the "Meeting of the Waters"? Her last concert, *Sunrise Sonata in F Minor*, also looms large in the memory of the whole city, though no doubt recalled with greatest intensity by that boy, now so ancient.

Senhor de Mato's psychological condition remains undiagnosed. Will he turn out to be merely a mythomaniac? Simply suffering from somniloquy? A victim of a crisis of delirium tremens? What he saw, or said he saw—will it prove to have been lunatic delusions? A resident of the Praça São Sebastião swears that she saw a pregnant woman dragging herself into the Opera House. Yesterday's thunderous downpour didn't cause her to veer from her course for a minute, said our informant, who, we should point out, is a regular reader of this weekly column, *The Truth is a Seven-Headed Animal.*

Translated from the Portuguese by Ellen Doré Watson

107

Funerals in our village are short and to the point.
While the mourners are finding their seats
Etta Andrews plays "Now the Day Is Over."
No one is ashamed to wipe his or her eyes.
Then the Reverend stands up and reads
the Lord's Prayer with the mourners
speaking it with him. Then there is a hymn,
usually "Rock of Ages" or one chosen by
the wife of the deceased. The deceased,
I might say, is never present, except for
an urn prepared by Mr. Torrant, who is
always squinting. Next there are remarks
by the Reverend. He is a kind man and
can be relied upon to say something nice
about the life of the departed, no matter
how much he may have been scorned or even
disliked.

The Reverend's eulogies are so much the
same, with appropriate readings from Scripture,
that I gave up listening to them years ago,
instead, unheard, I eulogize myself,
the real picture of how I've been in
the village. I admit that I was self-satisfied
and arrogant. I didn't go to much pains
to provide diversions for my wife. When
the children and grandchildren came for visits
I lectured them and pointed out their faults.

I made appropriate contributions to the
local charities but without much enthusiasm.
I snubbed people who bored me and avoided
parties. I was considerate to the people
who worked in the post office. I complained
a great deal about my ailments. When I'm
asked how I'm doing, I reply that I'm
not getting any younger. This inveterate
response has become a bore in the village.

After the Reverend's eulogy is over
there is another hymn, and the benediction.
As they leave, everyone, except me, presses
the flesh of the bereaved with appropriate
utterances. But I get away as quickly as
I can. If they don't bore me I like
almost all the people in the village.
But as they go, I tick them off. I've
been to at least fifty funerals. When
will mine be?

Illness

is a kind of prison in which the doctor
is the warden and the nurses are the guards.
There are no bars on the windows. It's not a
gloomy place; flowers make it bright and
cheerful. No court jury sets the length of
the sentences. That decision rests with
the warden, who prides himself on his
humanity. There are rules in his mind
which often seem arbitrary or confusing
to the prisoners. They can never tell
how long their incarceration will last.
It can be only a few days or it can be
a month or two. And there are some
prisoners who are never released at all;
dangerous cases. It is whispered on the
wards that they end up in the morgue.
I'm hoping that my stay will be short.
Though my cell is the most comfortable
I've ever had it's hard to bear or understand
Why I'm in it.

AND HOW COME I REMEMBER NOW . . .

one day he said something, I recall, something about women, no, no, you women he said, and I was offended, angry, don't be angry he said, obviously you want to yell again, but hush and listen, I am sick and tired of all this yelling he said, and I don't know why I agreed to remain quiet then, I shouldn't have when he said you women, but I did something stupid, just as I have all my life, had I not been this stupid I would not have let his father in, may God bless his soul, may he rest in peace, the poor man, the only one who truly loved me, and I didn't marry him, couldn't marry him, that cursed accident took him from me, had I not been stupid neither would I have married Reshit, that is, if the thing, if he had not happened, who knows, I could have been better off, no, perhaps worse off, still, all on account of him, all because I loved him, because I was madly attached to him even before he was born, from the first time I felt him inside, kicking, for him I accepted the pastry man's hand and he shuts me off, attempts to silence me, even though it was impossible for him not to love me, even though I knew it was impossible for him not to love me, even though he knew he could find no other woman, or even another man, ever to love him more than I do, he gave me grief, shut me off, how I agreed to remain silent that day, how I didn't kick him out of the room, how I didn't cast myself in the sea, and he says you women, you women, as if I were just any woman, you women, when you get attached to something you get blind and don't see any flaw even if it hits you in the eye, you don't see, he says, I am not saying you can't see, I am not saying you pretend not to see, I am saying you don't see, you don't because you're blind, he says, supposedly I didn't see his flaws, as if I didn't see his flaws, as if I didn't silence my heart and take in each day like poison and spend sleepless nights, and I'd still stay quiet, say nothing, was it because I didn't see his flaws, of course I pretended not to see, and he knew it too, and still he dares to say, I am not saying you pretend not to see, I am saying you don't see, because if you had the eye to see you wouldn't be a woman he says, for him to call me woman, to call his mother woman, after I carried him in my womb and endured everything just for him, of course I am a woman, I am but I shouldn't be in his eyes, besides, what's left of the woman ever since he took shape in my womb, you don't see because you're blind, he says, yes, those days are gone, gone and over with, far away from me, distances came between us, between our bodies, our rooms, our meals, between our warmth, even though he has no one else besides me and I have no one else besides him, even though we seemingly lived slept woke up in the same house, he distanced himself from me and then one day, out of nowhere he returned, our paths crossed again, you know how they tell of rats abandoning a sinking ship, just like that, everybody apparently abandoned him, and when he was left all alone I came to his mind, perhaps he realized he was falling ill, my baby returned to me, my goodness, I had not thought of this until now, I thought he became ill when he returned and saw me, I thought he couldn't bear the fact that he had to come back to me, I thought he couldn't stand me, it never occured to me, forgive me God, forgive me for wronging my son, I don't know perhaps I am mistaken but, no, I am certain, certain that he knew he was falling ill, he sensed he was falling ill and returned to me, and I tried to show him I was hurt, it's my fault, my sin, dear God forgive me, I totally forgot him, was seized by my womanness, my eyes grew blind, I didn't see what I should have seen, what I should have been able to see, he was right perhaps, he, too, was right but, forgive me dear God, I still can't get it out of my mind that he fell ill as soon as he returned to me, I say illness even when talking to myself, I don't want to let any word besides illness cross my mind and what he had was an illness, his mind got all scrambled, he went mad, he was afraid to go out on the street, they'll kill me, he was saying, don't you hear the voices, the uproar, he was saying, there is a war going on outside God is punishing the world he has released the devil to punish the world all men will die I don't want to die only the pregnant women will survive and bear children but not all are good women not all are good but the children ought to be good and they will defeat the devil and recover the path to God become men loved by God the women won't die, my God, how his words still ring in my ears, as if he were saying them by my ear just now, then the guns and cannons slowly hushed, and he calmed down, no longer anxious, dear God, he was saying, no one besides the children can find you any more, no one besides the children whose eyes are not sullied by the foul earth can reach you, by then he was walking around the house, we didn't keep him in bed, but whenever someone came by, as soon as he heard the doorbell ring, he'd run to his room, lock his door and stay inside, in those times I'd be seized by fear, though I knew he wouldn't answer if I knocked on his door, so I'd peek through the keyhole, see him crouched in one corner, sitting on the floor, I'd given up hope for his recovery, forgive me dear God, I had given up on you as well, forgive me, forgive me,

later he kept rambling about glasses, wherever he saw glasses he would break them, saying that the blind had no use for glasses, then one day he asked for his own glasses, you broke them I told him but he couldn't remember, how did I break them, mommy, he asked, I realized then that he'd recovered from his illness, I thanked You, dear God, again You had taken me by my hand and lifted me, I prostrated myself, dear God, forgive me, when I saw he no longer hated me, I didn't know what to do out of joy, so I was blind, I was truly blind not to see that he didn't hate me, it was illness that had overtaken him, that's why he had acted so, he had started quarreling as soon as he had returned to me, he would call me mother and then fight me, then he got ill, then recovered, but he left me again, five streets came between us, this time five streets and thirty-nine doors, he comes by and I also go to him but he doesn't want to move back home, when he visits he doesn't even go near his room, as though his madness is locked in the room and waiting for him, he is afraid of the room, of its door even, but what matters is he is calm now, he stays in his place, writes and reads, works too, comes by every month, saying, dear mother, here is your money, and leaves me something, I am happy, happy that he is well, he leaves the money, doesn't stay long, asks me when I'd visit him, I tell him when and his face lights up, though I don't want to trouble him with frequent visits, and he still calls me when I delay going, dear God, why couldn't he move back in, he'd even have a different room, the house is mine after all, it's Reshit's greatest gift to me,

114

it provides me with enough income to go on living, may God bless his soul, Reshit was plenty good to me, true, I am speaking ill of him, though much of my life's burden is also on account of him, in any case, no reason to talk of Reshit yet,

he doesn't want to come back now, but I wait, hope that he'll come some day, he'll grow tired, exhausted, of everything and then return to me, full of dejection but no longer ill, my God will forgive and send him back to me, full of dejection he'll arrive and my arms will still be open, he knows how I wait for him, he knows he knows he knows,

how come I remember now that day, I still can't forget his words, and I just remember on whose account we got to fighting, on account of his friend, he used to prefer his worthless friend over me, perhaps he still does but he no longer comes to talk to me about those he loves, probably he thinks I am not jealous any more, he no longer taunts me with every one of his affairs, he used to, he now thinks I've given up being jealous, whereas I am still, I am still jealous, how can I not be jealous of all his friends and lovers, all those with whom I must share his love, but when have I made it known to him, whatever I told him I told out of concern for him, how could I agree to his falling in love with just any man, when I was able to like at the most one or two among them, besides, didn't all abandon him, did any one of them visit when he was ill, besides, none ever loved him, he loved, burned, lost sleep, tried all he could for them, ruined his days and nights in their name, having them around was enough for him, he never wanted to be loved, didn't I know this also, but now he no longer tells me anything, peace, he says now and then, peace, he says and smiles, if he could also learn being loved, back then he used to tell me, you're jealous, shame on you, he'd tell me, when I wouldn't admit even to myself that I was jealous, how he dared to utter those words, saying, all you women, so this was our flaw, true, we wouldn't want our loved one to be flawed, and if he were, we would overlook his flaw, but, no, he said, we were blind and that's why we wouldn't see, I disagreed that day, I told him that one woman can see truths better than ten men can, he refused to believe, he didn't understand, besides, he never listened to me back then, then again, when did he ever want to, he used to do all the talking, and if I ever attempted to say something, he'd quickly want to cut me off, of course, I wouldn't mince my words, when I'd tell him you're

115

angry because I am telling the truth, he'd blow his top, spew every which word that reached his mouth and poison the day for both of us, besides, when did I ever tell him something false, when did I ever say anything uncalled for, but obviously he couldn't stand hearing the truth, they all wanted me to tell lies, all my life, first his father and I lived a life of lies, and how hard I tried to keep him from discovering, from hearing about the lies, if it were up to me, I wouldn't even want him to talk to others, but Reshit, and the poor man really tried to be a father to him, and how he loved him, and Mushfik, too, almost respected him, though not once did he give him a hug, smile at him or call him father, not even to please him, as though he knew, but he couldn't have known, how could he have known, later when he was ill, he kept saying things but I didn't dwell on them, goodness, I hadn't thought of them till just now, I also must have forgotten what he said, but he couldn't have known, well, he was a suspicious child, his father, his father was an exceptional man, he loved me a great deal, neither he nor Reshit ever found fault in anything I said, yes, there were days when we were cross with each other and Reshit always knew that I preferred remaining silent rather than saying something wrong, and when I did talk he'd understand it was true and tell me that I knew best, but Mushfik, my very own son, he never wished to tell me anything like this, if you asked him, everything I said was wrong, everything crooked, but never mind, the dear Almighty must have wanted to test me that day and made my son say all those things,

why am I obsessing over this, anyway, I don't know, it just occurred to me, all you women are blind when you love a man, you don't see even the slightest of his flaws, no, he didn't say, the slightest flaw, he said something else, you don't see any of his flaws but let him commit the slightest indiscretion against you, yes, that's what he said, then another sort of curtain falls over your eyes and he is the worst man in the world, even if he tried and caught a bird with his mouth just to please you, and that's no lie, I agree, if someone is good he is good, bad if he is bad, can any good come from someone who breaks your heart, now he broke my heart plenty of times but he is my son, I tolerate him no matter what, forgive him, love him as always, of course, it'd be better if he didn't break my heart, but which son doesn't, and if the mother loves her son as much as I do, though could you even find mothers who love their sons as much as I do, who among them sacrificed herself as much as I have, who among them gave up her youth on account of her son, ah, how come these thoughts surge to my mind, my sleep lost, where do they come from, now, in the middle of the night, does he know that I still lose my sleep, toss and turn in bed for him, even if he knows, does he understand, perhaps he gets angry, but, no, he doesn't, he no longer would, perhaps he has learned being loved, perhaps he has learned the peace of being loved, just the other day, we were both lost in thoughts, and suddenly, mother, he said, love is the only path to God, both of us have sought it all our lives, you couldn't find it but I did, the right way to eat, drink, dress, sleep, to love a singular person, to offer one's heart's burden to God as a debt of gratitude, all this you have sought and I found at last, can anyone say such things unless he has learned being loved,

but even if he now knows how to be loved, he still wouldn't understand, still wouldn't want me to lose sleep over him, my blessed mother, may she rest in peace, why did she visit me in my dream, is something going to happen again, there I was, our house had plenty of windows overlooking the sea but I loved one in particular, when sitting on the sofa, I'd see the entire coast, all the way from Hisar to Arnavutköy, I had Mushfik in my lap, I was breastfeeding him, he was making these gurgling sounds while enjoying my milk and even though I was afraid he'd choke himself I couldn't pull my breast off his mouth, his eyes would slide, squint, and close from pleasure each time he swallowed, I couldn't look at him enough, I was crying, thinking about his father who didn't get to see his baby, Reshit must not have been around yet, I must not have been married to him yet, I was all alone in the room, ships were passing in the distance, though few used to pass in front of our mansion, suddenly a ship appeared on the pier, blew its horn, it was death, the ship, it had come to take my baby away, Mushfik still wouldn't let go of my breast, I was holding him tightly, the ship blew its horn again, it was a piercing, rending sort of sound, I must have been all alone in the house, after the ship blew its horn one more time, it suddenly began moving, when I looked out the other window, I couldn't see it anymore, then the door to the room opened, my mother entered, I was startled, I kept pressing Mushfik against my breast, my mother, mother dearest came near me, with her pure white face, her delicate snow-white hair and pitch-black dress, don't

117

be scared my child, she said, no one can take your baby away from you, what woman has ever lost her son to others, I've never heard such a thing, a woman would rather die than give up her child, then she looked at his face, this child is full, don't you see, she said, why are you still feeding him, he's sleepy and about to fall asleep, give him to me, I looked at my mother's face, the woman in front of me wasn't my sweet-faced mother, she was a conniving stranger with an evil face who wanted to take my child away, Mushfik's eyes were closed but from pleasure, he wasn't full yet, he was still sucking, I could still feel the milk oozing off my bones and pouring into my breast, how could I let him go, I told her, didn't you just say that a woman would rather die than give up her child, that she'd protect him even if she had to die, then she laughed, then I suddenly found myself in the middle of the meadow, she was laughing, chasing me, Mushfik was still in my arms sucking my breast, there was no milk coming anymore, my son started crying, I was running, chased by the woman, her laughter mixed with my son's cries, then I saw my mother in the distance, her arms were open, she was calling me, hurry, come, she is exhausted, can't catch up with you, I was climbing the hill, panting, the woman remained far below, I was almost in my mother's arms, Mushfik was crying incessantly, mother, I said, my milk dried up, she nodded, just when

I reached her, she suddenly disappeared, vanished, Mushfik stopped crying, bit my breast, then turned his face, I woke up, drenched in sweat, lost my sleep, when Mushfik had turned his face toward me, his eyes seemed to say, you are a bad mother, your milk dried up, how can a mother's milk dry up from fear, what was my fault, when did I ever turn him down, was I at fault whenever I warned him against mixing with those boys, did I ever open my mouth and say a word whenever he brought them home, even though they were rude and bad, yes he loved the boys but I always could see their flaw, is that why women are wrong, is it because they speak the truth, ah, I wish I could sleep a little, I should go and see him tomorrow, I should kiss and caress his hair and overlook all his flaws, forgive him, dear God, forgive me, if I am a woman, am I not still a mother?

long ago, just to please him, I used to tell tales to him and his friends, once I was cross with him, he was four at the time, I was leaving him at home and going out, he was looking behind me, I saw him from the corner of my eye, his face full of wrinkles as if he was about to cry, suddenly a terrible aura of hopelessness came upon him, if you leave me, he said, I will call the Arab and ask him to devour me, what would it take, what would it take for him to say the same thing now, to ask me, mother, how about a fairy tale, what would it take?

Translated from the Turkish by Aron R. Aji

MEMENTO MORI

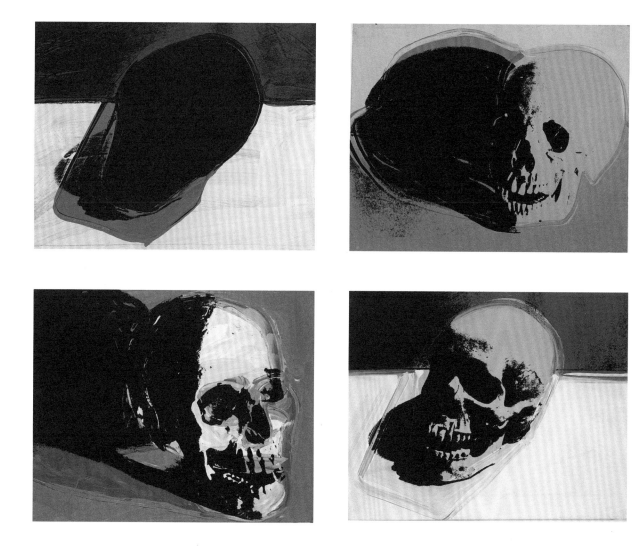

RAYMOND PETTIBON
No Title
(*Every Knucklehead Has Parents*),
1997.

EVERY KNUCKLEHEAD HAS PARENTS.

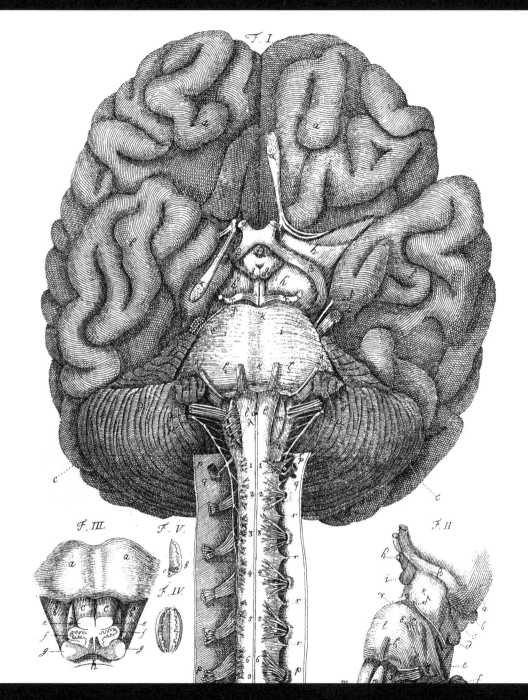

JANE KRAMER | BRENDA MILNER

Brenda Milner is the kind of woman who used to be called a dame—as in, "Some dame!" She is seventy-nine years old. She talks straight. She works hard. She loves clothes. She doesn't particularly care for cats. She is one of the most important neuropsychologists in the world. Her office is on the sixth floor of the Montreal Neurological Institute at McGill University, and it's where we met. We talked for three hours, and then moved on to the bar of the Ritz Carlton Hotel and talked some more.

Somebody once described Brenda Milner's field as "at the border between the brain and the mind." Milner studies the brain, but what she seems really to be after is that elusive signature of the person, in its ongoing articulation of what she sometimes calls autobiography," and other times "history." Specifically, she looks at how we make and retain memory. She has spent nearly fifty years studying how the brain fixes the information it receives; how it transforms that information into memory; where different kinds of memory are located; how memory is lost and gained and processed into the consciousness of a particular set of details and experiences that describe a person and a life.

The case that made Brenda Milner's name was the case of a twenty-seven-year-old epileptic known today in the literature of neuropsychology as H.M. H.M.'s hippocampus and the medial aspects of his temporal lobes—areas of the brain crucial to memory, had been removed in an admittedly radical effort to control his seizures, and while he remembered his pre-operation self perfectly well, he couldn't retain or remember anything else. His memory had stopped with his operation. He had literally lost himself.

When Brenda Milner met H.M., in 1955, she had already distinguished between the memory functions of the two cerebral hemispheres. After H.M., she started to look more closely at the sources and sites of the different kinds of memory she was beginning to identify—to dissect the act of remembering, to locate and understand its stages and its variety. She confirmed, for one thing, that the hippocampal region, storing and fixing information, starts the process by which information becomes memory—in the case of her most famous patient, becoming the "H.M." that the patient was able to remember. She confirmed, for another, that the same H.M. who couldn't remember her from one visit to the next, or even for the space of a short distraction, could nevertheless "remember" the often complicated skills she taught him—like making a mirror-drawing of a star.

It is thanks in large measure to Brenda Milner's work that neurosurgeons today can avoid repeating what she calls "the tragedy of H.M." Today, when they cut into a patient's brain, they are able to cut "around" memory instead of cutting "into" memory and thus taking the terrible risk of curing someone who will not even remember that he has gotten better.

Jane Kramer

126

Jane Kramer: How did you become interested in memory?

Brenda Milner: Because the patients we studied had memory impairment. Initially, I was particularly interested in visual perception. I was looking for perceptual disturbances in the patients with temporal-lobe lesions because there was evidence of this from lesion work in monkeys. But when you have patients who come and tell you that they have trouble with their memory, you'd be rather foolish to say, "Well, don't tell me that; I want to study perception. I'm not interested in memory." The patients determine what you study, to a certain extent.

I'm currently interested in how one recalls from memory where objects are in the world; in spatial relationships. In people, of course, you have the further interesting thing that the two halves of the brain are not doing quite the same thing. I find that it's more often the right, the non-dominant, the non-speaking part of the brain, that plays a bigger role in this kind of nonverbal spatial memory.

Jane Kramer: Is this where spatial memory, skill memory resides?

Brenda Milner: No, skill memory is not the same as spatial memory. Skill memory is the sort of learning that you acquire by increments, the learning that you can't really introspect on and say what you've learned. If your stroke at tennis (I'm not a tennis player) or golf gradually improves, you can't really put into words what you've learned to do, and if you try to teach it to somebody, they can't learn it by sitting in an armchair or reading a book. They learn it by doing it. It's like learning to pronounce a foreign language, the sorts of things that you learn best when you're very young, and that stay remarkably stable. And they stay stable from season to season. I mean it's very impressive that, you know, we swim in the summer and we ski in the winter and there are all these months in between, but we don't forget those skills. But this is not the sort of thing you can introspect about. You can't say in words what it is you've learned, really. There are some rules, of course— how to hold your tennis racket for example, these basic things—but the transformation from the clumsy performance to the skilled performance, you can't describe what you're learning.

Jane Kramer: As in the case of H.M., whom you taught to do that mirror drawing—which I tried to do and couldn't.

127

Brenda Milner: Yes, of course, but you would learn. And he learned. The amazing thing there was that I took these two learning tasks down from Montreal, I'd gone over to our psychology lab, and gotten these two tasks; a mirror drawing and a maze. And I got on the train to Hartford, got there early in the morning, and I had just three days to work with this patient. I had already done the preliminary studies on him; I had the feel of his memory impairment, and now I wanted to see what he could learn. I was very self-critical as I was doing this, because of course he wasn't learning the maze, where he had to learn a series of "choice points." In retrospect, nobody would expect such a patient to master twenty-eight choice points; it was silly. At the beginning of each new trial he had no idea which way to go. I thought it was going to be the same thing with the mirror drawing. We started the mirror drawing and, as you say, it's terribly difficult at first. And I thought, "Well, I am really crazy. I'm going to spend three days showing that this man can not learn these things, and couldn't I be doing something better with him?" But instead, with the mirror drawing, he showed this beautiful learning curve. And at the end he had no idea he had ever done it before. He had done thirty trials over three days, perfect performance in the end, and he had absolutely *no* sense of familiarity, *no* awareness that he had ever done it before. Which is an amazing dissociation.

Jane Kramer: To what extent is our recovery of stored memory provisional? I'm not talking about trauma memory loss, but about ordinary people who discard a whole chunk of learned information because it's not so useful in their lives because in the meantime they've filled their minds up with something else. I've had one or two moments like

that and I've always been curious about it. After a year of physics for instance—I did very well in physics and the day after I took my last exam it left my mind completely. I couldn't tell you a thing.

Brenda Milner: Did it happen with anything else?

Jane Kramer: Well, it did *not* happen with biology, which I keep to this day.

Brenda Milner: Well, you keep being involved in it.

Jane Kramer: No, not actively involved in it.

Brenda Milner: Well, biology's more verbal, or maybe you have a different kind of representation of it. I went to university to study math and physics and I certainly don't remember the things that I did except in the most schematic way, though they do help as a framework, not as consciously remembering something. I realize that I can follow a lecture that maybe somebody else wouldn't follow, not a completely mathematical lecture but a lecture that just has these little bits of assumptions of knowledge of basic mathematics that I assume that everybody knows, but of course they don't. So, it hasn't left you totally. But I think you do have to use information to retain it. Even with languages.

Jane Kramer: Yes, I've wondered about how learned information can get discarded, maybe because I have a lay person's notion of memory as a bureau with drawers that you occasionally empty out. You do housecleaning.

Brenda Milner: No, no, I think you need to do a kind of updating of memories—when you think about things, when you read something in the newspaper that reactivates facts that you knew before. My first encounters with amnesia were in patients that I myself had tested before and then after their surgery and then later in follow-ups. What was fascinating there was that there were people who knew things before the surgery and also in the early post-operative period—I'm talking now about their semantic knowledge, their facts and information which are not affected after the surgery. But when you see these patients in follow-up—these are young people—a year or two later, their concepts about certain things, like what the Vatican is and what the distances are between a and b and so on had become much vaguer, as though we ourselves are updating our knowledge a little bit all the time as we live, as we talk about things, as we listen to the news. You start talking to me about Washington state or British Columbia and I start picturing this relationship. These accretions keep those memories alive and I think that without what we call "rehearsal update," these patients' concepts get a little vaguer.

Jane Kramer: Does that happen to unimpaired people, too, though, to a certain extent?

Brenda Milner: Yes, I think so, yes. But you know, we are bringing in different factors here now. I'm sure that now, at my age—I'm 79 and I was doing my physics when I was 18—I'm sure if I were to sit down now and try to learn physics I would do a lousy job of it because my brain is very different and I'm not as smart at 79 as I was at 18, nobody is. But if you were to think of me when I was, say, 30 and had not done any physics or math since I had switched to psychology and you put me with another person who was in psychology but had not had any background in physics and you said, "We want you both to take a course in physics; we think for the next stage in your

work physics is going to be useful so we'd like to put you through this," I would probably do much better than the other person; I wouldn't be starting from the bottom in physics—and neither would you. We would be starting with something to build on.

Jane Kramer: Where do you suppose symbolically, metaphorically—in terms of the literature of the mind in a literary sense, not a scientific sense—the notion of a cluttered mind comes from?

Brenda Milner: Well, when you say cluttered, are you using it in a pejorative sense?

Jane Kramer: As in things milling around, as in a stuffed drawer.

Brenda Milner: Yes, well. I think this means that you don't have a very well-organized brain, in the sense you don't deliberately organize new information as you acquire it. I think it's wonderful to have a very stuffed mind, I don't think you can overstuff it, any more than I believe the statement that you use only a small percentage of your brain most of the time. I think you need all your brain, and I think that the more varied and rich the things you've learned the more possibility there is for interaction among them. But a cluttered mind calls up the idea of something like my office. My office is cluttered but I hope my mind isn't.

Jane Kramer: I guess what I'm getting at in some of these questions is the interplay between mysterious self-editing processes and very bedrock physiological processes. For instance, you wrote about memory, or you answered questions about memory being one's autobiography—

129

Brenda Milner: Well, it is more than one's autobiography.

Jane Kramer: To what extent do we edit that autobiography? To what extent does one edit the material of memory differently to construct a different autobiography out of basically the same material.

Brenda Milner: It's not the same. The brain is getting modified all the time by your experience, but you can only retain what your brain is educated to process. There are all these stories about scientists going to visit a tribe in some remote part of Africa where the native guide can tell that a particular animal has passed this way by some disturbance of a blade of grass. But they can't really say how they know this; it is presumably some little perceptual cue they've picked up, but they have enormously educated minds. They've been looking, these things have been important to them all their lives, but again this is a skill, this is a perceptual skill—it would almost certainly not be affected by the lesions in an amnesiac patient like H.M. It is not a memory in the sense of your autobiography, but their brains are changed by their accrued experience. We can't acquire it just by having the person who is skilled say, "But look, there, can't you see?" Because we haven't yet educated our brains to see those things. I think that with our autobiography, too—a brain is changed by it all the time, unless we have a brain lesion that impairs the system—our brain is changed constantly without any effort on our part. The reason that deep temporal-lobe lesions are so devastating is that this is a system we feel we can count on; it's not like making the deliberate effort to concentrate and solve something, or remember something, where there are other parts of the brain

that come in and make you concentrate. It's something that is constantly turned on: you remember how you came up University Street and how you came into this hospital and how you got up here and it's totally unimportant that you should be able to remember this but you can't help but remember, it's a system you can count on. Your whole life is sort of built up in this way and if this system is lacking then you no longer have any continuity, that's why I find it really sad.

Jane Kramer: It's tragic. What constitutes, then, a sense of identity or self?

Brenda Milner: You see, the patients [with temporal-lobe lesions] have a sense of identity, fortunately, because they don't lose the past experiences. They may have some retrograde memory loss for events leading up to the surgery but essentially, they know who they are. It's not like somebody who goes on a fugue and doesn't know who he is: they know very well who they are. But they don't build up and modify past experiences; they're stuck and as they get older it's really sad to see the discrepancy between the physical change consequent on the person's natural aging and the stories and the things they talk about and think about which are right back in the time before the operation or injury, or what caused their amnesia.

Jane Kramer: You were about to mention a film. . .

Brenda Milner: Oh yes; there was a scientific film festival in Montreal some years ago, and they asked me to give a lecture about memory and to do so by commenting on a documentary made in England. It was about a gifted young man at Cambridge who was going to be a lawyer, very brilliant apparently, and he had a stroke which resulted in him having this memory impairment. I'm sure from seeing him and seeing this documentary about him that he was not as totally incapacitated as my patient H.M., because some of the things he was able to do, I don't think H.M. would be able to do. But it was an extremely moving film because this man constantly wrote down everything that was happening; of course he couldn't go on training to become a lawyer, but he wrote down everything that was happening and you saw him doing this. And in his living room, he had a huge trunk, a box about the size of the space here under my desk and it was filled with the transcriptions. He would dictate, as soon as he had an experience, and then he would transcribe it and this was his memory. Seeing this huge box was very moving.

Jane Kramer: Has the surgery that's being done here, the work you do with the surgeons—has it become refined enough now not to pose some of the moral problems I imagine you once had of a choice between the risk of severe seizure and the risk of memory loss.

Brenda Milner: Oh, for a long time now. Initially, if you go back to the time when I was working with Dr. Penfield[*], the ways of visualizing the brain were very primitive. You could only get a rough idea of where there was brain atrophy, but they really couldn't see into the brain. I felt I was very privileged to be working in a situation in which you could actually see what the surgeon was doing, because most neurologists working with stroke patients had really no idea or only a very limited idea of what the damage was in these patients they were studying. The EEG, the electrical recording, which was such an important guide to the localization of the epileptic discharge, was still very primitive, you see, it was just the beginning, so you could be misled. With patients with temporal-lobe seizures, Dr. Penfield operated on the side that the EEG seemed to be telling him was where the seizures were coming from. And then after the operation in certain cases the patients developed amnesia; as I say there were two patients like that before my first encounter with H.M. and we speculated as to why we were seeing this memory loss. Obviously if this kept occurring, Penfield would have to stop doing temporal-lobe surgery because this is elective after all—epilepsy is not a deadly disease, it is a social handicap. These cases coming in had their injury going back to the earliest period of life and there's no reason why that injury wouldn't be in both hemispheres. The assumption is you are only going to operate if the damage is on one side and the other side is working—you can manage with one kidney or one eye, but you don't want to lose both. The same is true in the brain. We speculated that these patients had damage on the unoperated side, so that when Penfield operated, he effectively gave them bilateral lesions. That is what we reported in Chicago in 1955 and that report led Dr. William Scoville[*] in Hartford to tell us that he had seen this with his operations, too.

Now we have this wonderful MRI, the magnetic resonance imaging, which gives us such an incredibly clear picture of the brain. This was first developed in England. I still remember when they came over from England, and showed us these pictures. We couldn't believe that you could get such

---

[*] Dr. Wilder Penfield, who pioneered the surgical treatment of epilepsy in Montreal.

[*] The surgeon who originally operated on H.M.

a good picture of the brain, and it's got much more refined since, so that you can really measure quantitatively the atrophy and now we know that if you see the atrophy in certain structures—if you see it bilaterally—you'll have to restrict the scope of your operation.

But even before we got those good pictures, the Amytal procedure* enabled us to discover which side was dominant for language. After we ran into this trouble with Dr. Penfield's patients, Dr. Theodore Rasmussen—who was Dr. Penfield's successor and with whom I worked very closely—suggested that it would be possible to adapt the Amytal procedure to studying memory, that we might develop special memory tests such that when you anesthetized one side of the brain you might produce an H.M.–like effect for a few minutes and if so that would be an indication of malfunction in the temporal region of the opposite hemisphere

Jane Kramer: Of where language resides?

Brenda Milner: Well, not language in this case. We did in fact adapt the procedure to study memory and it turned out to be very useful. Of course it is much trickier than with language for two reasons: one reason is that anybody's concept of memory suggests some change over time, even if it is a short time interval and this drug only acts for a matter of minutes so that almost from the moment you inject the drug the patient is beginning to recover.

---

* In 1960, doctors began testing left-handed and ambidextrous patients before brain operations in an effort to determine which of the two hemispheres of the brain controlled speech. To do this, they temporarily knocked out one of the hemispheres by injecting the barbiturate sodium Amytal into the carotid artery on one side. Milner adapted this technique in 1963 to test memory functions in patients scheduled for epilepsy operations.

The other problem is whereas you know from the anatomy of the vascular system that when you make this injection you are going to get the drug to the speech areas, if there are speech areas in that hemisphere, and if you see that you have produced paralysis on the opposite side of the body, with memory it's much trickier because these critical structures deep in the temporal lobe are irrigated from two different sources so that you may or may not knock out enough of this region to be confident of the validity of the memory test. Of course we do it now with vascular control and EEG control, so everything is getting more and more refined. Surgery itself is of course much more refined than it used to be. So these technological changes have really helped.

But to return to your question, the Amytal tests can lateralize language to one hemisphere but they can't tell you anything about the localization of language function within each hemisphere. They can't tell you anything about such questions as how the presence of a brain tumor or injury has changed the situation within that hemisphere.

Jane Kramer: Can you describe some of the choices you've had to make when you are evaluating a patient who elects to have surgery and there are risks involved?

Brenda Milner: Risks for memory?

Jane Kramer: Yes.

Brenda Milner: Well, absolutely nobody today would do an operation which bore a clear risk of producing an amnesiac patient like H.M. For a patient with epilepsy from a well-circumscribed lesion in one temporal lobe, where there is no question of them becoming amnesiac but where there will probably be some accentuation of pre-existing memory problems, surgeons consider the trade-offs. For example, a lesion from early childhood in the temporal lobe of the left hemisphere, which is normally the dominant hemisphere for speech, doesn't usually result in speech developing on the other side because the left temporal region is not a critical zone for language development. A patient who grows up with a badly functioning left temporal lobe doing the best it can will have some difficulty with verbal memory, for example, that is memory for lectures you listen to, for books you read. Think of somebody who is in his twenties and bright and yet, in spite of studying hard, is not remembering things as well as his colleagues. Today, psychologists will see this, and can measure it, before the surgery—a memory impairment associated with this abnormally functioning area. And this abnormal electrical activity from the seizures can interfere with the functioning of the healthy areas of the brain. So the surgery will have two effects depending on how many seizures the patients have and how active the abnormalities are: first, the epilepsy is treated, and you may see that their general intellectual achievement which was quite variable before the operation, is enhanced, because the damaged area is not inert—you don't get epilepsy from an inert area, you get it from a poorly functioning, abnormal area. So what are the choices? If everything goes well the general intelligence certainly doesn't go down and it may go up. Even H.M.'s general intelligence went up after his radical surgery.

The reason for the improvement is that you have taken away the interfering effect of the seizures and you let the rest of the brain function normally. But there's no magical way by which, once having removed this temporal lobe, you can restore its function. You've taken it out. After a removal from the left temporal lobe the patient will often experience some increased difficulty with verbal memory along with an overall gain in general mental lucidity and concentration. It's not a bad trade-off if you consider that the epilepsy is brought under control as well. I'm taking the left temporal lobe as an example because patients rarely complain of those deficits we see with the right temporal lesions, where the result is impaired memory for faces, places, and melodies. Usually people take that in stride.

Jane Kramer: Can the left temporal lobe compensate for what is lost in the right temporal lobe?

Brenda Milner: No, I don't think one compensates for the other. It's just that we live in such a verbally dominant society so the verbal handicap is more evident. People come in and say, "I have a terrible memory," and then you test them and find out that it's not true, that they don't have a terrible memory in the general sense, they remember the events of their lives, they remember people's faces. They are just not remembering what they read and what they hear, so they say they have a terrible memory but it's a material-specific one. It's specific to verbal material, it's not amnesia.

But with a right-side lesion, you can, for example, show the patients an array of unfamiliar faces and then later show them a bigger array and ask them to pick out the faces they saw before. They tend to do this very badly because they try to do it by verbal labeling, and that's no way to try to remember a face—by thinking that someone has long hair or an eyebrow that goes up—a face is much too complex and idiosyncratic to be coded in a few simple words and therefore they do poorly at the subsequent recognition test.

Jane Kramer: But the opposite lobe does not generate any kind of compensatory ability.

Brenda Milner: It can, but only to a very limited extent. In a case like that of H.M. who has the damage in the medial temporal region in both sides, you see, he is much worse on both verbal memory and face memory than someone who has damage on just one side. So there is certainly overlap of function. I wouldn't describe it as compensation by one lobe for the loss in the other. But the effects of unilateral temporal-lobe surgery are slight when the opposite side is undamaged, how much it disturbs you depends on what your profession is—imagine if you are an actor trying to learn lines and suddenly your left temporal lobe gets damaged, you'd be handicapped. In general the only thing the patients will complain of is in the case of an operation affecting the left temporal lobe, where they complain that their memory is bad but you can show that it was bad before the surgery; afterward, it's only a little bit worse. And again, it is only one aspect of memory. You warn the patients beforehand that they may have trouble with memory for words now and that it may get a little worse. But because they have bad verbal memory and they don't write this down, they don't always remember what you told them.

Jane Kramer: What are your views, from what you have learned as a scientist, of all the recovered memory claims that are being exploited now?

Brenda Milner: Well, I have tried to keep away from this, but of course I am interested in it. Obviously it is a can of worms. I am very, very skeptical—I think people can only remember what their brains were capable of storing in the first place. I think in some cases these false memories have been exposed partly by the breakdown of these people when they were really challenged in a systematic way, not just allowing them to say, "I remember such and such," but comparing it with real memories. I *am* getting a little sorry for the people who are being accused of doing terrible things. Of course, there is terrible abuse, we know that from some of the scandals.

Jane Kramer: At what point in development is the brain physiologically capable of storing detailed memories of the kinds of abuse that are being described where someone says, "I was six months old and my mother's husband walked into my room and—"?

Brenda Milner: No, no, you can't. This is really nonsense.

Jane Kramer: What about the questions of collective memory? At what point does the memory die with the people who remember? At what point do you count on collective cultural "memory"? At what point does history stop existing for people? At what point does denial set in?

Brenda Milner: I was really astonished when I first realized how widespread the denial of the Holocaust can be. That is, I don't know how you can deny things that are so well documented. It doesn't surprise me at all that an individual can have these paranoid delusions; what's hard to believe is that such large groups can embrace these theories.

Jane Kramer: But if you're like some of the people I've dealt with in Europe or some of the right-wing extremists in the U.S., if you believe in a conspiracy, then all proof that is not *your* proof is part of the conspiracy. It is fabricated. If you believe that six Jewish bankers just bought the United Nations, then you are going to believe that the Holocaust archives are in a sense Jewish Hollywood making movies.

Brenda Milner: But it is so strange that so many people can believe this; this is what I find disturbing.

Jane Kramer: What is the physiology of people who cannot accept the evidence of their own experience? How would you account for those people? We can explain it in a million ways, but we're still left with people for whom the actual memory is not functioning. Or how about people who are diagnosed paranoiacs: can you relate this to your work and say that memory is functioning differently for people like that?

Brenda Milner: I think memory isn't it, it's perception, it's the interpretation. I mean the interpretation of what happens around them. They misinterpret what they see. I think in schizophrenia people misinterpret. It's a disturbed perception of reality, not a memory impairment.

Jane Kramer: So that's what we're seeing in, say, these right-wing extremists?

Brenda Milner: Yes, yes, I think it's a disturbed perception of reality. It's not that they see it and then forget it, or distort it in their memories. They *perceive* it differently.

Jane Kramer: Do you find that the more you discover, the more maddening it is not to know it all?

Brenda Milner: Well, each step is exciting. I find it exciting that we'll never run out of things to explore.

NANCY SPERO:
SPERM BOMBS AND JOUISSANCE

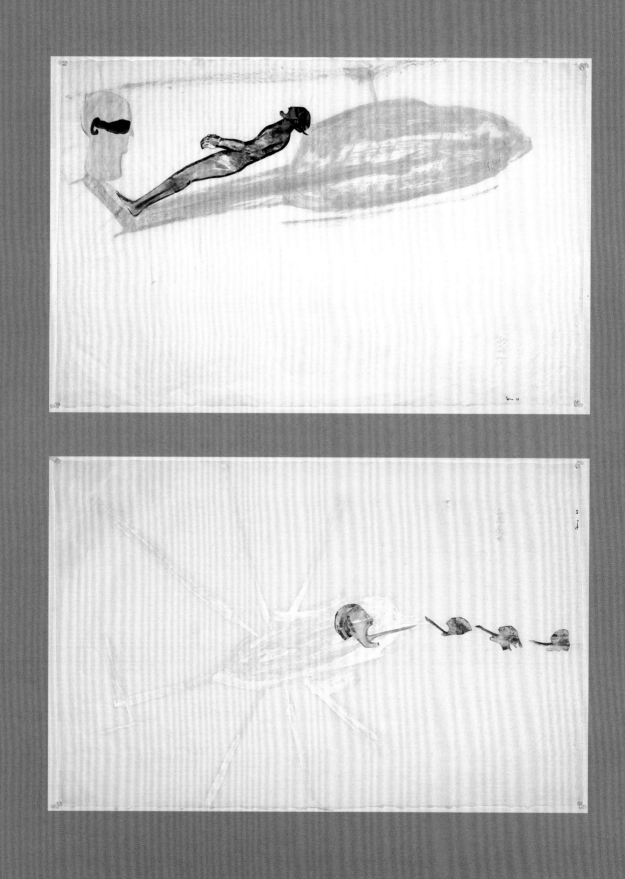

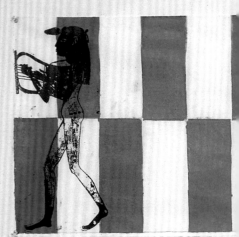

PAGE 137 (TOP):
Pilot/Gunship, 1968.

PAGE 137 (BOTTOM):
Helicopter, Pilot/Blinding Victims, 1968.

ABOVE:
Helicopters & Victims in River of Blood, 1967.

PAGE 138–139 (BOTTOM) AND PAGE 139 (TOP):
Black and The Red III (details of
installation), 1994.

138

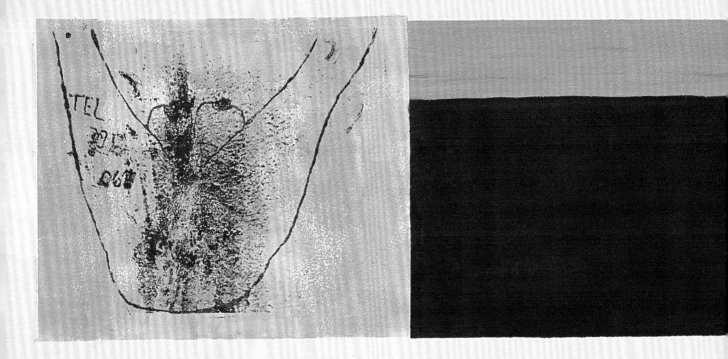

Black and The Red III (detail of installation), 1994.

Nancy Spero

Except for the principles of Eros and Thanatos, what is the meaning of Nancy Spero's juxtaposition of her *War Series* paintings from 1968 next to the imprinted scrolls of *Black and The Red* from 1994? What is the meaning of the encounter of violence and eroticism in her abundant textual and visual language?

Distressed by the increasing U.S. military involvement in Vietnam, Spero expressed in the *War Series* her anger at the craziness and obscenity of war. Releasing in paint on paper her *Nightmare Demons*, *Sperm Bombs*, defecating helicopters, *Body Counts*, dismembered victims, and bloody skulls, the artist denounced the essential structure of war and the nonlocatable, omitted, or altered relation between body and voice, "between the collective casualties that occur *within* war, and the verbal issues . . . that stand *outside* war."[*]

When the pain of war is articulated in the realization of artifice, a painting, a poem, a language occurs where there had been silence. It is in this process of externalization, Spero's move out into world, through the scrolls of *Black and The Red*, that the interior world of pain and imagining, invisible to anyone outside the boundaries of her body, begins to be sharable. A celebration of bright colors and the erotic gestures of female bodies, the lengthy scrolls develop the feminine lexicon of a complex story without beginning or end. Her method is a kind of dialectical imagining; she works not so much to make the art object, but to remake human sentience and alter perception. Spero's *Black and The Red* is a vital utopia in progress, uncertain and unpredictable: a procession of the maternal and the feminine in a loose choreography. Even more than a utopian manifesto it is an homage to creation, and to its continual potential for self-revision and challenge of existing social and cultural orders. Her generous paintings, with their power of reciprocation, exist both to celebrate the reinvention of language and to assist us in the understanding of the act of creation itself.

Catherine de Zegher

---

[*] From Elaine Scarry, *The Body in Pain: The Making and Unmaking of the World* (Oxford University Press, 1985), p. 63.

Orchard of Far Worlds

This is the land of small rain.
Because it is round, I still need you.
The men move amongst their stones.
Because it is holy, the air is uneasy
with memories of things that are gone,
bats whirling out of the trees,
a cobra's slow-rising hood,
mangoes that ambered the blood.
You could have run further.
There are pockets given to frost
where portions of birds lie frozen.
Where the outside extends to within
on a vein that cuts itself open.
Where minerals fail in the quiet
to live otherwise than rich,
and jade keeps revealing its strings,
mica, more fragile planes,
to no one, to nothing.
Where breath will suffer to be music,
where skin turns infrared—
they say you hurried for the end.
A sudden recollection lights the wind.

Sanctuary

Who loves the world? The sleeper does.
Where he is, the jungle is still large.
The things that sing, sing flight into his heart,
and sky, and sun, and sounds so glad
he thinks his mother was a bird,
but singing, warn him, as she didn't,
of the scourge to come, and feed him,
not as she did, warm against her plumes,
thistles, moths and worms,
but a hundred false beginnings
so the true one will be watered down,
will barely hurt him, scourge,
the true one, whose coming will ignite
like Babylon the great, in whose hold
he'll perish like a river in a cherished bed,
slowly turning pebbles, tossing mud
and weed, and fling himself
at last, like parrots leaving trees
for cages made of brass, too fresh and green,
too real once, to dream of real things.

Salad Days

DAVID MAMET

Thirty years ago I'd go to the Waverly Theater in the afternoon with a large cup of coffee with a little milk in it and a pack of Camels and I'd skip acting school to watch a double feature and come out only to go to work in the evening, which was work as an usher, then house manager, then assistant stage manager, for The Fantasticks. After work I would walk home the seventy or so blocks across upper Sixth Avenue and across the corner of the park to Seventy-first Street and Columbus.

On the weekends the fellows in the show would take me out for brunch at the Pam Pam on Seventh Avenue, or between shows on Sunday for a drink, a Bloody Mary or two, at Asher's on Christopher Street, and I suppose they were trying to court me, though I must have seemed to them a rather unformed thing, but perhaps that was the point.

My roommate at that time was studying dance at Juilliard and he kept bringing home perfect sixteen-year-old ballerinas. He got the bedroom and I got the couch in the living room. One night long tall Jenny Hobs stopped by at eleven o'clock and flung a cat in the door and said, "He's yours. His name is Leonard." I kept him a short and difficult while and finally ditched him somewhere.

One night I woke up at four to hear that they had shot Bobby Kennedy on the radio I'd left on all

night. I must have fallen asleep to the radio. I was fairly lonely in those days. One night in the middle of the night I was listening to the WMCA Good Guy Sweatshirt Offering on some call-in program and they asked the name of the pretty French girl on the Gary Moore Show and I knew it was Denise Darcoux and I called in and said so and a month later there was a sweatshirt stuffed into my mailbox and I was overcome by its compressibility.

Across the hall lived two exceptional young women, both small, one very muscled and she was a flier in the circus and the other petite and Irish and I longed for her through a very lonely year and at the end of which and upon my exit I discovered she'd had a similar pash for me. I moved out as I'd gotten a job in summer stock out on the tip of Long Island and it may have been the only, at least one of the few times I was ever hired as an actor. And then I left Seventy-first Street.

I remember food being very important up there. Days I would exist on a bowl of rice and beans which came with a small basket of bread. And when I was more flush I'd get a cup of café au lait and occasionally the prized maduros fritos. And weekends I lived on a quart of milk and a package of Milano cookies.

How I envied those glimpsed from afar who had

145

it seemed their society intact, their support intact, their prospects and their careers before them. I moved in a daze. I was happiest on the walk up Sixth Avenue. What did I think of? Fame, success, love, being accepted. I ran into the cop and the kids having a snowball fight at midnight in Washington Square, New Year's Eve, 1967.

And I remember one of the players in *The Fantasticks* and we went out for a drink one night on Bleecker Street and he bought me a margarita and he told me he wanted me to remember that it was he who bought me my first one and I do remember.

I remember afternoons at the Cafe Figaro, and the jazz at the Top of the Gate, and Kenny Lanken at the Bitter End and Steve Martin at the Bitter End and running the old complicated cross fade at the end of *The Fantasticks* on the rheumatic rheostat stick board in the lighting booth at the show and plunging everyone into darkness. Someone wrote, as I read long ago, that artists moved to Greenwich Village in the twenties because the streets were short and winding and the bill collector had a difficult time finding his way.

It occurred to me years later that that was nonsense and that no one is more persistent than a bill collector. That they're infinitely more persistent than artists and that the artists must have come into the Village for another reason. Perhaps they came for love, for good coffee, and for the influx and availability of adventure minded youth, and the permitted wistfulness of the whole damn thing.

If I could go back would I do it differently? Well, I can't go back. And I remember Thompson Street in bed with a lovely young woman asleep and we'd let the candle burn down too low and I woke up and the walls and the Indian bedspread on the walls and the mattress were in flame and we were out on the street naked and shivering and I can't recall what happened next.

I remember my father coming down to visit me once or twice and going to hear jazz with him after my show at the Top of the Gate. Some of the fine times I remember that we had together.

And I remember envying those who took life easy, who were happy in love, who were happy in their work, with themselves, with their life.

If I could go back would I do it differently? Well as I said I can't go back. The altimeter seems to unwind and my past life and the remainder of my life rushes before my eyes and I have become one of the fellows it seemed I looked at longingly when I was a youth and there you have it.

A.R. AMMONS

Mucilage

Led off the arena with a noose around my neck,
bearing the leash of cowering humiliation &
degradation, I thought to myself, hey, between

facing one death and another is this interlude,
life, and having escaped the first may I not
by grace or god, device or dare, sidestep

the second: by the time I hit the stoneshade
of the periphery, I believed in hope again:
the crowd was already rolling in some other

emotional slush:
                              you may wonder, as I often have
and sometimes do, what I mean by all these

statements: well, of course, I mean the
statements as gestures, actions, jots and tittles
of possibility, nods, smiles, words, thoughts,

things which, summed up, will take on ambiance,
milieu, intermediacy, flow, these representing
existence which evidences certain values—

a willingness to be nearly honest, if that
state is nearly approachable (if I go on too
long about this you will think I don't

mean it): anyway, that's what I've been doing
and tricks like this are unworthy of you:
what I really really mean to do, though, is

to dissolve encrusted certainty: I believe in
definition, in limits and being fairly certain
about things, but I want ongoingness to have

always this power to break through bringing
upheaval and growth: I would like to have just
enough structure so that when change hit it I'd

be left with a shambles: I can get along
with a shambles; I can prop it up or knock
a leg from under it or gradually replace it: I

don't want a steel cell but on the other hand
I don't want to settle down in hurricanes or
floods: I like the mild passion of thinking

something reasonably so, or not: anyway,
they took me off, washed, scraped, oiled,
pounded and kneaded me, spritzed me with

aromatics so witchingly fine you'd have to
get your nose nearly to the skin to be sure
scent was there, and they strapped me,

arms and legs, on a kind of tilted catafalque,
a gold and silk fabric knotted around my waist
and falling open below: lutes in tiers and

files of naked women lifted the dome of the
high place with spangled light and sweetest
sound: when the women swayed and turned,

their arms rising and falling into waves by
their sides, I felt an unquenchable rush which
I could not reach to hide: what is a man to

do, his lust visible and no permissions
granted or sought: a most beautiful face
began to rise from my waist toward my face, and

I looked directly into a pair of eyes and lips
so open and pure and gorgeous that I was
already swimming in dreams when the hand lightly

moved upward along my thigh, and then the face
went back where it came from and raptures
dreams can't conceive touched me: past the

cresting ecstasy, my heart subsiding, I saw
the face again, peeling itself away, shining
hair, eyelashes, glowing lips and revealing

the emperor, the very magnificence that had
spared me even against the wishes of the crowd
(you take the word *fucking*—as in, who cut

the fucking tree down—a blustery effect that
almost hides fear from courage; a useful
word, for isn't everything a pretense or a

substitution, integrity the biggest cover-up
of all: I know this woman, lady-like, lately
met, her first move is grinning obsequiousness,

this the paranoia alert, and sure enough she
comes up with trifle after puzzling trifle till
the bulldozer that is her true nature

chugs: poor little thing, all she wants to
do is push the world off a cliff: beware such
who haunt you with niceties till your guts

form a lasso or a noose, one for you, one
for her): the *f* word, tho, used
too frequently loses its force: why? *the*

doesn't lose its force: but then one hardly
ever notices *the*, whereas, in polite society,
fucking is strong tonic, not, of course, in high

society: those fuckers don't care what they
say and can back up their vulgarity with moldy trust
funds: the slavish behave slavishly, even while

they wait to bulldoze the upper crust away:
& those of us (I mean, you) with a million a
year income should recall from time to time the

splitting fine edge of the guillotine: walk
upon the bottom of your trust fund if you want
to cross the river of life: lake, I mean: the

river has a bad reputation: on the other side,
it's a gray area: walk along the bottom of the river
and you may have a non-round trip: my wife

says she feels sorry for this man she met the
other day: he had the look of someone who has
said yes all his life when he wanted to say no,

somebody like a suit salesman or accommodating
real estate salesman or professor or possibly
a L-A-N-G-U-A-G-E poet, for, you know, a

language poet will think twice about anything if
he thinks it will get closer to the truth: yes,
yes, you're right, I'm only kidding: I'm not

typing or even talking, I'm yapping, and almost
anything will outlast this measly rhyme: it's
metrical time for memory and next time around

maybe I'll take that up: but this time it's
free verse for me: who wants to remember this
century's mess: I think the main reason,

though, that I don't have any subtle gestures,
withery gracious moves, is that I came from a low
religious caste, holy roller, where anything

under a shout is insincere; I never sat in any
cool Presbyterian pew and considered the
startling differences in effect between $3\frac{1}{4}$ and

$3\frac{1}{2}\%$ interest over time: even Baptists held it down
a little: they even held it under, and their
preachers talked just like they'd met somebody

on the road, neighborly like: my kind were afire
with the fire of the pentecost, although what
they were actually lit up about was where the

next meal or rag for their children would
come from: the surface tells the truth every
time, but you have to know how to read it right.

SANTU MOFOKENG

BLACK PHOTO ALBUM /

LOOK AT ME : 1890 - 1950

156

Santu Mofokeng

PAGE 152:
(LEFT) Mmiletswa Sepobe (standing, left) with friends. No more information is known to the respondent, Krause Sepobe, who is a distant relative of the subject living in Pimville, Soweto. Photographer: Lydenburg Studios, Lydenburg, 1926. Silver-bromide print.

(RIGHT) Cleophas and Martha Moatshe. Cleophas and his wife Martha came from Boshoek, where he was a moderator in the breakaway Anglican church. He died in 1923 from "drie dae" influenza. This information was supplied by a relative living in Mohlakeng, Randfontein. Photographer unknown, Boshoek, c. 1900s. Albumen print.

PAGE 153:
(LEFT) Rozetta Dubula and friends. Rozetta Dubula, born Duma, was born in Thaba-Nchu in 1901. Her granddaughter, who was named after her, knows little about her life. Photographer: H.F. Fine Studio, 26 West Str., Johannesburg, c. 1910s. Albumen print.

(RIGHT) Tokelo Nkole with friends. Tokelo Nkole was a dedicated follower of Marcus Garvey and also worked with Alan Paton at the Diepkloof Reformatory School. He died in 1940. This information was supplied by Emma Mothibe. The photograph belongs to the Ramela family of Orlando East, Soweto. Photographer unknown, Johannesburg, c. 1900s. Silver-gelatin print.

PAGE 154:
(CLOCKWISE FROM TOP LEFT) Moeti and Lazarus Fume. Biographical information is not known to the respondent, Emma Mothibe. The photograph belongs to the Ramela family of Orlando East, Soweto. Photographer unknown. Silver-bromide print.

Elizabeth and Jan van der Merwe. Elizabeth and Jan were siblings born to a family of "inboekselings" in Lindley, Orange River Colony (now called Orange Free State). Inboekseling, loosely translated, means forced juvenile apprenticeship in agriculture. This information was supplied by Emma Mothibe. Photographer unknown, Johannesburg, c. 1900s. Silver-bromide print.

Moduetha and Maria Letsipa. See below for Maria's background story. There is little information about her husband Moduetha. They all came from Orange Free State. Photographer unknown, c. 1900s. Silver-bromide print.

Ouma Maria Letsipa and her daughter, Minkie Letsipa. Maria was born into a family of "inboekselings" in Lindley, Orange River Colony. Her family became prosperous livestock and grain farmers at the turn of the century. This information was supplied by Emma Mothibe. The photograph belongs to the Ramela family of Orlando East. Photographer: Scholtz Studio, Lindley, Orange River Colony, c. 1900s. Albumen print.

PAGE 155:
P.G. Mdebuka. At the back of this print is written and stamped "A present from [P.G. Mdebuke - Location School, Aliwal North] to Jane Maloyi." P.G. Mdebuka was a hymn composer and minister of the Methodist church. Photographer: Aliwal North Location School, c. 1900s. Albumen print.

PAGE 156:
Bishop Jacobus G. Xaba and his family. Bishop Xaba was the presiding elder of the AME Church in Bloemfontein from 1898–1904. The Church was active in the events leading up to the formation of the South African Native National Congress in 1912. Photographer: Deale, Bloemfontein, Orange River Colony, c. 1890s. This photograph and the photograph on P. 155 were found in a wooden box labelled (in Afrikaans) "Aan M.V. Jooste van die persooneel van Die Vaderland." In the box there were 68 images, including one of "Their Most Gracious Majesties, Edward VII and Queen Alexandra—In Their Robes of State." The box belongs to Moeketsi Msomi, whose grandfather, John Rees Phakane, was a bishop in the AME Church. Albumen print.

The Black Photo Album/Look at Me: 1890–1950

These are images that urban black working- and middle-class families commissioned, requested, or tacitly sanctioned. Some were left behind by dead relatives. Some hang on obscure parlor walls in the townships. In some families they are coveted as treasures, displacing totems in discursive narratives about identity, lineage, and personality. And because to some people photographs contain the "shadow" of the subject, they are carefully guarded from the ill will of witches and enemies. Sometimes they are destroyed

with other rubbish during spring-cleaning because of interruptions in continuity or disaffection with the encapsulated meanings and history the images convey. Most often they are rotting through neglect, lying hidden in chests, cupboards, cardboard boxes, and plastic bags.

Some of them may be fiction, a creation of the artist insofar as the setting, the props, the clothing or pose are concerned. Nonetheless there is no evidence of coercion. When we look at them we

157

believe them, for they tell us a little about how these people imagined themselves. How we see these images is determined by the subjects themselves, for they have made them their own.

They belong and circulate in the private domain. That is the position they occupied in the realm of the visual, in the nineteenth century. They were never intended to be hung in galleries as works of art. They were made in a period when the South African state was getting entrenched and the government's policies on the "native question" were being articulated. It was an era mesmerized by the newly discovered life sciences such as anthropology, when pernicious racial theories were given scientific authority.

Officially, black people were frequently depicted in the same visual language as the flora and fauna; represented as if in their natural habitat, for the collector of natural history; or invariably relegated to the lower orders of the species on occasions when they were depicted as belonging to the family of man.

Images informed by this prevailing ideology are enshrined in the public museums, galleries, libraries and archives of South Africa. In contrast, the images in this display portray Africans in a very different manner. Yet, all too often these images run the risk of being dismissed or ignored as evidence of pathologies, or bourgeois delusions.

It should be pointed out that from the turn of this century and even earlier there were many Black Africans who spurned, questioned, or challenged the government's racist policies. Many of those integrationists were people who owned property or who had acquired Christian mission education, and they considered themselves to be "civilized." These people, taking their model from colonial officials and settlers, especially the English, lived a life in manner and dress very similar to those of European immigrants. The images depicted here reflect their sensibilities, aspirations and sense of self.

Santu Mofokeng

The Act of Naming

Santu Mofokeng is a lyric poet of the photographic mood; of fugitive traces that haunt both mind and memory. To encounter his own darkly printed images is to look at pictures that, for all that they may reveal, speak as much of what they fail to reveal— of the evanescent, the liminal, and the indeterminate. Taciturn and difficult in the wonderful and frustrating way that artists with rich imaginations often are, Mofokeng is a peripatetic and intense figure who talks about his work in discontinuous ways, leaving gaps, as he often does in his pictures, for the mind to fill.

His latest project, which has occupied him for the last four years and is still ongoing, is the

accumulation of hundreds of photographs of Africans taken in South Africa from the end of the nineteenth century up to the period when apartheid became official policy. *Black Photo Album/Look at Me: 1890–1950* is Mofokeng's brilliant meditation on the nature of identity and the individual's sole possession of its conclusive defintion. In this work, race, politics, desire, and photographic representation subtly converge to unsettle the archive and jar memory. It is an extraordinary investigation into an area now occupying many South Africans as they attempt to build possible futures and construct new narratives.

Okwui Enwezor

greguerías

RAMÓN GÓMEZ DE LA SERNA

There are sighs that connect life with death.

Earphones are the dark glasses of the ears.

Each word has an inedible bone: its etymology.

The only bad thing about death is that one's skeleton is so easily mistaken for another's.

A pencil writes only the shadow of words.

The most terrible thing about our address book is that it will be used, inevitably, as the means of communicating our death to friends and relatives.

It was one of those days when the wind was trying to speak.

There some matches that light a little while after they have been struck, as if they had momentarily forgotten what to do.

The cypress is a well that has become a tree.

Time is nourished with dead clocks.

His knees were laughing.

There are railway stars, shining near stations, that give out more cold than other stars.

The blind man waves his white stick to take the temperature of human indifference.

Rivers do not know their names.

The courtyards of lunatic asylums should be roofed over with glass to prevent the contagion from spreading.

Streets are longer at night than by day.

If they were to invent a watch with a special alarm to sound the penultimate hour of life, nobody would ever buy it.

The Last Trumpet is the echo of the echo of the repeated echo of the First Trumpet.

If we were only to count the number of steps from here to there, we should never go there at all.

Dry fountains are the pantheons of water.

If we couldn't sigh, we'd drown in our own lives.

After all is said and done, the only immortal butterflies are those which the lepidopterist has stuck through with a pin.

You must choose very carefully, because virtually nothing can be exchanged.

Translated from the Spanish by Philip Ward

Caves

REBECCA SOLNIT

Sometimes walking past the carcasses

being unloaded into butcher stores or seeing a particularly graphic medical photograph, one is reminded again that beneath the blank wall of the skin is another world of meat and processes, marvelous and unnerving. Carlsbad Caverns had something of that revelation of the otherworld under a deceptive surface, and the landscape above it was as featurelessly flat as, say, the expanse of skin on a belly. The entrance to the caves is perched on a steep rise that looks southward across the last arid flatness of southeastern New Mexico to the Guadalupe Mountains on the otherwise flat horizon of Texas.

We bought tickets in the Visitor Center and descended along a walkway of signs and barriers, half amusement park, half national park, that took us around a bend to a vast gaping mouth in the earth. I cannot say how vast, however: one of the odd things about the cave was that it warped and undermined one's sense of scale. Once we had left daylight behind, I felt no size at all, only wandered in and out of the wildly varying sizes of the cave. In the first chamber, one was always heading downward, so that the cave behind rose up and ahead dropped down great distances, and at certain junctures one could see an astounding way in either direction. The air was, as air in caves generally is, 56° and 90% humidity: so comfortable and, once past the guano-scented entrance, so scentless that one's body almost seemed to disappear for a long while, but for uneven footing and the occasional drip of water on one's head.

And of course all the strange forms we saw suggested other forms: it seemed impossible to look without associating these nameless, shapeless stones with items from the upper world, particularly with bodies. In the first long chamber, the soft-looking folds of rock reminded me of flesh and in the second of bone—but we wondered about the way people always need to compare the unknown to something known, and often the overwhelming to something banal.

A lot of the place names had to do with food—popcorn formations, soda straw stalactites—and a lot of the people around us brought up pop culture resemblances. The familiar always forms a bridge to, or a bridge back from, the unfamiliar, and this is one of the useful functions metaphor performs: to let us enlarge the world without getting lost in it. But there's a danger of domesticating the wildest things by this process, and it seems to be part of a larger artillery of conquest of the sublime. Although we were down there with nothing but the path to direct us, the majority of other visitors had rented audio equipment—strange black wands like a cross between police batons and cordless phones that they waved near the sides of their heads. The wands provided a sort of spoken accompaniment triggered along the way by plastic signs and caused their listeners to march at a set pace, ignoring their companions, with the slightly glazed expression of television watchers. The stray phrases I overheard suggested all the other cave tours I'd been on: stuff about dates and sizes and names that reined the wild in far more strictly than the associative acts in which our group engaged in. And sometimes it seems to me that one major touristic agenda is to stage such attacks on the unfamiliar: to go halfway around the world only to eat hamburgers, to see the grandest spectacles of the organic world, only to reduce them to banal, quantifiable and thereby dismissible phenomena. The corniest remarks on earth are made on the rim of the Grand Canyon, and cave formations are always tamed by reference to religion and art; to crosses and altars and brides and wedding cakes and doll theaters.

The eighteenth century refined to an astounding degree the voluptuous pleasure of seeing scenery through a practice of making oneself intentionally susceptible, of murmuring to oneself the possibilities of terror, the magnificence, the resonances, and I think I induced in myself a similar state, with help from my responsive companions—graduate students in a seminar on metaphor I was teaching at UNM come to look at a real cave before we were swallowed up by cave allegories. Of course there is no denying that the eighteenth-century dip in the sublime was no less an artifice than, say, the overexplanatory tone of audiotours today—but I think the former was if nothing else more fun. (Later on my students nearly came to blows over the subject of whether consumer culture denies people the fullest experience and whether we could deplore it—which most of the midwesterners among them thought was undemocratic and uncouth—but we were harmonious while we walked along the railed path through the cave.)

Maybe all those wedding cakes and altars are attempts to clothe the naked stone in garments of propriety, but these caves look like flesh anyway, a constantly varying scale of flesh, recalling not only the obvious metaphor of the cave as womb full of phallic stalactites and stalagmites, but also every kind of tissue and fiber and structure. The main caves opened into long chambers wandering off in every direction into the velvety darkness beyond the lighting of the principal features, and sometimes they looked like throats up there in the roof. One was stained reddish and dripping with formations and looked violent, like a birthing womb, and other holes were pits dropping down through the floor for hundreds of feet. Some of these throats were no bigger than those of animals, some could have swallowed large houses without choking. There was one perfect hemispherical pale upright pointing breastlike stalagmite about three feet high, amid all those dangling fingers and phalli, all those gaping mouths and throats and wombs in a whole structure that seemed to make literal the phrase the bowels of the earth—and it was acknowledged as a nipple, in a break from the decorum and dissociation of the rest of the signage. Sometimes the texture of the walls resembled the crenelations of the brain and the villi of the intestinal walls, of surface maximized, and sometimes of the spongy insides of the long bones. Sometimes the walls hung in folds, sometimes curved into sockets and angled lengths, and the same formations that sometimes looked to others like broccoli and like tiers of trees looked to me at times like teeth with long roots showing; other formations looked more like fangs—the stalactites evenly spaced across an aperture—and mouths were everywhere in this monstrous beauty. The rock seemed alive, and could one slow down one's moments to millenia, perhaps one would see the stone grow and warp and bloom and drip itself into this infinitely complex form, see rock as malleable as silk and honey.

The entire repertoire of form was here, but without the context and order that makes it coherent above ground. All forms were jumbled together here in the underworld, as though this were an experimental zone, a place where all the patterns for the surface of the earth were worked out. It seemed like a laboratory or a mine from which not materials but shapes and textures came, and this sense of a raw, primordial workshop was enhanced by the lack of color. Other than the reddish formation in one of the shallower caves, there was no color but the slight variety from alabaster to amber to brown, with the deep shadows cast by the lights and the depths beyond the lights an inky black. But scale, texture, shape, depth, height were all here in infinite variation. There were places where the gloss of the dripped rock was so gleaming it seemed slimy, or like a pile of slime. Sometimes the shallow pools reflected the stone above so that it seemed to be going far down into the depths, and a few of the depths fell into such darkness that they might have gone on forever. The forms were strangely stirring, both erotic and terrifying. Some places had perfectly clear shallow lakes into which a droplet would fall every so often, sending out ripples across the floor, and many had flat crusts through which time and force had broken through.

After a few hours in this humid cool air which seemed soft and neglectful on the skin after months in the arid air of New Mexico, and after a few hours of walking through this visual vocabulary of the body, it came to seem incredibly perverse that all these almost obscene forms could only be looked at; that in this hole of sensuality, the rules forbade us to touch or of course taste; politeness forbade us to test echoes; and though I leaned close and sniffed at various formations that seemed as though they should smell of dust or slime or something, nothing had a scent—only the heavy pleasure of humidity in dehydrated nostrils. It was a superb exercise in contradiction, this realm in which one's actual body seemed almost to disappear amid so many images of the body. After a long time on the sometimes wet and often tilted paths looking through the dark at illuminated formations that had dripped down according to gravity but then had been tilted by later geological shifts, one's sense of balance and uprightness disappeared too, and it became easy to get dizzy. And for days afterward I seemed to live in a world in which everything was more vivid and more intense. It seemed almost an after effect, a hangover from the cave, that the night I reached my temporary home in northern New Mexico, there was a great comet in one side of the sky and a lunar eclipse in its heights.

AFTER THE FACT

Sophie **Ristelhueber** | Sophie **Calle** | Willie **Doherty**

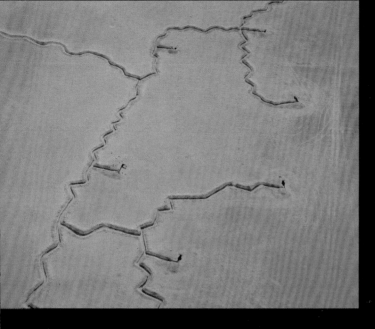
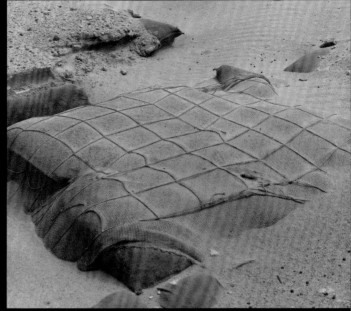

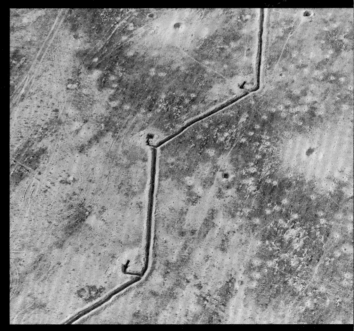

PAGES 169, 170, AND 171: Sophie Ristelhueber, from *Fait*, Kuwait, 1992.

The engine continues to run. The scene is interrupted by a male voice which speaks a short phrase. At this point the scene ends abruptly and cuts to the opening shot. This sequence is repeated, each time ending with a different phrase.

AT THE END OF THE DAY THERE'S NO
GOING BACK
WE'RE ALL IN THIS TOGETHER
THE ONLY WAY IS FORWARD
WE HAVE TO FORGET THE PAST AND
LOOK TO THE FUTURE
WE'RE ENTERING A NEW PHASE
NOTHING CAN LAST FOREVER
LET'S NOT LOSE SIGHT OF THE ROAD AHEAD
THERE'S NO FUTURE IN THE PAST
AT THE END OF THE DAY
IT'S A NEW BEGINNING
LET'S NOT REPEAT THE MISTAKES OF THE PAST

Charles Merewether

After the fact: to represent that which is no longer and that which remains. The work of these artists stands against the pictorial traditions of landscape photography. It represents a form of the anti-sublime: it offers nothing heroic, nothing grandiose to which one can appeal. Like an excavation that exposes the incomplete fragments and traces of what has disappeared or been erased, their photographs expose the memory of a time of war and violent change.

In the photographs of Sophie Ristelhueber, Willie Doherty, and Sophie Calle, the landscape is revealed as a desolate memory, scarred by signs of a traumatic past. Doherty returns again and again to sites of demarcation, borderlands where vision and bodies are brought to a halt. Ristelhueber's photographs show us horizonless wastelands littered with half-buried debris. Calle records the scars left behind in concrete and stone when monuments and memorials are excised from the public landscape, leaving only the imprint of their presence.

In Sophie Ristelhueber's 1992 series of photographs, Fait, the desert that was the theater for the battle of Kuwait has become a burial ground for the detritus of war. The half-buried trenches, armaments, and the stuff of everyday life left like abandoned bodies in the sand are a memory of the landscape's occupation and desertion. The work distances itself from the images in tourist guides, as well as from those ubiquitous television and magazine images constructed for the tourists of war that we have become. Ristelhueber addresses each scene by posing the questions: How do we return there without repeating the act of surveillance, the aerial or panoramic point of view that presages subsequent destruction? Where is a standpoint that will allow another perspective, a place from which to view the devastation? Ristelhueber captures the still-burning desert as one oil rig after another brightens the night sky with its column of fire. There is no distance in her photographs. They abolish any notion of scale. No horizon line can be found that is not ruptured.

Sophie Ristelhueber, from Fait, Kuwait, 1992

For Willie Doherty, the border is the limit of vision, the threshold of perception. It is the frontier between night and day, between city and country, between states, between cultures, self and other, life and death. What we see in the space between the moment just passed and the moment to come are the warning signs of potential violence. What we see in a photograph of a blind corner, a dark thicket, or a road that loses itself in a blanket of darkness, is disturbed by what we cannot see. The object eludes the eye, exceeds the camera's attempt to capture within the frame, to make visible the unseen, the unknown. In Doherty's video work, as well, we are suddenly surrounded by the unfamiliar, the unrecognizable. The viewer stumbles upon the scene, finds himself in the wrong time and place, and discovers himself to be a foreign element— someone who does not belong. The observer becomes the one who is being watched, the object of attention, the subject of surveillance. The landscape allows no privilege for the viewer. What seems innocent becomes suspect: an effect of the violence that informs everyday life in Northern Ireland.

Willie Doherty, *Wasteground*, 1992

Sophie Calle, *Relief and Child* (detail), from *The Detachment*, 1994.

The photographs in Sophie Calle's series, *The Detachment*, document the traces of monuments and memorials removed from their place. Accompanying the photographs are the stories, often contradictory, told by those who remember the people and events these vanished monuments once commemorated. Their fitful memories are cobbled together into a narrative where the statue and its subjects merge and separate in the recounting—as if the representation had already replaced that which it memorialized. We are reminded of how every regime marks and controls the landscape with representations of its heroes and leaders. And of how history is remade and falsified by the erasure of these figures from public squares, from books, from archives, and by the rewriting of history in the light of new leaders and new beliefs. Can history begin again? Calle's work captures the moment after the slate is wiped clean, after the fact, before the future.

The work of each of these artists is concerned with the phantasmic afterlife of what is left behind by the events that make history. In the memory of place, the legacy of a time of war is its imprint on the landscape—physical traces which function as an index of past trauma. Photography is, as Roland Barthes has suggested, essentially commemorative. Yet we may say that, in describing events that erase the past in their wake, such images as these exist as emblems of the uncertain present in which we live. In recognizing the past, they charge their audience with being a witness to these events and their aftermath.

The Pathetic Fallacy

A cautionary mister,
the thaumaturge poked holes in my trope.
I said what are you doing that for.
His theorem wasn't too complicated,

just complicated enough. In brief,
this was it. The governor should peel
no more shadow apples, and about teatime
it was as if the lemon of Descartes
had risen to full prominence on the opulent skyline.

There were children in drawers, and others trying to shovel them out.
In a word, shopping had never been so tenuous,

but it seems *we* had let the cat out of the bag, in spurts.
Often, from that balcony
I'd interrogate the jutting profile of night
for what few psalms or coins it might
in other circumstances have been tempted to shower down
on the feeble heathen oppressor, and my wife.

Always you get the same bedizened answer back.
It was like something else, or it wasn't,
and if it wasn't going to be as much, why,
it might as well be less, for all anyone'd care.
And the ditches brought it home dramatically
to the horizon, socked the airport in.

We, we are only mad clouds,
a dauphin's reach from civilization,
with its perfumed citadels, its quotas. What did that
mean you were going to do to *me?*
Why, in another land and time we'd be situated, separate
from each other and the ooze of life. But here, within
the palisade of brambles it only comes often enough to what
can be sloughed off quickly, with the least amount of fuss.
For the ebony cage claims its constituents

as all were going away, thankful the affair had ended.

Gentle Reader

Abruptly, unassertively, the year starts,
as freeways close and roofs collapse,
and all kinds of incidents give nervure to the map:
a stitch in time, a local hero here,
boys falling in tune with the ageless argument.

So out of the turquoise turmoil a name
implodes like a star, having made its point.
And the seasons, welcome as you know,
are seen packing it in. Maybe add some rust
at a crucial jointure, no? But who am I
to be telling you your business. Next, young and beautiful,
emerging from a door, casting your essence
along the face of today's precipice, you see "there's no tomorrow,"
only avatars waiting in the wings, more or less patiently.
This is what it takes for you to do what's best,
covering all the exits.

Oh, there is a danger there?
Who would have thought it in today's heat?
But on the other hand, why just be standing
while its morose page rolls over,
an encumbrance to all, not just ourselves?
And when twilight licks appreciatively at the sky,
your answer will be there in the circuitry,
not bypassed. For you to hold,
to genuflect with.

A shadow of a flagon crossed your face:
The cease-fire is improving?
And in this starting to be in something, what had the older
children been doing? Taking lessons still to be paid for,
impinging on what comes next. Comes now.

Soon there is something to be said for everything,
he said, whiplash, whippets; why even my identity
is strange to me now, a curiosity. When someone comes later,
who will I be talking with? The erroneous vision
make no mention of this. Its conquering agenda is complete,
and we, of course, are incomplete, destined to ourselves
and its fitful version of eternity:
the one with chapter titles.
More worldliness to celebrate. And yet, someone
will take it from you, needy thing.

CHRIS MARKER

Dial Ⓜ for Memory

A PROJECT

Hélène Chatelain, Davos Hanich in LA JETÉE (1962)

"The directors of the Experiment tighten their control. They send him back. Time rolls back again. She is near him. He says something. She doesn't mind, she answers. They have no memories, no plans. Time builds itself painlessly around them. As landmarks they have the very taste of this moment they live, and the scribbling on the walls."

Japanese worshipper in **SANS SOLEIL** (1982)

"Brooding at the end of the world, on my Island of Sal, in the company of my pouncing dogs, I remember that month of January in Tokyo, or rather I remember the images I filmed of the month of January in Tokyo. They have substituted themselves for my memory, they *are* my memory. I wonder how people remember things who don't film, don't photograph, don't tape. How had mankind managed to remember. . . I know, it wrote the Bible. The new Bible will be the eternal magnetic tape of a Time that will have to reread itself constantly, just to know it existed."

Bosnian refugee in **PRIME TIME IN THE CAMPS** (1993)

"We want to hold on to this moment. The part of the project which concerns our memorial is based on that : how to keep hold of a moment to keep it for a time yet to come? So many things we've seen have not been recorded… "

Catherine Belkhodja in **LEVEL FIVE** (1997)

"If someday an ethnologist of the future sees these images, he will draw conclusions on the funeral rites of these bizarre tribes at the end of XXth Century. And I'll be too happy to provide him with details. Yes, it was customary among these tribes to rely on a familiar and protective spirit they used to call a computer. They used to consult him about everything, he was the keeper of their memory—in fact they had no memory anymore, *he* was their memory."

Chris Marker

To acknowledge Chris Marker as one of the indispensable figures of the postwar world cinema is to state a truth that only begins to comprehend his artistic project. Born in 1921 outside Paris, under a different name, Marker has worked for decades, obscured by a deep modesty that has paradoxically won him a legendary, even mythical, status. That he politely refuses to be interviewed, photographed, or to participate in public recognitions has only attracted further honors. Yet, beginning with his assumed identity, his readers and viewers encounter no ego, only alter ego. Small surprise that his favorite film is Alfred Hitchcock's *Vertigo*.

A refracted recognition came to him in 1995, with the release of Terry Gilliam's *Twelve Monkeys*, inspired by Marker's peerless 1962 film *La jetée*, a *ciné-roman* consisting almost entirely of still photographs, with a voice-over narration (the book version was published by Zone Books in 1993). Drawn as much to the word as to the image, Marker virtually invented the modern form of the film-essay, wandering the globe as an insomniac dreamer and reporting back with a self-effacing, questioning and doubting bemusement.

Author of a postwar novel, *Le coeur net*, and a critical study of Jean Giraudoux, Chris Marker founded Editions du Seuil's influential Petite Planète series in 1954, text and photo travel books that today are prized collector's items among artists and photographers. His own two-volume *Commentaires* (1961) consists of scripts of films he actually made and films he only dreamed, using the book form to recall the world of images just as his films aspire to speak with an essayist's precision.

More recently, Marker has been pursuing Mallarmé's vision of "the book to come" by turning to the tools of digital imaging. In 1997 he produced an inarguable masterpiece of the CD-ROM format, *Immemory*, presented as his initial ordering of seven decades of personal memory. Openly echoing Proust (Marker: "I claim for the image the humility and the powers of a *madeleine*"), *Immemory* takes advantage of the CD-ROM form's capabilities to incorporate clips from his own films and from those of his friends, written materials, cartoons, and drawings, and homages to figures past and present. Marker remains astonishingly prolific and inventive in the challenges he sets for himself, and with *Immemory*, he has become the first artist whose authoritative *Pléiade* edition will be coming to us, over time, on disc.

For this portfolio, Chris Marker chose a single still from each of four of his films.

Bill Horrigan

189

Not About Nightingales

TENNESSEE WILLIAMS

Not About Nightingales is a newly-discovered play by twenty-seven-year-old Tom Williams; it is the first long drama he would sign as "Tennessee." Radicalized by the Depression and by three years of work in a St. Louis shoe factory, Tom Williams had come to the University of Iowa in 1937 to study drama. His first assignment was to write a short sketch based on a news story which described a hunger strike at the Stateville, Illinois prison. The sketch, "Quit Eating," was given a classroom production, then forgotten as he turned to other assignments. In September 1938, after graduating jobless and penniless, he read about another hunger strike at a Holmesburg, Pennsylvania prison in which 25 convicts had been locked into a steam-heated cell. When the warden gave orders for the heat to rise to the boiling point, four of them were roasted alive. It was the one of the worst prison disasters in American history and Tom Williams reacted by expanding his "Quit Eating" sketch into the full-length play, *Not About Nightingales*.

Years later he wrote, "I have never written anything since then that could compete with it in violence and horror."

An excerpt from the play follows here.

Allean Hale

CAST OF CHARACTERS

Mrs. Bristol	**Schultz**	**Oliver White (Ollie)**	**Shapiro**
Eva Crane	**Butch O'Fallon**	**Jeremy Trout (Swifty)**	**Goldie**
Jim Allison (Canary Jim)	**The Queen**	**Mex**	**Guards, Troopers,**
Boss Whalen, *the warden*	**Joe**	**Chaplain**	**Convicts**
Jack Bristol (Sailor Jack)	**McBurney,** *a guard*	**Reverend Hooker**	

The action takes place in a large American prison during the summer of 1938.
The conditions which the play presents are those of no particular prison but a
composite picture of many.

OPENING

LOUD-SPEAKER: "Yeah, this is the Lorelei excursion steamer. All-day trip around Sandy Point. Leave 8 A.M. return at midnight. Sightseeing, dancing, entertainment with Lorelei Lou and her eight Lorelights! Got your ticket, lady? Got your ticket? Okay, that's all. We're shoving off now. Now we're leaving the boat dock, folks. We're out in the harbor. Magnificent skyline of the city against the early morning sunlight. It's still a little misty around the tops of the big towers downtown. Hear those bells ringing? That's St. Patrick's Cathedral. Finest chimes in America. It's eight o'clock sharp. Sun's bright as a dollar, swell day, bright, warm, makes you mighty proud to be alive, yes, Ma'am! There it is! You can see it now, folks. That's the Island. Sort of misty still. See them big stone walls. Dynamite-proof, escape-proof! Thirty-five hundred men in there, folks, and lots of 'em 'll never get out! Boy, oh, boy, I wonder how it feels t' be locked up in a

place like that till doomsday? Oh, oh!! There goes the band, folks! Dancing on the Upper Deck! Dancing, folks! Lorelei Lou and her eight Lorelights! Dancing on the Upper Deck—dancing! —Dancing!—Dancing. . . [*Fade.*]

[*Flash forward to end of play. Light fades except for a spot on Eva, clutching Jim's shoes.*]

LOUD-SPEAKER: Aw, there it is! You can see it now, folks. That's the Island! Sort of misty tonight. You'd see it better if there was a moon. Those walls are dynamite-proof, escape proof—Thirty-five hundred men in there—some won't get out till Doomsday. —There's the band!—Dancing on the Upper Deck, folks! Lorelei Lou and her eight Lorelights! Dancing —dancing—dancing. . . [*Fade.*]

[*Music comes up. The shoes fall from Eva's hands, and she covers her face.*]

BLACKOUT

[. . . .]

ACT ONE: EPISODE TWO

ANNOUNCER: *"Sailor Jack."*

Musical theme up: "Auprès de ma Blonde." Fade.

There is a spot on a cell. Electric lights from the corridor throw the shadow of bars across floor. The cell is empty except for the figure of Sailor Jack, slumped on a stool with the shadow of bars thrown across him. His face has the vacant look of the schizophrenic, and he is mumbling inaudibly to himself. His voice rises—

Sailor: Where? Port Said! —And not one of 'em but woulda done it 'emselves if they'd 'ad ha'f a chance. [*He begins to sing hoarsely.*]

> *Auprès de ma blonde*
> *Il fait bon, fait bon, fait bon!*
> *Auprès de ma blonde*
> *qu'il fait bon dormir!*

No chance for advancement, huh? What would you say if I told you that I was Admiral of the whole bitchin' navy? [*He laughs.*]

> *Je donnerai Versailles,*
> *Paris et Saint Denis—"*

> [*Sounds are heard: a shrill whistle in hall and the shuffle of feet: the door of the cell clangs open and Joe, Butch, and the Queen enter.*]

Schultz: Lights out in five minutes.

Butch: Ahh, yuh fruit, go toot huh goddam horn outa here. Mus' think they runnin' a stinkin' sweatshop, this workin' overtime stuff. Git yuh task done or come back after supper. Goddam machine got stuck. Delib'rate sabotage, he calls it. I'd like to sabotage his guts. [*To Queen.*]: What happened to you this mornin'?

Queen: [*in a high tenor voice*]: I got an awful pain in the back of my neck and flipped out. When I come to I was in the hospital. They was stickin' a needle in my arm—Say! What does plus four mean?

Joe: Christ! It means—

Butch: Pocket yuh marbles!

Queen: Naw. Is it bad?

Joe: We're in swell sassiety, Butch. A lunatic an' a case of the syph!

Queen: The syph?

> [*A whistle is heard: the lights dim in the corridor.*]

Queen: Naw! [*He tries to laugh.*] It don't mean that!

Sailor: *Auprès de ma blonde*
> *il fait bon, fait bon, fait bon*
> *Auprès de ma blonde—*

Schultz: Cut the cackle in there! It's after lights.

Butch: Goddamn it, can't you see he's blown his top?

193

Joe: Yeah, get him out of here!

Schultz: He's putting on an act.

Sailor: *Je donnerai Versailles,*
 Paris et Saint Denis

Schultz: You take another trip to Klondike, Sailor, it won't be on a round-trip ticket!

Butch: It's Klondike that got him like this. He's been ravin' ever since you brung him upstairs. You must've cooked the brains out of him down there, Schultz.

Sailor: *La tour d'Eiffel aussi!*

Schultz [*rapping the bars*]: Dummy up, the lot of you! One more squawk an' I'll call the strong-arm squad!

Queen: Mr. Schultz!

Schultz: Yeah?

Queen: What does plus four mean?

 [*Schultz laughs and moves off.*]

Butch: If I wasn't scared of losin' all my copper⋆ I'd reach through and grab that bastard. I'd rattle them pea-pod brains of his 'n roll 'em out on the floor like a pair of dice. The trouble is in here you gotta pick your man. If I rubbed out a screw I'd never git a chance at the boss. —What time is it?

Joe: Ten-thirty.

⋆ A reduction in a prison sentence, accruing from the inmate's good behavior.

Butch: Mac comes on duty now.

Joe: You think he'll take the Sailor out?

Butch: I'll tell him to.

Queen: Naw. It's nothin' that serious or they woulda kept me in the hospital. It's just indigestion. That's what I told 'em, I said the food is no good. It don't set good on my stomach. Spaghetti, spaghetti, spaghetti! I said I'm sick a spaghetti!

Sailor: *Auprès de ma blonde*
 Il fait bon, fait bon, fait bon!
 Auprès de ma blonde
 qu'il fait bon dormir!

 [*Butch clips him with a fist.*]

Joe: What did you do that for?

Butch: You wanta tangle with the strong-arm squadron on account of him?

 [*A whistle is heard: doors clang.*]

They're changin' now. [*He goes to the bars.*] Who's 'at? McBurney?

Mac: What do you want, Butch?

Butch: For Chrissakes git this kid outta here.

Mac: Which kid?

Butch: Sailor Jack. He's been stir-bugs since they brung him upstairs a week ago Tuesday.

Mac [*at the door*]: What's he doing?

Butch: He's out right now. I had to conk him one.

Joe: What did they tell you about roughin' up the boys?

Butch: Roughin? ME? Lissen! —Ask Joe, ask anybody, ask the Canary—the kid had blown his top —Schultz was gonna call the strong-arm squad an' have us all thrown in Klondike cause he wouldn't quit singin' them dirty French songs! Ain't that right, Joe?

Joe: Sure, Mac.

      [*Whistle.*]

Mac: Where's his stuff?

Butch: Here. I got it tied up nice.

Mac: Well, it's no put in of mine. He should've done his task in the shop.

Butch: He done his task pretty good.

Joe: That boy worked hard.

Mac: Not hard enough to suit the Boss.

      [*Enter guards.*]

Awright, git him outta here. Put him in isolation tonight an' have him looked after tomorrow.

Queen: Mr. McBurney, what does plus four mean? Mr. McBurney—

      [*Mac goes out with guards carrying Sailor. Bird calls are heard in the hall.*]

Voice: [*in hall*]: Goodnight, Mac.

Mac: G'night, Jim.

Butch: Who's at? Allison?

Joe: Yeah. It's the Canary.

Sailor [*from down the hall*]:
    Auprès de ma blonde
    Il fait bon, fait bon, fait bon!
    [*The sound fades.*]

Butch: Hey, Canary! Allison!

      [*The spot shifts to include Allison's cell.*]

Jim: What do you want, Butch? [*He is shown removing his shirt and shoes.*]

Butch: Next time you're in a huddle with the boss tell him the Angels in Hall C have put another black mark on his name for Sailor Jack.

Jim: I'll tell him that.

Butch: Tell him some day we're going to appoint a special committee of one to come down there an' settle up the score. —You hear me, Stool?

Jim: I hear you.

Butch: Just think—I used to be cell mates with him. I lie awake at night regrettin' all the times I had a chance to split his guts—but didn't!

195

Joe: Why didn'tcha?

Butch: That was before he started workin' for the boss. But now he's number three on the Angel's Records. First Whalen, then Schultz, and then the Stool! You hear that, Stool?

Jim: Yes, I hear you, Butch. [*He rolls and lights a cigarette.*]

Butch: That's good. I'm glad you do.

Jim: I know you're glad.

Joe: What's he say.

Butch: He says he knows I'm glad.

Joe: He oughta know. Wonder he don't go stir-bugs, too. Nobody have nothin' to do with him but Ollie.

Butch: He'll blow his top sometime, if I don't git him first. You hear that, Stool? I said you'll blow your top sometime like Sailor Jack—I'm lookin' forward to it.

Joe: What's he say?

Butch: Nothin'. He's smokin' in there.

Joe: We oughta tip 'em off.

Butch: Naw, I never ratted on nobody. Not even that Stool.

Queen: Allison! Hey! Jim! What does plus four mean?

Jim: Who's got plus four?

Queen: I have. What does it mean, Jim?

Jim: It means your physical condition is four points above perfect.

Queen [*relieved*]: Aw. These bastards had me worried.

Butch [*climbing on a stool by the window*]: Foghorns. It's thick as soup outside—Lissen!

Joe: What?

Butch: Excursion steamer.

Joe: Which one?

Butch: The Lorelei.

Joe: Lookit them lights on her, will yuh. Red, white, green, yellow!

Butch: Hear that orchester?

Joe: What're they playin'?

Butch: Roses a Picardy!

Joe: That's an old one.

Butch: It come up the year I got sent up. Why, I remember dancin' to that piece. At the Princess Ballroom. With Goldie. She requested that number ev'ry time I took her out on the floor. We danced there the night they pinched me. On the way out— right at the turnstile—them six bulls met me—

six of 'em—that's how many it took—they had the wagon waitin' at the curb.

Joe: Last time it was four bulls. You're gettin' less conservative, Butch.

Butch: Roses a Picardy. I'd like to dance that number one more time. With Goldie.

Joe: Maybe it was her that put the finger on you.

Butch: Naw. Not Goldie. I bet that girl's still holdin' the torch for me.

Joe: Keep your illusions, Butch, if they're a comfort to yuh. [*He removes his shoes.*] But I bet if Goldie was still holdin' all the torches that she's held before an' after you got put in the stir she'd throw more light across the water than a third-alarm fire!

Queen: Where's my manicure set?

Butch: I wonder if a guy is any good at sixty?

Joe: What do you mean?

Butch: You know. With women.

Joe: I guess it depends on the guy.

Butch: I'll still be good. But twenty years is a lot of time to wait.

Queen: Has anybody seen my manicure set?

Butch: You know there's a window in Boss Whalen's office from which a guy could jump right into the Bay.

Joe: Yeah. The Quick Way Out.

Butch: I was thinkin' that it would be a good way to kill two birds with a stone. Rub him out an' jump through that window for the getaway. Providin' you could swim. But me I can't swim a goddam stroke. I wish that I'd learned how before I come in here.

Joe: Wouldn't do you no good. Nobody's ever swum it yet.

Butch: I'd like to try. —They say some people swim instinctive like a duck.

Joe: You'd take a chance on that?

Butch: Naw. I'm scared a water.

Queen [*excitedly*]**:** I put it here last night. Butch, did you see it?

Butch: What?

Queen: My manicure set.

Butch: It's gone out wit' the slop bucket.

Queen: What did you do that for?

Butch: It stunk up the place. Smelt like rotten bananas—What's this on Sailor Jack's bunk?

Joe: A package a letters from his ole lady.

Butch: Aw.

Joe: She said she was comin' from Wisconsin to see him in the last one.

197

Queen: All my life I've been persecuted by people because I'm refined.

Butch: Somebody oughta told her how the Sailor is.

Joe: Well, she'll find out.

Queen: Because I'm sensitive I been persecuted all my life!

Butch: Yeah, she'll find out.

Queen: Sometimes I wish I was dead. Oh, Lord, Lord, Lord! I wish I was dead!

[*Musical theme up. Fade.*]

BLACKOUT

[. . . .]

ACT ONE: EPISODE FOUR

ANNOUNCER: *"Conversations at Midnight!"*

The spot lights two cells.

[. . . .]

Queen: Be quiet, you *all*. I'm sick. I need my sleep. [*He mutters to himself.*]

[*A searchlight from river shines on the window.*]

Joe: Where's that light from?

Butch [*at the window*]: Anudder boat load a goddam jitterbugs. Dey're trowin th' glims on us. Whaddaya think this is? Th' Municipal Zoo or something? Go to hell, yuh sons a bitches, yuh lousy—

Schultz [*rapping at the bars with a stick*]: After lights in there!

Butch: Someday it's gonna be permanuntly 'after lights' for that old screw.

Joe [*twisting on bed*]: Oooooo!

Butch: Bellyache?

Joe: Yeah, from them stinkin' meatballs. By God I'm gonna quit eatin' if they don't start puttin' in more digestible food.

Butch [*reflectively*]: Quit eating, huh?—I think yuh got something there.

Joe: Oooooo—Christ! [*He draws his knees up to his chin.*]

Butch: You ever heard of a hunger strike, Joe?

Joe: Uh.

Butch: Sometimes it works. Gits in the papers. Starts investigations. They git better food.

Joe: *Oooooo! We'd git—uh!—Klondike!*

Butch: Klondike won't hold 3,500 men.

Joe: No. But Hall C would go first on account of our reputation.

Butch: Okay. We'll beat Klondike.

Joe: You talk too big sometimes. You ever been in Klondike?

Butch: Yeah. Once.

Joe: What's it like?

Butch: It's a little suburb of hell.

Joe: That's what I thought.

Butch: They got radiators all aroun' the walls an' there ain't no windows.

Joe: Christ almighty!

Butch: Steam hisses outa the valves like this. [*He imitates the sound.*] Till it gits so thick you can't see nothing around you. It's like breathin' fire in yer lungs. The floor is so hot you can't stand on it, but there's no place else to stand—

Joe: How do yuh live?

Butch: There's an air hole about this size at the bottom of the wall. But when there's a bunch in Klondike they git panicky an' fight over the air hole an' the ones that ain't strong don't make it.

Joe: It kills 'em?

Butch: Sure. Unless the Boss takes 'em out. And when you beat Klondike you beat everything they've got to offer in here. It's their ace of spades!

Queen [*rising sleepily on his bunk*]**:** What's that about Klondike, Butch?

Joe: Nothing. He's talking in his sleep.

Queen: I dreamed about Klondike one night.

Joe: Did ja?

Queen: Sure. That was the night I woke up screaming. Remember?

Joe: Sure. I remember. —Oooooo! Uhhhhhh! Ahhhhhh! Jesus! [*He springs out of bed and crouches on the floor, clasping his stomach.*]

BLACKOUT

[. . . .]

ACT ONE: EPISODE SEVEN

ANNOUNCER: *"Butch Has A Dream."*

Theme up: "Roses of Picardy." Fade.

Goldie: Hello, Butch.

Butch [*half-rising on his bunk*]**:** Goldie!

Goldie: Yes, it's me.

Butch: How didja get in here?

Goldie: Walls ain't thick enough to keep us apart always, Butch.

Butch: You mean you walked right through? They couldn't stop you?

Goldie: That' right, honey.

Butch: It's marvelous, marvelous!

Goldie: Sure. I never was an ordinary bim. There was always something unusual about me. You noticed that. How light I was on my feet and always laughing. A girl that danced like me, all night till they wrapped up the fiddles and covered the drums, that never got tired, that always wanted one more of whatever was offered, is something kind of special. You know that, Butch. You don't buy us two for a quarter at the corner drug.

Butch: Yeah, I know that, Goldie. I always had that special feeling about you, kid. Honey, I used to try to find words to tell yuh what you did to me nights when you opened your mouth against mine and give me your love. . .

Room twenty-three! That was yours. Six flights up the narrow stairs with brass tacks in an old red carpet and bulbs at the end of the hall. Fire escape. We used to sit out there summer nights and drink iced beer till all we could do was giggle and then go to bed.

Day used to come so slow and easy through the long white blinds. Maybe a little wind making the curtains stir. The milk wagons rattled along, and out on the East River the fog horns blew. I never slept, I lay and watched you sleeping. Your face was like the face of a little girl then. A girl no man ever touched. I never told you about those times I watched you sleeping and how I felt toward you then. Because I wasn't good at making speeches. But I guess you knew.

Goldie: Of course I knew. I knew you loved me, Butch.

Butch: I wonder if your face still looks like that when you're sleeping.

Goldie: I haven't changed. You oughta know that, Butch.

Butch: You don't go out with other fellows, do you?

Goldie: No. You know I don't. I been as true as God to you, Butch.

Butch: But how do you live, how do you get along now, Goldie.

Goldie: As good as a girl can expect. I still work days over at the Imperial Dry Cleaners and nights I work at the Paradise, Butch.

Butch: I wanted you to quit the Paradise, Goldie.

Goldie: What for?

Butch: I don't like other guys dancin' witcha.

Goldie: They don't mean nothing. Just pasteboard tickets, that's all they are to me, Butch. I keep the stubs an' turn 'em in for cash. And that's as far as it goes.

Butch: But when they hold you close sometimes when the lights go out for the waltz—you don't ever close your eyes and blow your breath on their necks like you done for me, Goldie?

Goldie: No. Never.

Butch: You wouldn't lie to me, Goldie?

Goldie: Of course I wouldn't. Some of the girls say one man's as good as another. They're all the same. But I'm not made like that. I give myself, I give myself for *keeps*. And time don't change me none. I'm still the same.

Butch: The same old Goldie, huh?

Goldie: The same old kid. Running my dancing slippers down at the heels. But not forgetting your love. And going home nights alone. Sleeping alone in a big brass bed. Half of it empty, Butch. And waiting for you.

Butch: Waiting for me!

Goldie: Yes! Waiting for you! [*She begins to fade into the shadows.*]

Butch [*reaching toward her*]**:** Goldie!

Goldie: So long, Butch. So long. . .

Butch [*frantically*]**:** Goldie! Goldie! [*She has completely disappeared.*]

Joe [*sitting up on his bunk*]**:** What's the matter, Butch.

Queen: He's talkin in his sleep again.

Butch [*slowly and with terrific emphasis*]**:** God—damn!

BLACKOUT

[. . . .]

ACT ONE: EPISODE NINE

ANNOUNCER: *"Explosion!"*

The spot comes up on the cell. We should feel a definite increase of tension over the preceding cell scenes. Butch paces restlessly. The others sit sullenly on their bunks, the Queen with an old movie magazine, Swifty anxiously flexing his legs.

[. . . .]

Joe: Maybe our friend the Canary forgot to spill.

Butch: He'd never forget to spill anything.

Joe: Then maybe the Boss don't care how we feel about cold beans for supper.

Butch: He wants to call our hand.

Joe: Sure. He's got an ace in the hole. —Klondike!

Butch: We've got one, too.

Joe: Hunger strike?

Butch: You named it, Brother.

Joe: Two guys can't hold the ace of spades.

Butch: Once I sat in a game where that was the situation.

Joe: How didja solve it?

Butch [*producing his razor*]**:** Wit' this.

Joe: You better quit flashin' that thing.

Butch: Ev'rybody knows I got tough whiskers [*He laughs and replaces razor in his belt.*] "Fawchun's always hid-ing—

       I looked ev'rywhere!"

    [*Bird calls are heard from the hall.*]

Here it comes, it's th' Canary. [*He gives a shrill whistle.*] Hello, Canary. How's them solo flights you been makin? You know—out there on the mountain tops wit' nothing around ja but the stars? [*He and Joe laugh.*]

Ollie: [*from the next cell*] Don't pay 'em no mind, Jim.

Jim: Never mind about that. I got something to tell you.

Butch: Tell us about Goldilocks and the bears.

Joe: I like Goody Two-shoes.

Jim: Come outside for a minute.

Butch: You wanta fight?

Jim: No, I wanta talk.

Butch: You allus wanta talk, that's your trouble. If you got something to spill come in here.

Jim: I know what happened last time I got in a cage with you, Butch.

Butch: I'm glad I made that good an impression.

Jim: Are you coming out?

Butch: Naw. Are you coming in?

Jim: Yeah. I will. Soon as they douse the glims.

Queen: Better not, honey. Butch has got tough whiskers.

Jim: Yeah, I know what he cuts 'em with.

Butch: Why dontcha spill it, then?

Jim: I never deliberately ratted on nobody, Butch.

[*A whistle sounds. The lights dim.*]

Okay. I'm coming in now. [*He unlocks the cell and enters.*]

Queen: Now, Butch—

Joe: Watch, yourself. It's not worth getting jerked to Jesus for.

Butch: Naw, Canary, my respect for you is increased two hundred percent. I never thought you'd have what it takes to step inside here.

Jim: It's like what I was telling Ollie last night. We've all got walls around ourselves, Butch, that we can't see through—that's why we make so many mistakes about each other. Have a smoke?

Butch: Naw. Just say what you got to say and then take a double powder. I don't wanta lose control.

Jim: I know what you've got in mind.

Butch: What?

Jim: Hunger strike.

Butch: What of it?

Jim: I don't recommend it, Butch.

Butch: Did Whalen tell you to say that?

Jim: Naw, this is on the level, Butch.

Butch: Yeah, about as level as the Adirondacks.

Jim: I'll admit I've made myself useful to him. But I haven't forgotten two weeks we spent in the Hole together, and those visits he paid every morning to inquire about our health. He was even more solicitous about mine than yours, Butch. Things like that can make a common bond between men that nothing afterwards can ever—

Butch: Come to the point!

Jim: All right. I'm coming up for parole next month.

Butch [*rising*]: You are, huh?

Jim: There's a chance I might get it. And if I do I'm going to justify my reputation as a brilliant vocalist, Butch. I'm going to sing so loud and so high that the echo will knock these walls down! I know plenty from working in the office. I know all the pet grafts. I know all about the intimidation of employees and torture of convicts; I know about the Hole, about the water cure, about the overcoat—about Klondike! — And I know about the kind of food—or slop, rather! —that we been eating! You wait a month! That's all!

203

When I get through Whalen will be where he belongs—in the psychopathic ward with Sailor Jack! And I promise you things will change in here—look—here's an article about the Industrial Reformatory in Chillicothe!—that's the kind of a place this'll be!

Butch [*throwing the paper aside*]: I don't want no articles! —Allison, you're full of shit.

Joe: Take it easy, Butch. [*To Jim.*] So you don't want us to go on hunger strike?

Jim: No. It won't do any good. The Boss'll throw the bunch of you in Klondike. Do yourself a favor. Work with me. We can case this jug. But not if we keep on going opposite ways.—Give me your hand on it, Butch.

Butch: Fuck you!

Jim: It's no dice, huh? What do you say, Joe? Swifty?

Butch: They say what I say! Now git out before I lose my last ounce a restriction!

Jim: Okay. [*He goes out.*]

Joe: Maybe he *was* on the level.

Butch: He will be on the level when he's laid out straight underground. [*He slaps Swifty's rump.*] Git up! It's supper time!

Swifty [*his face buried in the pillow*]: Leave me alone. I'm sick. I'm not hungry.

Butch: You're coming along anyhow. We need you to help make some noise in case the kitchen boy was right about supper.

Joe: Noise?

Butch: Yep, *plenty* of noise

[*The bell rings in the hall.*]

Butch: Come along, youse! [*He shoves Queen and jerks Swifty to his feet.*] Hell's bells are ringin'! Come on, boys! Before them biscuits git cold! T-bone steaks for supper! Smothered in mushrooms! Come and git it!

[*A whistle is heard and the lights dim out. Theme up: "1812 Overture." Fade.*]

[. . . .]

ACT ONE: EPISODE TEN

ANNOUNCER: *"Hell—an Expressionistic Interlude"*

The following scene takes place on a dark stage. The shuffling of feet is heard and continues for several moments. A whistle sounds.

Voice: TAKE PLACES AT TABLES! [*More shuffling is heard.*] Set down!

> [*Now we hear the scrape of chairs or benches as the men sit.*]

Voice: Start eating!

> [*A low yammering commences.*]

Voice: Start eating, I said! You heard me! Start eating!

> [*Very softly, in a whisper, voices begin to be heard, transmitting a message from table to table with rising intensity.*]

Voices: Quit eating—quit eating—quit eating—quit eating—don't eat no more a dis slop—trow it back in deir faces—quit eating—quit eating—we don't eat crap we're human—quit eating—QUIT EATING—

[*The chorus grows louder, more hysterical, becomes like the roaring of animals. As the yammering swells there is a clatter of tin cups. The lights come up on Butch and others seated on benches at a table. Each has a tin cup and plate with which he beats time. [. . . .] The lights fade. There is a loud ringing of bells: a whistle sounds; then a sudden dead silence. The lights fade and come up on Schultz and the guards, entering cellblock. The prisoners are back in their cells.*]

Schultz: Now you boys are gonna learn a good lesson about makin' disturbances in mess hall! Git one out of each cell! Keep 'em covered!

Joe [*to Butch*]: You started something all right.

Queen: Oh, Lord!

Schultz: Ollie! Shapiro! Come on out, you're elected! Mex!

Shapiro: What for! Distoibance? I make no distoibance!

Mex: [*He protests volubly in Spanish.*]

Ollie: What you want me fo', Mistuh Schultz?

Schultz [*at the door of Butch's cell*]: Stand back there, Butch. [*He prods him with a gun.*] Who's in here with you? Joe? Queenie?

Butch: I started the noise.

Schultz: I know you started the noise. But we're saving you, Butch. You're too good to waste on the Hole.

Queen: I didn't make any noise, Mr. Schultz. I was perfectly quiet the whole time.

Schultz: Who's that on the bunk? Aw, the new boy. Playing Puss-in-the-Corner! Come on out.

Queen: He didn't make noise, Mr. Schultz.

Schultz: Come out, boy!

Swifty [shaking]: I didn't make any noise. I was sick. I didn't want any supper I've been sick ever since I come here.

Schultz: Yes, I've heard you squawking! Git in line there.

Swifty: I wanta see the Warden. It makes me sick being shut up without exercise.

Schultz: We'll exercise you! [He blows a whistle.]

Swifty [wildly]: The Hole? No! No!

Schultz [prodding him roughly with a billy]: Git moving! Krause! Alberts! Awright, that's all! —Two weeks in the hole, bread an' water—maybe we'll finish off with a Turkish bath. —Step on it, Mex!

Mex: [He swears in Spanish.]

Shapiro: Distoibance? Not me. Naw.

Schultz: Hep, hep, hep—[A slow shuffling is heard as the lights begin to dim.]

Joe: Christ!

Queen: Swifty won't make it! They'll kill him down there!

> [The whistle is heard, then the distant clang of steel.]

Butch: [whistles a few bars then sings out]:
> They fly so high, nearly reach the sky
> Then like my dreams they fade an' die!
> Fawchun's always hiding—I looked
> ev'rywhere!

> [Theme up and dim out.]

Mex: [He protests in Spanish.]

Schultz: Fall in line! March! Hep, hep, hep—[The voice diminishes as they move, heads bent, shoulders sagging, shuffling down the corridor.]

BLACKOUT SLOWLY

ACT ONE: EPISODE ELEVEN

ANNOUNCER: *"Hunger Strike!"*

A spot comes up on the office. Eva enters.

Warden: Had your supper?

Eva: Yes.

Warden [*watching her as she crosses downstage*]**:** Hate to keep you overtime like this—but with the boys in Hall C kicking up such a rumpus, we got to have all our books in perfect shape—just in case the professional snoopers git on our tails about something!

Eva: Yes sir. [*She removes the cover from the typewriter.*]

Warden [*watching her closely*]**:** Hope working nights don't interfere too much with your social life.

Eva [*tiredly*]**:** I don't have any social life right now.

Warden: How come?

Eva: I've been so busy job hunting since I moved here that I haven't had much time to cultivate friends.

Warden: No boyfriends, huh?

Eva: Oh, I have a few that I correspond with.

Warden: Yeah, but there's a limit to what can be put in an envelope, huh?

Eva: I suppose there is.—Mr. Whalen, there seem to be quite a number of bad discrepancies in the commissary report.

Warden: You mean it don't add up right?

Eva: I failed to account for about six hundred dollars.

[*The warden whistles.*]

What shall I do about it?

Warden: I'll git Jim to check it over with you. You know a lot can be done about things like that by a little manipulation of figures. Jim'll explain that to you.

Eva: I see.

Warden: How long have you been working here?

Eva: Two weeks.

Warden: Gin'rally I git shut of a girl in less time'n that if she don't measure up to the job.

Eva [*tensely*]**:** I hope that I've shown my efficiency.

Warden: Aw, efficiency! I don't look for efficiency in my girls.

Eva: What do you look for, Mr. Whalen?

Warden: Personality! You're in a position where you got to meet the public. Big men politically come in this office—you give 'em a smile, they feel good—

207

what do they care about the taxpayers' money? — Those boobs that go aroun' checkin' over accounts, where did this nickel go, what's done with that dime —jitney bums, I call 'em! —No, Siree, I got no respect for a man that wants a job where he's got to make note of ev'ry red copper that happens to slip through his hands! —Well—policy, that's what I'm after! —Being political about certain matters, it don't hurt *ever*, yuh see?

Eva: Yes, I think so.

Warden [*pausing*]: What color's that blouse you got on?

Eva [*nervously sensing his approach*]: Chartreuse.

Warden [*half-extending his hand*]: It's right Frenchy-looking.

Eva: Thank you. [*She types rapidly.*]

Warden [*opening the inner door and coughing uncertainly*]: Look here.

Eva: Yes?

Warden: Why don't you drop that formality stuff? [*He crosses to her.*] How do I look to you? Unromantic? Not so much like one of the movie stars? —Well, it might surprise you to know how well I go over with some of the girls! [*He seats himself on a corner of the desk.*] —I had a date not so long ago —girl works over at the Cattle and Grain Market —'bout your age, build, ev'rything— [*He licks his lips.*] —When I got through loving her up she says to me —"Do it again, Papa do it again!" — [*He roars with laughter and slaps the desk.*] —Why? Because she *loved*

it, that why! [*He rises and goes to the inner door.*] You ever been in here?

Eva: No.

Warden [*heartily*]: Come on in. I wanta show you how nice I got it fixed up.

Eva: No.

Warden: Why not?

Eva [*rising stiffly*]: You're married, Mr. Whalen. I'm not that kind of girl.

Warden: Aw, that act's been off the stage for years!

Eva: It's not an act, Mr. Whalen!

Warden: Naw, neither was *Uncle Tom's Cabin* when little Eva goes up to heaven in Act III on a bunch of steel wires! [*He slams the inner door angrily, then laughs.*] You're okay, sister. You keep right on pitching in there.

Eva: Now that you know me better, do I still have a job?

Warden: Why, you betcha life you still got a job! [*He laughs and grips her in a fumbling embrace which she rigidly endures. Jim enters.*]

Jim: Excuse me.

Warden [*still laughing*]: Come on in, Jimmy boy. Want you to check over this commissary report with Miss Crane. She says there's a few—what you call 'em? Discrepancies! You know how to fix that up!

208

Jim: Yes, sir.

Warden: How's things in Hall C? Pretty quiet?

Jim: Too quiet.

Warden: How's that?

Jim: When they make a noise you know what's going on.

Warden: They're scared to let a peep out since I put that bunch in the Hole.

Jim: I don't think so. I got an idea they might quit eating tonight.

Warden: Quit eating? You mean—*hunger strike?* [*The words scare him a little.*]

Jim: Yes. They're tired of spaghetti.

Warden: Maybe a change of climate would improve their appetites!

Jim: Klondike?

Warden: Yeah.

Jim: Klondike won't hold 3,500 men.

Warden: It would hold Hall C.

Jim: Yes, but Butch is in Hall C.

Warden: What of it?

Jim: He's got a lot of influence with the men.

Warden: He's a troublemaker an' I'm gonna sweat it out of him.

Jim: I wouldn't try that, Boss. Hunger makes men pretty desperate and if you tortured them on top of that there's no telling what might happen.

Warden: Hunger strike's something I won't put up with in here. Creates a sensation all over the country. Then what? Cranks of ev'ry description start bitching about the brutal treatment of those goddamn mugs that would knife their own mothers for the price of a beer!

Jim: The easiest way to avoid it would be to improve the food.

Warden: Avoid it, hell. I'll bust it to pieces! Wait'll they see that gang we've got in the Hole—if that don't make sufficient impression I'll give 'em the heat!

[. . . .]

ACT THREE: EPISODE ONE

ANNOUNCERS: *"Morning of August 15!"*

A spot comes up on the office. The warden is at the phone. During the following episodes the theater is filled almost constantly with the soft hiss of live steam from the radiators—

Warden: Schultz? How hot is it down there now? 125? What's the matter? Git it up to 130! You got Butch O'Fallon in No. 3 aintcha? Okay, give No. 3 135 and don't let up on it till you git instructions from me. Hey! Got them windows in the hall shut? Good. Keep 'em shut an' let 'em squawk their goddamn heads off!

> [*Blackout. A spot comes up on Klondike. The torture cell is seen through a scrim to give a misty or steam-clouded effect to the atmosphere. The men are sprawled on the floor, breathing heavily, their shirts off, skin shiny with sweat. A ceiling light glares relentlessly down on them. The walls are bare and glistening wet. Along them are radiators from which rise hissing clouds of live steam.*]

Joe [*He coughs, too.*]: W'at time is it?

Butch: How in hell would I know?

Swifty [*whimpering*]: Water—water.

Joe: I wonder if we been in here all night.

Butch: Sure we have. I can see daylight through the hole.

Joe: How long was you in that time?

Butch: Thirty-six hours.

Joe: Christ!

Butch: Yeah. And we've just done about eight.

Swifty: Water!

Butch: Hey! Y'know what—what the old maid said to the burglar when she—she found him trying to jimmy th' lock on th'—

Joe: Yeah. [*He coughs.*]

Queen: Swifty's sick. I am, too. Why don't somebody come here?

Butch: Aw, you heard that one?

Joe: Yeah. A long time ago, Butch. [*He coughs, too.*]

Butch: You oughta know some new ones.

Joe: Naw. Not any new ones, Butch.

Butch: Then tell some old ones, goddamn it!! Dontcha all lie there like you was ready to be laid under! Let's have some life in this party—Sing! Sing! You know some good songs, Queenie, you got a voice! C'mon you sons of guns! Put some pep in it! Sing it out, sing it out loud, boys! [*He sings wildly, hoarsely.*]

Pack up your troubles in yuhr ole kit bag an'
Smile, smile, smile!

[*The others join in feebly* —]

Sing it out! Goddamit, sing it out loud!

What's the use of worrying
It never was worthwhile!

[*Joe tries to sing* — *he is suddenly bent double in a paroxysm of coughing.*]

Swifty [*in a loud anguished cry*]: Water! Water! Water! [*He sobs.*]

[*There is a loud shrill hiss of steam from the radiators as more pressure is turned on.*]

Queen [*in frantic horror*]: *They're givin' us more!* Oh, my God, why don't they stop now! Why don't they let us out! Oh, Jesus, Jesus, please, please, please! [*He sobs wildly and falls on the floor.*]

Swifty [*weakly*]: Water—water. . .

Butch: Yeah. They're givin' us more heat. Sure, they're givin us more heat. Dontcha know you're in Klondike? Aw, w'at's a use, yer crybabies. Yuh wanta go on suckin' a sugar-tit all yer life? Gwan, sing it out—

I'm forever blowing BUBBLES!
Pretty bubbles in the—AIR!

[. . . .]

Joe [*coughing*]: Lemme at the air hole.

Queen: You're hoggin' it!

Joe: Cantcha see I'm choking to death? [*He coughs.*]

[*The steam hisses louder.*]

Butch [*rising*]: We got to systematize this business. Quit fightin' over the air hole. The only air that's fit to breathe is comin' through there. We gotta take turns breathin' it. We done sixteen hours about. Maybe we'll do ten more, twenty more, thirty more.

Joe: Christ!

Queen: We can't make it!

Butch: We can if we organize. Keep close to the floor. Stay in a circle round the wall. Each guy take his turn. Fifteen seconds. Maybe later ten seconds or five seconds. I do the counting. And when a guy flips out—he's finished—he's through—push him outta the line—This ain't a first-aid station—this is Klondike—and by God—some of us are gonna beat it—Okay? Okay, Joe?

Joe: Yeah.

Butch: Well, git started then.

Swifty: Water!

Butch: Push the kid up here first.

[*They shove Swifty's inert body to the air hole.*]

Breathe! Breathe! Breathe, goddamn you, breathe! [*He jerks Swifty up by the collar—stares at his face.*] Naw, it's no use. I guess he's beating a cinder track around the stars now!

Queen: He ain't dead! Not yet! He's unconscious, Butch! Give him a chance!

Butch [*inexorably*]: Push him outta the line. [*As the lights dim. . .*] Okay—Joe—

[*Theme up: "I'm Forever Blowing Bubbles." Fade.*]

DIM OUT

[. . . .]

Once Again About My Father

LULJETA LLESHANAKU

Forgive me, father, for writing this poem
that sounds like the creak of a door
against a pile of rags
in a room with cobwebs in its armpits
a cold so bitter that it stops your blood.

The same old black and white television
deformed images in its chest
the same old threadbare bedspread
like the face of a menopausal woman.
Next to a lamp, Adam's shriveled apple,
a hunger in your washed-out eyes.

You remember to ask me about something
when a toothpick snaps between your teeth.

I know how it is with you now, father:
by now you are content with loneliness—
its corpse in minus four degrees centigrade
its aluminum siding
its brace of dust
its calm sterility, infinitely white.

Translated from the Albanian by Albana Lleshanaku and Henry Israeli

Fresco

Now there is no gravity. Freedom is meaningless.
I weigh no more than a hair
on a starched collar.
Lips meet in the ellipsis at the end of a drowning
confession; on the sand, a crab closes its claws hermetically,
and moves one step forward and two steps to the right.
It was a long time ago when I first broke into a shudder
at the touch of your fingers;
no more shyness, no more healing, no more death.
Now I am as light as an Indian feather, and can easily reach the moon,
a moon as clean as an angel's sex
on the frescoes of the church.
Sometimes I can even see asteroids dying like drones
in ecstasy for their love, their queen.

Translated from the Albanian by Uk Zenel Buçpapa and Henry Israeli

Peninsula

My shadow stretches over the street
peninsula of fear
with coordinates that shake in the wind
like last week's wet blankets
hung out to dry.

The frightened child, or the nervous woman
(the last brushstroke is missing)
the trembling border that separates them
is the zigzag of smoke
from a forgotten cigarette.

At first I had only one eye
big and blue and dilated . . .
Now I have two
and a strip of sand between them
that dries and thickens
from day to day.

And a wind constantly shifts directions
pursuing clues left by the fossils
of extinct fish.

Translated from the Albanian by Albana Lleshanaku and Henry Israeli

215

CILDO MEIRELES | MEMORY OF THE SENSES

PAGE 216:
Olvido (Oblivion), 1987–89.

PAGE 217:
Volatile, 1980–94.

BELOW:
Eureka/Blindhotland, 1970–75.

RIGHT:
Marulho, 1992–97.

PAGE 220:
Através (Through), 1983–89.

Cildo Meireles

Over the past thirty years, Cildo Meireles has been making art concerned with the senses and sensorial consciousness of being in the world. It is through the body that we make sense of the world: insofar as experience and cognition are mediated through the body, our subjectivity is an embodied subjectivity. As Maurice Merleau-Ponty observed in "Eye in Mind" (1964) "it is by lending his body to the world that the artist changes the world into paintings," and in the the work of the Brazilian neo-concrete movement in the sixties, especially Lygia Clark and Helio Oiticica, the body can be seen as the *location* of a work of art.

Insertions into Ideological Circuits: 1. Coca-Cola Project, 1970.

In a work from 1969, Meireles stood on a noisy street corner in Rio de Janeiro, closed his eyes and tried to hear sounds that were coming from as far away as possible, suggesting that while we do not *see* all that we hear, we sense it. This activity was part of an exploration that led Meireles to a series of artistic interventions and installations where the audience became a participant in the work, intervening in order to disrupt the transparency of communication. What becomes evident in his work is, as Meireles himself has suggested, the possibility of producing an "aesthetics as ethics" and an "ethics as aesthetics." This approach enabled him to produce a

series of works in the late sixties that engaged directly with life under a military dictatorship at a time when the global economy caused deepening conditions of impoverishment and dependency in Brazil. In the work *Inserções em circuitos ideólogicos* (Insertions into Ideological Circuits), Coca-Cola bottles and paper currency were inscribed with messages concerning the experience of political and social violence in Brazil and then placed back into circulation. Following Marcel Duchamp's concept of the ready-made, in which he inserted industrial objects into the art world, Meireles extended the strategy by re-inserting the altered bottles and currency back into the commodity system. Meireles's audience thus became an author of the work.

Such works recall the notion of *dematerialization*, a term coined to describe the disappearance of the art object in much work produced during the sixties. However, in Meireles's work, the participation of the subject entails a more intimate relationship with the phenomenal world, a relationship in which the subject's body is implicated. In the installation of 1970–75, *Eureka/Blindhotland*, Meireles created a space defined by a lightweight black netting, in which he placed two hundred black rubber balls of different weights, a soundtrack of the balls being dropped to the floor and at the center, a sculpture with a scale, weights, and two wooden bars and a cross. The viewer experiences both sensory confusion and a form of deprivation. No one sense seems adequate to experience the installation's components, nor is the body sufficient to account for its own relation to the world. The language of appearance and representation have no absolute authority. "Blind," in the title, refers to the density of experience, a field of sensory perception in which the difference between the weight and volume of the rubber balls is unclear. Hence the condition of meaning in Meireles's work is dependent upon a physical engagement with the work itself, an experience of the intertwining of subject and object.

"Sight," as Emmanuel Levinas has written, "maintains contact and proximity. The visible caresses the eye. One sees and hears like one touches." Meireles carries this idea further. His work forfeits the dominance of the visual not only as the language of art, but

out, the smell is of a harmless chemical compound. The danger passes.

The emphasis that Meireles gives to the non-visible offers the viewer a chance to enter the work, to make contact in a corporeal sense, demanding of the viewer a lingering attentiveness rather than the customary distanced gaze. One thinks as one hears, touches, smells. *Volatile* incorporates the living body

LEFT AND RIGHT: Insertions into Ideological Circuits: 2. Banknote Project, 1970–75.

also as a precondition to our being in the world. To challenge vision in this way is to question the idea that consciousness is tied to vision and that mastery is granted to the one who sees. In *Volatile* (1980–1994), the viewer enters a room seeing little more than the flame and soft light cast by a partially-buried candle. As one makes one's way toward the back it is virtually impossible to determine from sight, from sound, or touch, what the ground is composed of, except for the experience of a certain foreboding as one moves towards the light in the back of the small room. The strongest impression is of the smell of natural gas and the consequent sensation of danger prompted by the perception of the flame and gas together. This is the volatile situation to which the title refers, but "volatile" only insofar as it is produced by an accumulated memory within the body of the participant. As it turns

that, as it moves through space, provides perceptions shaped by recollection and anticipation that, in turn, disrupt consciousness.

This disruptive experience is essential to his installation *Através* (Through). Produced in 1983 and later in 1989, it is a maze comprised of velvet museum ropes, street barriers, garden fences, blinds, railings, and aquariums that act as a series of translucent screens. In the center of the space there is a large ball of crumpled cellophane about three meters in diameter, and the floor is covered with eight tons of broken plate glass. Underscoring Meireles's concept of the body as the ground of our acting in the world, the installation confronts the viewer with a powerful sensation of physical and psychological unease. The apparently transparent space provides a way through which the gaze can pass, yet the series of screens and rails and strewn glass creates a psychological barrier that impedes the body—representing a space of interdiction and enclosure, a limit. This sense of unease is heightened in the work by the cracking sound of the glass being stepped on. The danger is that of walking through unknown territory, where clear vision is perhaps not enough.

The participant encounters the world both through recognition and an estrangement of the senses. Controlled by the space through which the body moves, the subject is defined by the horizon of his consciousness, whether it be territorial, economic or mental: spaces of difference, circulation, and confinement. In *Olvido* (Oblivion) 1987–89, Meireles constructed a native tent painted black on the inside, covered with banknotes from countries of the Americas that had once been (or remained) inhabited by indigenous populations. The tent was placed in the middle of a circular area covered with bones and surrounded by a low wall of candles. The sound of a chain saw could be heard from inside it. Like the ashes or charcoal in some of Meireles's other works, the bones in *Olvido* then are, like memory, indissoluble. They represent a memory trace of what had been before, of those who lived and then disappeared, that remains opaque. The work offers a critique of our demand to *see*, of the privilege of the eye implied in the metaphor of light being brought into the world. The candles—which may be associated with Western tropes of illumination as knowledge and revelation as belief—cast their light on a place outside of representation, a place of forgetting. There is nothing more to be seen. Night

has fallen. What remains are bones given in exchange for capital, a sacrificial economy that fills the interior void, void of human life except the sound of the chain saw destroying the rain forest.

The work summons us, exposes us to a recognition of what lies between us and the other; it puts us face-to-face with mortality. And yet it is also the limits of language to which Meireles appeals in these works, insofar as it is the bodily experience which constitutes the work of art rather than the simple elements of its construction. He introduces what is both familiar and foreign to the senses, placing us in a more precarious situation, at risk as we summon an accumulated memory drawn from sensory experience. We remain as we do in the dark, swimming in an endless sea. And yet this is not a void or a negative space to which we are led, for we would then lose our way and return.

In a recent work called *Marulho*, which means "the sound of waves," Meireles constructed a wooden pier extending over a floor covered with hundreds of copies of a book, each opened to a color photograph of the sea. To this he added a soundtrack of voices of people of all ages and ethnicities, that came and went, washing over the viewer like waves. As the voices rose and fell, the work provided a sensory immersion in the world. From standing on a street corner, listening to the sounds around him, Meireles has moved to the image of standing on the pier surrounded by the sea with the world before him. Through such immersions, we become attuned to the language of difference, to others who speak, to the community of voices in which we find ourselves.

Charles Merewether

The Little Hand

When he was still an infant, Malaparte was sent to live with his wet-nurse Eugenia Baldi and her family in a working-class district of Prato, about fifteen kilometers from Florence. His mother would come and visit occasionally, but Malaparte continued to stay with Eugenia, her husband Mersiade, and their sons Faliero and Baldino for the next four or five years.

For the rest of his life he considered them, in many aspects, his real family.

When I was a boy, I loved to go with Faliero and Baldino to visit the rag shops—Sbraci's, Campolmi's, Cavaciocchi's, or Calamai's. And there, sitting underfoot among busy workers, I would rummage through the heaps of fabric, sometimes finding the most marvelous and unexpected things: shells, pieces of colored stones that seemed to be precious—green, purple, turquoise, and yellow—and some that the rag men called *moonstones*—as pale, smooth, and transparent as moonbeams. Or those red stones which the rag men said would bleed if you squeezed them hard enough, so we boys would bite them, or pinch them between our fingers, hoping for blood. Occasionally there were strange dried animals—some of them might have been sea horses, or mummified lizards, or mice. Others looked like fetuses with crushed heads.

It was a world unto itself: the whole city of Prato was a mountainous landscape of rags, though few people, aside from the rag men and us boys, took the trouble to explore these mysterious continents. Occasionally Faliero, Baldino, and I would be joined by some of the other kids from our street, via Arcangeli, out beyond the Santa Trinità gate, and as soon as we crossed the threshold of the shop, that smell of rags—dry and dusty, yet strong and intoxicating as fermenting fruit—would go to our heads and trigger a kind of ecstatic snowblindness.

The instant a bale was sliced open, the rags would pour out of the wound like yellow-red-green-turquoise intestines, and we would thrust our arms inside this flesh the color of blood, the color of grass, the color of sky, rummaging through the swollen stomach, the hot viscera, of those bundles of rags—the eyes of our hands searching in that dark world for some luminous treasure: a pearl, a shell, a moonstone. Then we would plunge headfirst into those cloth mountains the way we might dive into the rapids of the Bisenzio on a summer's day, slowly dissolving in the deep, sweet swirling odor of incense, of musk, of clove, the perfumes of India, Ceylon, Sumatra, Java, Zanzibar, the fragrances of the South Seas.

One time we found a large-mouthed snake covered in green and turquoise scales, smooth and thick as silken rope. Another time, a blue tortoise with golden claws and a Chinese mask of green porcelain. And then one day we found a woman's hand, its fingernails lacquered gold: a little hand, sweet and light as if fashioned of rosewood. It occurred to me to slip it into my pocket and take it home, where I hid it under the pillow of the big bed in which all five of us slept: Mersiade, his wife Eugenia, their sons Faliero, Baldino, and I.

They say the first thing to die are the eyes, and the last are the nails. Those nails were shiny, sharp, still alive.

I couldn't fall asleep, fevered from the thought of the hand under the pillow. I heard it moving, bending its fingers, sinking its nails into the sheets. Faliero and Baldino, who slept at the foot of the bed, had pulled their knees up against their chests, terrified of the horrible rustling. I don't know how I ever dozed off, but I dreamed that the hand was slowly crawling out from under the pillow, slithering along my shoulders, caressing my throat.

I awoke with a shout and sat bolt upright, drenched in a cold sweat. Mersiade gave me a slap to chase away the fright, but when he saw the little hand, which had in fact come out from under the pillow, he turned as pale as wax. Eugenia, though, seized it with the tips of her fingers and jumped out of bed.

"Calm down!" she said. "So much fear for a little hand!"

It was the first time it occurred to me that we might trust the dead more than the living, that we might have more to fear from the hands of the living than the hands of the dead. It was the first time I glimpsed that the dead may not be foolish, like the living, but prudent. And that while being alive exposes you to all sorts of dangers—forces you to sleep with your eyes open—if you are dead, you can rest peacefully with your eyes closed.

Eugenia opened the window, ready to toss the hand outside. The warm, rich, sweet smell of tomatoes poured into the room.

"Don't! It will shrivel up my vines," said Mersiade.

"It's your brains that are shriveled up!" said Eugenia.

And she flung the hand out into the garden, where we found it the next day, covered with ants. They were dragging it slowly through the tomato plants, toward the hedge of reeds.

We let it go.
It never came back.

Translated and adapted from the Italian by Walter S. Murch

No One Dies In This Life

Bare feet pad the kitchen floor
A shuffled youth tangos
In fires. Welfare homes
Catch temper and fall.

Sadly stands the raft
At midnight among
Bottles and wood
Cinder to spot a mind,

Hammer the fridge,
Interrupt the call. Your life
Had a suicide. Again
But no feet left the truck

Hit by your fear that badly passed
The blinking red light.

DEATH OF MARY THE HARLOT

MIROSLAV KRLEŽA

It all happened in a civilization, God forgive us, in which such events are noted in newspaper chronicles as something barely worth mentioning. On the same day the papers reported how the little harlot Mary poisoned herself in the hotel such and such, whole pages were devoted to His Majesty the King of Schiavonia's visit, to soccer games, to fraud inside government ministries, so that no reporter was inspired by the little harlot's death to dedicate a few lines to her and thus, amid the frantic madness of events, sensations, and pretense, at least for the twenty-four hours preserve all that sorrow that tore at that humble victim of an innocent girl.

Mary took poison early in the morning, around four, and her moaning was picked up through the closed door by a hotel page who went to the fourth floor in order to wake up a guest wanting to depart on the morning ship. At that time, when the first man heard the moaning of the poisoned girl through her locked door, it was more or less too late for any help, since the stomach acids already had fused with poison, and from the human standpoint there was simply nothing else to be done. But a few hours before that, when the hapless and weeping girl had knocked on the archimandrite's door, Room Number 74, all possibilities had still been open and so it seems not to be an exaggeration when we state that her whole wretched life had been in the archimandrite's hands, as a porcelain figurine broken in the paw of a drunken bear turning its rear to the whole world, snoring vulgarly, primordially, belching like a pig that beheld a rose in front of its snout. But since it is not our intention to write a puritanical thesis concerning this incident, wishing, instead, to report it duly as chroniclers, all these events should be presented in some sort of a chronological order, approximately the same order (quite independent of us) in which the story unfolded.

So it was late at night. The hotel was asleep, and the passengers from the last nightly express had already settled in their rooms, as in a steamship's cabins when only the groaning of the engine is audible, and the light flickers on the first foremast. Somewhere from deep inside, from the tavern, came music, muffled, as if from underneath a glass bell; at the end of the soft carpeted hallways there were shaded lamps, and from time to time an elevator would hum and then the silence would ensue, and then, after a slight pause, an elevator would again give a long drone.

The archimandrite, a big man in a fur-lined coat, with a precious gem cross hanging around his neck on a massive, jewel-studded chain, was not so drunk as to have forgotten (enclosed in the glass elevator box with a liveried boy) how the elevator's chain could snap and how all that, including his four hundred pounds, could plunge deep down. Once, years ago, he had read in the newspapers how an elevator plummeted in that way, taking with it all those sitting in the glass box. Since then, that unpleasant thought would not leave him, and so he sighed with relief when the liveried boy opened the glass door and when he felt the crossbeams and the solid concrete under his feet. And so the archimandrite, who occupied Room 74 on the fourth floor, a graying man with a beard, with the greasy wavy hair, like some classical figure of the Greek Orthodox confession (seen by Mussorgsky in a gentle scherzo, while Demjan the Poor sings of him as a spider with a swollen purple nose and a tall cap), this archimandrite opened the door to his room with a deep relief.
He quietly grunted some frivolous coachman's song, took off his fur coat, his robe lined with red silk, and, his digestion so badly upset, bent down belching, taking off his shoes with those swollen butcher's hands. One heavy, massive shoe fell off. One, and then the other and the archimandrite, the famed preacher, who had drank all night with three ministers, seven swindlers, burglars, shadowy figures, who all drank to the King and Country, and talked of millions and blood, the archimandrite, this notorious drunkard, stopped to think, Should he retrieve from his suitcase a box of sodium bicarbonate, take a teaspoon or two and thus wash away the unpleasant taste in his mouth? when he heard knocking on his door. The archimandrite was taken by surprise, wondering why anyone should be knocking upon his door.

At first, he thought it had to be a mistake. When he heard more knocks, and when it went on, timid and persistent, he got up and, in his underwear and heavy wool socks, went to the door.

There he saw a girl, a disheveled anemic girl, clad in silk. Her face was pale-green. She trembled as if in deadly fear.

"What is it? You must have come to the wrong door, miss!"

"No, I haven't! Please! This is by no means a mistake! I live here, in 73, next to your room. I already wanted to come to you before dinner! Please, I am begging you, this is a question of life and death to me."

"All right, all right! I understand! Quiet! Just be quiet! Why are you so upset? There's no need to get so upset! I understand you! Please! Do come in! Just keep quiet!"

The girl edged past him into the room; somehow managed to get to the chair, collapsed in it and started to sob. This weeping was so spasmodic that the archimandrite stopped, half naked, in socks, in the robe lined with red silk (so that his underwear and the bands around his ankles were revealed), having no way of knowing if those tears were real or not.

"If this is an act, my hat's off to you," thought the archimandrite, looking at the girl suspiciously. As the weeping went on, it seemed that time had stopped, and when the girl noticed the archimandrite did not move she threw herself on the floor and crawled on her knees to the priest. There, under his feet, she again started to weep.

The presence of a young, perfumed woman, the softness of her hair, the silk through which the warm body could be felt, all made the drunk's blood churn, and his voice quivered.

"My dear child! I don't understand all of this. I just cannot! Calm down! It's the middle of the night! You can hear the floor creaking in here! What's the point of this, here and now?"

The girl was very young, barely seventeen, and she wept like a child. She could not find words, so intense were the tears. The archimandrite stroked her face, feeling the flame of her cheeks, and then turned around, went to the washstand, poured a glass of water and gave it to her.

"Calm down, my child! Pull yourself together! What is the meaning of all this?"

"Dear sir! My dear sir, father! Please, I am so scared, I'm frightened, I'd like to make a confession, I'm terrified, I'm sick, dear sir!"

"I, to hear your confession, my child? And how am I supposed to do that? And why?"

The archimandrite, this philanderer and drunkard, did not believe in God. Ever since his Büchner-Darwinian times, his primary school days, the whole so-called supernatural superstructure remained for him unequivocally refuted, and as life later tossed him here and there, all of that lay in ruins in him and he lived in his priest's robe as an atheist and cynic. By his profession, he watched over the holy relics of the legendary saints and emperors, and when he got drunk, he would mock with these skeletons, spit at the icons, smash bottles on the crosses, vomit in the treasuries and lie in the church. And now, long past midnight, a whore, a drunken woman, reeking of cognac and homemade brandy, came to him, weeping under his feet and wanting to confess. The archimandrite wanted to laugh, to laugh in his healthy and deep bass voice so loudly that all the guests and travelers would run out of their cabins, as if there were a wreck and the hotel were sinking. As this unknown young woman was kneeling before him with her head bowed, he came down to her and with the routine of an old spiritual father, started caressing her hair, the top and the back of her head, and then beneath it, this downy gutter, her vertebrae, her shoulders, her neck, her back, this little bird, the poor baby, unhappy girl, weeping, in fear of God, confessing.

The girl wept on, burying her head in the red-lined robe, recounting some banal, everyday story of the drunkard of a father, of the mother sewing all night long, of the war that broke out and of her starvation while roaming the cities, saying she could not go on anymore. It was certain she could not go on like this anymore, and the fear of some ineffable architectural heaviness of the existing metaphysical superstructure, of some supernatural order, that she had no means of describing, calling it instead, and very unintelligently, "God's will," so this fear of a possible anti-Büchnerian order and world, it all made her go down in front of the archimandrite's feet, forcing her to confess, to unburden herself, to die clean. It is quite possible that in her seventeen-year-old child's organism there was a parallel, strong, and ineradicable impulse of deep and healthy liveliness, frustration, and that the act of knocking on her neighbor's door in the middle of the night was the act of a drowning person, desperately reaching—in the form of a last, helpless signal—for salvation.

And indeed, for a moment it looked as if the archimandrite was about to comprehend this and actively lend a hand and save the moral drowner. But, above all else, the pitiful artificiality of the story itself, the desperately naked banality of life of the anonymous, little city harlot, the very presence of a young woman, and all that wine and the sleepless night, all this suddenly looked profoundly false. And so this drunken, obdurate rhinoceros of lust and instinct awoke under his skin and he lifted the weeping girl into his lap, as he would do with a wounded man all in bandages. He stroked this desperate, unhappy child, caressed her with his hand, telling her of God, who was, apparently, good and eternal, and how he already had heard of thousands and thousands of such cases, and how there are no sinful and sinless people, but, instead, all people are equally sinful standing in front of God; and how God tells us we should live, and only live, and how living is not sinful, but holy, the only wisdom, the only salvation. And so the archimandrite spoke of God, feeling, under his butcher's hands, the womanly calves, thighs, and garters (those damn modern garters, tied around the waist), slurping the girl's tears, caressing her, quieting her until the room finally went silent.

It was still very early, and the first bluish daylight was emerging through the curtains when the archimandrite awoke from the heavy, leaden sleep. Outside, in the hallway, people were yelling, and many voices could be heard. So the archimandrite instantly sat in the bed, reaching in darkness for the woman.

"She's gone. What if she's robbed me?!"

Tired and dazed, half asleep, he reached for the night table, and when his fingers found the chain and the precious diamond cross, the golden watch in its buckskin pouch, and the wallet. He turned over, snoring away loudly, as if all those movements had been somnambulent or unconscious.

Outside, the hallway was buzzing with the commotion over the girl who had poisoned herself in the next room. Somebody hissed for the servants not to yell.

"Shhh! Quiet! The guests are still asleep."

—1924

Translated from the Croatian by Damir Biličić

233

CONTRIBUTORS

Aron R. Aji, born in Izmir, Turkey, is an associate professor of Comparative Literature at Butler University in Indianapolis. He is the editor of *Milan Kundera and the Art of Fiction* (Garland Press) and has published articles on Salman Rushdie, Milan Kundera, Chinua Achebe, and others.

A.R. Ammons's most recent book of poetry is *Glare* (Norton 1997).

John Ashbery's new collection of poems *Wakefulness* will be published this spring by Farrar, Straus & Giroux.

Nina Berberova was born in St. Petersburg, Russia in 1901. She attended the Institute of Art History in Moscow before leaving the country in 1922. She then lived in Germany, Czechoslovakia, and Italy, settling finally in Paris in 1925, where she attended the Sorbonne. After moving to the United States in 1951, she worked as a language instructor at the Berlitz school, as a radio announcer for the "Voice of America," as an office machine-operator, and finally as an instructor at Yale University and later at Princeton University. She is the author of *The Tattered Cloak and Other Novels*, *The Accompanist*, *Three Novels*, her autobiography *The Italics Are Mine*, and a biography of Pyotr Tchaikovsky, among others. In 1989, she was honored as a Chevalier of the French Order of Arts and Letters. She died in Philadelphia, Pennsylvania in 1993.

Damir Biličič was born in 1966 and lives in Duga Resa, Croatia. He has translated numerous English-language works into Croatian, including David Guterson's *Snow Falling on Cedars*.

Uk Zenel Buçpapa is an Albanian poet and translator living in Tirana, Albania. His translations include "The Wasteland," and "Howl," as well as various poems by Rudyard Kipling, Robert Frost, Ezra Pound, Octavio Paz, and Yehuda Amichai. In 1992, he received a Fulbright Scholarship and a residency at the International Writers Program in Iowa. His books include *My Daughter Speaks, Weeps, and Laughs With Elez Aba*, and *Gray Days*.

Sophie Calle was born in Paris in 1953. Her work has appeared most recently in group exhibitions at the Musée National d'Art Moderne, Centre Georges Pompidou, Paris, the Louisiana Museum of Modern Art, Humlabaek, Denmark, and in the 1995 Istanbul and 1997 Johannesburg Biennials. Solo exhibitions of her work have been held at the Museum Boymans-van Beuningen, Rotterdam, the University Art Museum, University of California, Santa Barbara, the Tel Aviv Museum of Art, Tel Aviv, and the Centro Cultural de la Fundació, Barcelona. In 1998, solo exhibitions of her work will be held at the Tate Gallery, London and the Centre Nationale de la Photographie, Paris. She lives and works in Paris.

Marc Cohen is the author of *On Maplewood Time* and *Mecox Road*, published by Groundwater Press. He lives in New York City.

Willie Doherty's photographs and video projections have presented images from his native Derry, Ireland since 1985. Doherty has been the subject of several one-person museum exhibitions in Paris, Toronto, Lisbon, Bern, and Munich. He was short-listed for the Turner Prize in 1994 for *The Only Good One is a Dead One*, a two-screen video projection which was first shown in the United States at the Grey Art Gallery and is currently being presented in the traveling six-person exhibition *Being & Time: The Emergence of Video Projection*. He will have a major solo exhibition at the Tate Gallery in the fall of 1998 and at the Renaissance Society, Chicago, in the spring of 1999.

Okwui Enwezor is a poet, critic, and curator, and is the publisher and founding editor of *Nka: Journal of Contemporary African Art* copublished with the Africana Studies Center at Cornell University. His writing has appeared in many art magazines, as well as in exhibition catalogues including *Future, Present, Past* (47th Venice Biennial), and *Transforming the Crown: African, Asian & Caribbean Artists in Britain, 1966–1996* (Studio Museum in Harlem and the Bronx Museum of Art). Enwezor was the artistic director of the 1997 Johannesburg Biennial and curated *In Sight: African Photographers, 1940 to the Present* at the Guggenheim Museum, New York. He divides his time between Johannesburg and New York.

Louis Fernandez was born in Oviedo, Spain, in 1900. The *Skulls* are among his later works, dating from 1953 to the early 1970s. He was a perfectionist who worked slowly and produced relatively little: his first solo exhibition, at the Galerie Pierre in 1950, was not followed by a second show until his 1956 exhibition at the Galerie des Cahiers d'Art. In 1965 he showed at the Galatéa Gallery in Turin, and in 1972 at the Centre National d'Art Contemporain, Paris. He died in Paris in 1973.

Allean Hale recently edited *The Notebook of Trigorin* by Tennessee Williams (New Directions 1997), an adaptation of Chekhov's *The Seagull*. She has written widely on Tennessee Williams and currently teaches theater at the University of Illinois at Urbana.

Milton Hatoum was born in 1952. He studied architecture in Brazil and literature in Paris and now teaches at the University of the Amazon in Manaus, Brazil. His novel *The Tree of the Seventh Heaven* was published by Atheneum in 1994.

Bill Horrigan is the curator of Media Arts at the Wexner Center for the Arts at Ohio State University in Columbus which commissioned Chris Marker's video installation, *Silent Movie*, in 1995. Marker's CD-ROM installation, *Immemory*, will be on view there in 1998. Horrigan has also commissioned projects from Mark Dion, Todd Haynes and Christine Vachon, Beth B, and Bruce and Norman Yonemoto.

Henry Israeli has published poetry in *Black Warrior Review, Fence, Fine Madness, Nimrod, Descant*, among others. He has translated and published many poems by Luljeta Lleshanaku, and the Israeli poet, Ronny Someck. His co-adaptation of *Henry VI* was produced at the Joseph Papp Public Theater in 1996.

Bilge Karasu was born in Istanbul in 1930. Upon receiving his degree in philosophy from the College of Literature at Istanbul University, he worked at the National Office of Publications and at the Foreign Correspondence division of Ankara Radio. He held a Rockefeller Grant from 1962 to 1963, and in 1974 he assumed a faculty position at Hacettepe University in Ankara. Karasu's translation of D. H. Lawrence's *The Man Who Died* won the Turkish Language Association's translation award. Among his works in Turkish are *Death in Troy* (1963), *A Long Day's Evening* (1970), *The Garden of Migrant Cats* (1979), *The Kiosk Called Kismet* (1982), and *The Guide* (1992). In 1991, his novel, *Night* (Louisiana State University Press), won the International Pegasus Award. Karasu died in 1995.

Jane Kramer writes the "Letter from Europe" for *The New Yorker*. Her last book was *The Politics of Memory* (Random House 1996) and her next will be about a militia community in northwestern Washington state. She lives in Paris and New York.

Miroslav Krleža (1893–1981) was one of the most versatile Croatian writers of the twentieth century. He wrote poetry, short stories, novels, plays and essays and was the founder of several literary magazines. He was recommended for the Nobel Prize in literature in 1961. His works include collections of poetry (*Pan*, *Three Symphonies*, and *Croatian Rhapsody*), plays (*In Agony*, *The Glembays*), and the novels *The Return of Filp Latinovicz*, and *Banquet in Blitva*, among many other titles. "The Death of Mary the Harlot" was first published in the magazine *Književna republika* (Literary Republic) in 1924, and appears here through the courtesy of the Croatian Academy of Arts and Sciences.

James Laughlin was born in Pittsburgh, Pennsylvania in 1914. In 1936 while a sophomore at Harvard, he began a life-long commitment to publishing experimental poetry and prose with the first of his New Directions anthologies. These volumes appeared each year until 1991, introducing American readers to the work of Delmore Schwartz, Dylan Thomas, Thomas Merton, John Hawkes, Denise Levertov, James Agee, Céline, Cocteau, and others. His New Directions publishing house revived difficult-to-find work by such authors as

Gertrude Stein, Nathanael West, as well as Hesse, Nabokov, and Pasternak. Collections of Laughlin's own poems include *In Another Country* (1979), *Stolen and Contaminated Poems* (1985), and *The Bird of Endless Time* (1989). He was an avid skier all his life, and in later years contributed articles on professional skiing for *Town & Country*, *Harper's Bazaar*, *Vogue*, and *Sports Illustrated*. Laughlin died in November 1997. A new book of his poetry, *The Secret Room*, will be published by New Directions in April 1998.

Marie Claire Leng was born in Ontario, Canada. She is currently pursuing her MFA at the Bennington Writing Seminars, where she received the first Jane Kenyon Poetry Scholarship.

Phillis Levin is a poet and translator. Her books of poetry are *Temples and Fields* (University of Georgia Press, 1988) which won the Poetry Society of America's Norma Farber Award for best first book of poetry, and *The Afterimage* (Copper Beech Press, 1995). Her poems have also appeared in *Best American Poetry 1989* and the forthcoming *Best American Poetry 1998*, edited by John Hollander. In 1995 she was a Fulbright Fellow in Slovenia. Her poems have appeared in *Grand Street*, *The New Yorker*, and *The Nation*.

Luljeta Lleshanaku, born in Elbasan, Albania, began publishing her work in 1991 after the overthrow of the Stalinist regime. Her books of poetry are *The Sleepwalker's Eyes* (1993), *Sunday Bells* (1994), and *Half-Cubism* (1996). English translations of her work have appeared in *Seneca Review*, *Modern Poetry in Translation*, *Anthology of American Verse & Yearbook of American Poetry 1997*, and *Visions-International*.

Albana Lleshanaku is Luljeta Lleshanaku's sister and has translated her work into English. She lives in Brooklyn and is currently studying architecture.

Curzio Malaparte was born Kurt Suckert in 1898 near Florence, Italy, to a German father and an Italian mother. He served in combat in World War I, was wounded several times and decorated by both the French and Italian governments. Associating himself early on with the Fascist movement, he achieved success as a journalist, playwright and poet, and counted Benito Mussolini as a patron. In 1931 Malaparte left Italy for France, where he broke with Fascism, and on his return to Italy was imprisoned for having attacked Hitler and Mussolini in the French and British press. His harrowing World War II novel, *Kaputt* (Northwestern University Press 1995), was drawn from memoirs he kept while covering the war for *Corriere della Sera* from 1941 to 1943. "The Little Hand" is adapted from *Maledetti Toscani* (1956), a memoir of his childhood in Prato, outside Florence. Malaparte died in 1957.

David Mamet is the author of various plays, including *American Buffalo*, *Speed-the-Plow*, *Glengarry Glen Ross* (for which he won the Pulitzer Prize), *Oleanna*, and *The Old Neighborhood*, which is currently on Broadway. His films include *The Verdict*, *The Untouchables*, *House of Games*, *Hoffa*, and most recently, *Wag the Dog*. His most recent books include the novel *The Old Religion* (Free Press 1997), and two books on acting, *True and False: Heresy and Common Sense* (Pantheon 1997), and *Three Uses of the Knife* (Columbia University Press 1998). He lives in Vermont and Massachusetts.

Chris Marker was born in 1921. After an early career as a mediocre student, soldier, jazz pianist, and social activist, Marker turned to filmmaking where his innately impractical disposition somehow passes unnoticed. Fascinated by the computer, he recently issued a CD-ROM called *Immemory* and is waiting for the new technology, DVD, to do the sequel. He loves cats and owls.

Cildo Meireles was born in Rio de Janeiro in 1948. His installations have appeared at the Museu de Arte Moderna, Rio de Janeiro, the Museum of Modern Art, New York, the Institute of Contemporary Art, London, the Capp Street Project, San Francisco, and the Centre d'Art Contemporain, Thiers, France. A 1995 retrospective of his work, organized by IVAM, Centro Julio Gonzalez, Valencia, Spain, traveled to the Fundacão de Serrávales, Porto, Portugal and the Institute for Contemporary Art, Boston. His work has been included in exhibitions at El Museo del Barrio, New York, the Musée National d'Art Moderne, Centre Georges Pompidou, Paris, the Kanaal Art Foundation, Kortrijk, Belgium, and P.S. 1 Museum, New York, and in the 1997 Johannesburg Biennal. A solo exhibition of his work is scheduled to open next year at the New Museum for Contemporary Art, New York.

Charles Merewether is curator of Spanish and Portuguese–language cultures at the Getty Research Institute. He has taught at the Universidad Nacional de Bogota, the University of Sydney, the Universidad Autonoma, Barcelona, and the Universidad Ibero-americana, Mexico City. He is the author of the forthcoming *What Remains: Ana Mendieta*, as well as *Art and Social Commitment: An End to the City of Dreams 1931–1948* (Art Gallery of New South Wales 1984). He has written extensively on the reinvention of modernism in non-European cultures, especially in Latin America and is currently writing a book on art and the archive.

Brenda Milner was born in Manchester, England and was educated at Cambridge University. At the end of World War II, Milner moved to Canada, where she took up a teaching position at the newly formed Institut de Psychologie of the Université de Montréal. In 1950, Milner came to the Montreal Neurological Institute to study patients in whom Dr. Wilder Penfield was

237

carrying out unilateral brain operations for the relief of focal epilepsy. She has remained there ever since, obtaining her Ph.D. in physiological psychology from McGill in 1952 and going on to establish a laboratory of neuro-psychology at the Institute where she is currently the Dorothy J. Killam Professor of Cognitive Neuroscience. In 1964, Milner was appointed a Career Investigator by the Medical Research Council of Canada. She and her students have demonstrated the important role played by the right hippocampal region in spatial memory and by the frontal cortex in the temporal ordering of recent events. She has received numerous honors including the Isaak Walton Killam Award, the Hermann von Helmholtz Prize from the Cognitive Neuroscience Institute, and the McLaughlin Medal from the Royal Society of Canada. In recognition of her research achievements, Milner will be inducted into the Canadian Medical Hall of Fame in 1998.

Santu Mofokeng was born in Johannesburg, South Africa, in 1956. He began his career as a freelance photographer in 1982, as a member of the Afrapix Collective, and is a documentary photographer for the Institute of Advanced Social Research (formerly the African Studies Institute) at the University of the Witwatersrand, Johannesburg. His work was included most recently in the group exhibitions *Colours: Contemporary Art from South Africa*, at the Haus der Kulturen der Welt, Berlin, *In-Sight: African Photographers, 1940 to the Present*, at the Solomon R. Guggenheim Museum, New York, and in the 1997 Johannesburg Biennial. He lives and works in Johannesburg.

Murathan Mungan was born in 1955 in Istanbul, Turkey, and spent his childhood and early youth in Mardin. Mungan holds a master's degree in Theater from Ankara University. He currently lives in Istanbul. Mungan has published novels, poetry, plays, screen-

plays, essays, film and theater criticism, and political columns. His prose works include *Battle Stories, Forty Rooms, Last Istanbul, Lal Tales*, and *Before the Mount Kaf*, and *The Mesopotamian Trilogy* is among his dramatic works. He is the author of ten books of poetry and five collections of short stories including, most recently, *This Side Of Legends*. The work in this issue is drawn from *Murathan 95*, a selection of previously published and unpublished work in a semi-autobiographical framework, published in Istanbul by Metis.

Walter Scott Murch has been a film editor and sound designer since 1969. He collaborated on the early films of Francis Ford Coppola and George Lucas (THX-1138, *The Godfather* (Parts I and II), *The Conversation, American Graffiti*, and *Apocalypse Now*). His most recent work was editing and mixing Anthony Minghella's *The English Patient* for which he won two Academy Awards. He is currently working on a re-edit of Orson Welles's *Touch of Evil* based on recently discovered notes by Welles.

Walter Tandy Murch was born in Toronto, Ontario in 1907. He studied the violin for 15 years, attending the Toronto Conservatory of Music in 1922 and 1923. In 1925, he enrolled in the Ontario College of Art, and two years later moved to New York City to study at the Art Students League and the Grand Central School, where his instructor was Arshile Gorky. Murch had his first one-person show in 1941 at Betty Parsons's Wakefield Gallery, and through his continuing association with Parsons, met Barnett Newman, Theodoros Stamos, Mark Rothko, and Jackson Pollock. Murch made his living as a freelance commercial illustrator, and his work appeared on the covers of *Scientific American, Forbes, Fortune*, and *Vogue*. In 1966, a retrospective exhibition of Murch's work opened at the Rhode Island School of Design and subsequently traveled to other institutions. He died in 1967.

238

Peter Nagy is an American artist who is based in New Delhi. The most recent exhibition of his works was held in June 1997 at the Nicole Klagsbrun Gallery in New York. From 1982 to 1988, he was the director of Gallery Nature Morte in New York City's East Village. He has recently resurrected Nature Morte as a commercial curatorial project in New Delhi, combining Indian and international contemporary art.

Pablo Neruda was born Ricardo Eliezer Neftali Reyes y Basoalto in Parral, Chile, in 1904. A career diplomat for Chile starting in Rangoon in 1927, he was a consul in Java, Thailand, Cambodia, as well as Buenos Aires, Madrid, and Mexico City, during the 1930s. He was elected to the Chilean Senate as a Communist in 1944, and was politically active to the point of being expelled from the country in 1949. His volumes of poetry include *Crepusculario* (1923), *Twenty Love Poems and One Song of Despair* (1924), *Residence on Earth and Other Poems* (1933), *Canto general* (1950), and *Elementary Odes* (1954). In 1971, he was awarded a Nobel Prize in Literature. Neruda died in Chile during the week of the 1973 military coup.

Philip Nikolayev's poems have most recently appeared in *Verse*, *Exquisite Corpse*, *Culture Front*, *The Formalist*, *The Dark Horse*, and other literary magazines. His second collection of poems, *Dusk Raga*, is forthcoming in India.

Suzan-Lori Parks's plays include *The Death of the Last Black Man in the Whole Entire World*, *Imperceptible Mutabilities in the Third Kingdom*, and *The America Play*. She has won two OBIE awards and has received grants from the Kennedy Center Fund for New American Plays, The Cal Arts Herb Alpert Foundation, two National Endowment for the Arts grants, and others. In 1996, she received a Lila Wallace–Reader's Digest Fund grant with which she established the

HarlemKids Internet Playwrighting Workshop. Two collections of her plays are available from Theatre Communications Group: *The American Play and Other Works*, and most recently *Venus*. Her first feature film, *Girl 6*, was directed by Spike Lee. She is a new regular columnist for *Grand Street* and is currently working on two commissioned plays and a screenplay, as well as a novel.

Raymond Pettibon was born in Tucson, Arizona, in 1957. His work has been included in the 1993 Whitney Biennial and the seminal group exhibition, *Helter Skelter: L.A. Art in the 1990s*, at the Museum of Contemporary Art in Los Angeles. Solo exhibitions of his work will open in 1998 at the Philadelphia Museum of Art, Philadelphia, and the Renaissance Society at the University of Chicago. He lives and works in Hermosa Beach, California.

Pablo Picasso was born in Malaga, Andalusia, on the Mediterranean coast of Spain in 1881. The painting on page 121, *Skull and Pitcher*, represents, perhaps, a transition between the ominous works of the wartime years such as *Guernica* (1936) and *The Charnel House* (1945), and that of later years. Picasso died in his sleep in 1974, at the age of 94.

Giovanni Pontiero (1932–1996) was José Saramago's English translator. He died on his 64th birthday while correcting proofs of *The History of the Siege of Lisbon*. Final revisions on his translation of *Blindness* were completed by Margaret Jull Costa.

Neil Printz is writing a doctoral dissertation about Andy Warhol titled "Other Voices, Other Rooms." He is the co-editor of the *Andy Warhol Catalogue Raisonné of Paintings, Sculptures and Drawings*.

239

Sophie Ristelhueber was born in Paris in 1949. Her work was included most recently in exhibitions at the Victoria and Albert Museum, London, the Museum of Modern Art, New York, the Neue Gallery, Graz, Austria, P.S. 1 Museum, New York, and the Musée National d'Art Moderne, Centre Pompidou, Paris, as well as at the 1993 Venice and 1997 Johannesburg Biennials. Solo shows of her work have been held at Le Magasin, the Centre National d'Art Contemporain, Grenoble, France, the Imperial War Museum, London, the Centraal Museum, Utrecht, Netherlands, the Cabinet des Estampes du Musée d'Art et d'Histoire, Geneva, and Le Consortium, Dijon, France. Her series *Fait*, which is excerpted in this issue, will be shown in its entirety at the Albright-Knox Art Gallery, Buffalo, in April 1998. She lives and works in Paris.

Alastair Reid is a poet, prose writer, traveler, and translator. He has been a staff writer at *The New Yorker* since 1958. In addition to his own writing, he has translated the work of many Latin American writers, Jorge Luis Borges and Pablo Neruda among them.

Tomaž Šalamun, a Slovenian, has published extensively since his first two books, *Poker* (1966) and *The Purpose of the Cloak* (1968), appeared in samizdat. His books translated into English include *Selected Poems* (Ecco Press), edited by Charles Simic with an introduction by Robert Hass, and *The Four Questions of Melancholy: New and Selected Poems of Tomaž Šalamun* (White Pine Press), edited by Christopher Merrill.

José Saramago was born in Portugal in 1932. He is the author of *Baltasar and Blimunda*, *The Year of the Death of Ricardo Reis*, *The Gospel According to Jesus Christ*, and *The History of the Siege of Lisbon*, as well as plays, poetry, short fiction, and essays. *Blindness*, the novel from which the excerpt in this issue was taken will be published in the fall of 1998 by Harcourt Brace.

Marian Schwartz has translated three volumes of Berberova's fiction in addition to the story collection that will include *The Big City*, and a novel, *The Book of Happiness*, both forthcoming from New Directions. She is the recipient of a Translation Fellowship from the National Endowment for the Arts. Her most recent translation is *Conversations With Joseph Brodsky: A Poet's Journey Through the Twentieth Century* by Solomon Volkov (Free Press).

Ramón Gómez de la Serna was born in Madrid in 1888. He was a regular contributor to *El Sol* and to José Ortega y Gasset's *Revista de Occidente*, while writing numerous novels, essays, and poetry, as well as his greguerías, a literary blend of simile and aphorism based on Japanese haiku and the Arab-Andalusian qasida. In 1936, he fled the Spanish Civil War for Buenos Aires, where he lived with his wife, the Russian writer Luisa Sofovich. He was awarded a Premio March one year before his death in 1963. There are some ten thousand greguerías in his 1,592-page *Total de Greguerías*, published by Aguilar, Madrid in 1962.

Tony Smith was born in South Orange, New Jersey, in 1912. He attended Georgetown University for two years before moving to New York in 1933 to take classes at the Art Students League. In 1937, he enrolled at the New Bauhaus in Chicago, and between 1938 and 1939 he worked with Frank Lloyd Wright. Smith had a successful architectural practice of his own from 1940 to 1960, designing private houses for clients that included the art dealer Betty Parsons and the painter Theodoros Stamos. During these years, he continued to work on his own painting. Smith was 48 years old when he began creating the geometric sculptures for which he is best known, which were shown for the first time in the 1964 show *Black, White, and Gray* at the Wadsworth Atheneum in Hartford. Between 1946 and 1980, he taught art and design at New York University, Cooper Union School of Art, Pratt Institute, Bennington College, and Hunter

College as well as other institutions. His work has been included in major exhibitions including *Primary Structures*, at the Jewish Museum, New York (1966), *Scale as Content*, at the Corcoran Gallery of Art, Washington D.C. (1967), *The Art of the Real, USA 1948–1968*, at the Museum of Modern Art (1968), and *A Century of Modern Sculpture: The Patsy and Raymond Nasher Collection*, at the Dallas Museum of Art (1987). A retrospective of his work will open at the Museum of Modern Art in the summer of 1998. He died in 1980.

Rebecca Solnit is a contributing editor to *Art Issues* and *Creative Camera*. Her books include *Savage Dreams: A Journey into the Landscape Wars of the American West* (Verso) and *A Book of Migrations: Some Passages in Ireland* (Verso). She is currently at work on a book about walking. She strays from San Francisco.

Nancy Spero was born in Cleveland in 1926. She received her BFA from the School of the Art Institute of Chicago in 1949 and spent the following year in Paris studying at the Ecole des Beaux-Arts and Atelier Andre Lhote. She lived in Chicago until 1956, when she moved to Italy with her husband, the artist Leon Golub and her two sons. Since the 1960s, Spero has concentrated on social and political themes in her work, producing the *War Series* between 1966 and 1970, *Codex Artaud* from 1971–72, and *Torture of Women*, 1974–76. A traveling retrospective of her work was organized in 1987 by the Everson Museum of Art, Syracuse, and in 1994 *Leon Golub and Nancy Spero: War and Memory* was organized by MIT List Visual Arts Center, Cambridge, Massachusetts. Her work has been shown at the Haags Gemeentemuseum, the Netherlands, The Studio Museum in Harlem, The Whitney Museum, and the Museum of Modern Art, New York, the 1986 Sydney Biennial, the 1997 Lyons Biennial, and the 1997 Documenta X, in Kassel. She lives and works in New York.

Robert Storr is an artist and critic, and a curator in the Department of Painting and Sculpture at the Museum of Modern Art, New York. The exhibitions he has curated include *Bruce Nauman, Mapping, Robert Ryman: Paintings 1955–1993, DISLOCATIONS, Projects 61: Franz West, Willem de Kooning: The Late Paintings, Chuck Close,* and *Tony Smith: Part and Whole* (opening in July 1998), all at the Museum of Modern Art, New York, as well as *Susan Rothenberg: 15 Years — a Survey*, Rooseum, Malmö, Sweden. Storr is the author of *Philip Guston* (Abbeville), and *Chuck Close* (Rizzoli).

Larissa Szporluk teaches at Bowling Green State University in Ohio. The poems in this issue will appear in her collection *Dark Sky Question*, to be published by Beacon Press in May 1998.

Philip Ward is a writer, poet, translator and author of numerous works, including novels, travel books, and anthologies. He is the author of *The Oxford Companion to Spanish Literature*. The greguerías in this issue appear in his translation of *Greguerías: The Wit and Wisdom of Ramón Gómez de la Serna*, published by the Oleander Press (Cambridge, England).

Andy Warhol was born Andrew Warhola, in Pennsylvania in either 1928 or 1930. The images here are from a series of skulls he did in 1976, following his immensely successful series of celebrity portraits. Warhol died in 1987.

Ellen Doré Watson has translated eight Brazilian novels including *The Tree of the Seventh Heaven* by Milton Hatoum. She has also translated the work of the Brazilian poet Adélia Prado for which she received a National Endowment for the Arts Translation Fellowship. A poet herself, Watson's *We Live in Bodies* was published in 1997 by Alice James Books. She is an editor at *The Massachusetts Review*.

241

Tennessee Williams was born in 1914 in Columbus, Mississippi. He studied at the University of Missouri and at Washington University before graduating from the University of Iowa in 1938 where he wrote his first plays, including *Not About Nightingales*. He worked at various odd jobs in the following years, living in New Orleans, New York City, California, Florida, and Mexico while writing *The Glass Menagerie* (1945), and *A Streetcar Named Desire* (1947) for which he won the Pulitzer Prize. He wrote over a dozen full-length plays and many collections of one-acts, as well as short stories, verse, and a novel, *The Roman Spring of Mrs. Stone* (1950). His play *Cat on A Hot Tin Roof* won the Pulitzer Prize in 1955. In his later years, he settled in Key West, Florida, continuing to write into the 1970s. He died in 1983. *Not About Nightingales* was discovered by Vanessa Redgrave in 1997 and had its world premiere in March 1998 at the Royal National Theatre in London, directed by Trevor Nunn. It will be published by New Directions later this year.

Catherine de Zegher was born in Gronigen, the Netherlands in 1955. She studied archaeology and art restoration at the State University of Ghent, Belgium, and from 1977 to 1985 she worked as an archaeologist, doing inventories and restorations of historic monuments. Since 1985 she has been the director of the Kanaal Art Foundation, in Kortrijk, Belgium, a center for contemporary art of which she was a co-founder. In 1995 she became a visiting curator at the Institute of Contemporary Art, Boston, and organized *Inside the Visible*, an exhibition of 37 twentieth-century women artists, for the ICA's sixtieth anniversary in 1996. She lives and works in Belgium and the United States.

Grand Street would like to thank **Dr. Eric Kandel** for recommending the interview with **Brenda Milner**, and also **Barbara Epler** for her assistance with the **Tennessee Williams** excerpt. We are grateful to **Mladen Urem** and to **The Croatian Academy of Arts & Sciences** for providing the story by **Miroslav Krleža**. We also thank **Sarah Auld** for her help on the **Tony Smith** portfolio.

Grand Street would like to thank the following people for their generous support:

Edward Lee Cave
Cathy and Stephen Graham
Dominic Man-Kit Lam
The New York State Council on the Arts
Betty and Stanley K. Sheinbaum

ILLUSTRATIONS

Front Cover
Sophie Ristelhueber, from *Fait, Kuwait*, 1992.
Cibachrome print, 39 3/8 x 51 3/16 in. Courtesy of the
artist.

Back Cover
Willie Doherty, *At the Border 5 (Isolated Incident)*, 1995.
Cibachrome on aluminum, 40 x 72 in. Courtesy of the
artist and Alexander and Bonin, New York.

Title Page
Walter Murch, *Grey Melon*, 1965. Mixed media on paper, 19
x 15 1/8 in. Collection of the Rhode Island School of
Design Musuem of Art, Providence, Rhode Island; gift of
Mrs. Murray S. Danforth. Photograph courtesy of Walter
S. Murch.

Table of Contents
Willie Doherty, *The Bridge* (diptych), 1992. Two black-and-
white photographs, each 48 x 72 in. Courtesy of the artist
and Matt's Gallery, London.

pp. 33–40 Peter Nagy, *Meltdown*. Titles and dates appear
on **p. 41**. **p. 33** Collection of the Musée Guimet, Paris.
Photograph by Peter Nagy. **pp. 33 (inset), 38, and
38 (inset)** Collection of Shamina Talyarkhan, New York.
Photographs by Oren Slor. **pp. 34 and 35** Photographs by
Jaroslav Poncar. **pp. 36 and 37** Photographs by Edward
Robbins. **pp. 39 and 40** Photographs by Douglas Bressler.

pp. 55–67 Tony Smith. Titles and dates appear with
images. **p. 55** Ink on paper, 11 3/4 x 17 11/16 in. **p. 56** Ink
on paper, 8 3/8 x 10 7/8 in. Courtesy of Matthew Marks
Gallery, New York. **p. 57** Oil on canvas, 18 x 14 in. **p. 58**
Pencil on paper, 10 3/8 x 7 7/8 in. **p. 59** Oil on canvas, 39

1/2 x 55 1/4 in. **p. 60** Oil on canvas, 44 x 28 in. Collection of
Bennington College, Bennington, Vermont. Photograph
by John Conte. **p. 61** Oil on canvas, 24 x 26 in. **p. 62 (top)**
Pencil and ink on paper, 6 3/4 x 3 3/4 in. **p. 62 (bottom)**
Ink on paper, each drawing 4 3/4 x 3 in. **p. 63** Ink on paper,
10 7/8 x 8 3/8 in. **p. 64** Painted steel, 204 x 374 x 216 in.
Permanent collection of the Massachusetts Institute of
Technology, Cambridge. Photograph by Herb Englesberg.
p. 65 Welded bronze, black patina 80 x 80 x 57 in. Edition
of six. Photograph by T. Charles Erickson. Courtesy of the
Paula Cooper Gallery, New York. **p. 67** Photograph by
David Gahr. **pp. 55, 56, 57, 58, 61, 62 (bottom), and 63**
Photographs by Thomas Powel. **pp. 59 and 62 (top)**
Photographs by Peter Berson. All images courtesy of and
copyright © Tony Smith Estate.

pp. 96–100 Walter Murch, *Monolith of Time*. Titles and
dates appear with images. **p. 96** Watercolor on paper, 29 x
32 in. Collection of the Chase Manhattan Bank, New York.
p. 97 Mixed media on paper, 20 x 27 in. Collection of
Frank Lavaty. **p. 98** Mixed media on paper, 29 3/8 x 33 3/4
in. Private collection. **p. 99** Mixed media on paper, 16 1/2 x
22 in. Collection of Mr. and Mrs. Carl L. Selden. **p. 100
(left)** Gouache and pencil, 29 x 23 in. Collection of the
Westmoreland Museum of American Art, Greensburg,
Pennsylvania; gift of the Women's Committee. **p. 100
(right)** Oil, pencil, and crayon on cardboard, 28 1/2 x 22 1/4
in. Collection of the Museum of Modern Art; Larry Aldrich
Foundation Fund. All photographs courtesy of Walter S.
Murch.

pp. 121–124 *Memento Mori*. Artists, titles, and dates appear
with images. **p. 121** Oil on canvas, 28 5/8 x 36 1/8 in.
Courtesy of the Menil Collection, Houston. Photograph by
Hickey-Robertson, Houston. **p. 122** Egg tempera on

canvas mounted on wood panel with incised lines, 18 1/8 x 15 in. Courtesy of the Menil Collection, Houston. Photograph by Adam Rzepka. **p. 123** Silk screen ink and acrylic on canvas, each 15 x 19 in. **p. 123 (top left)** Collection of the Baltimore Museum of Art. All images copyright © 1998 Andy Warhol Foundation for the Visual Arts/ARS, New York. **p. 124** Pen and ink on paper, 22 1/2 x 15 in. Courtesy of the artist, Regen Projects, Los Angeles and David Zwirner Gallery, New York.

p. 125 Georg Procháska, from *De Structura Nervorum*, 1779. Collection of the Biblioteca Medica, Centrale di Careggi, Florence.

pp. 137–140 Nancy Spero, *Sperm Bombs and* Jouissance. Titles and dates appear with images. **p. 137 (top)** Gouache and ink on paper, 25 1/2 x 39 in. **p. 137 (bottom)** Gouache and ink on paper, 24 x 36 in. **p. 138 (top)** Gouache and ink on paper, 24 x 36 in. **pp. 138–139 (bottom) and 140** Handprinting on walls and printed collage on paper, 22 panels, each approximately 19 1/2 x 96 1/2 in. Installation at Malmö Konstall, Malmö, Sweden 1994. Photographs by David Reynolds. All images courtesy of the artist.

pp. 152–156 Santu Mofokeng, *Black Photo Album/Look at Me: 1890–1950*. 10 archival photographs. Captions appear on **p. 157**.

pp. 169–179 *After the Fact*, titles and dates appear with images. **pp. 169, 170, 171, and 177** Seven photographs by Sophie Ristelhueber. Cibachrome prints, each 39 3/8 x 51 3/16 in. Courtesy of the artist and Galerie Arlogos, Paris. **pp. 172, 173, and 179** Five works by Sophie Calle. **p. 172 (clockwise from top left)** Color photograph, 47 1/4 x 35 7/16 in., and book. Color photograph, 39 3/8 x 29 1/2 in., and book. Color photograph, 39 3/8 x 29 1/2 in., and book. Color photograph, 29 1/2 x 39 3/8 in., and book. **p. 173** Color photograph, 34 5/8 x 44 1/16 in., and book. **p. 179** Color photograph, 29 1/2 x 39 3/8 in., and book. Courtesy of the artist and Galerie Arndt & Partner, Berlin. **pp. 174–175, 176, and 178** Three works by Willie Doherty. **pp. 174–175** Single-screen video installation with sound, dimensions variable. Collection of the Arts Council of England. Photograph by Mimmo Capone. Courtesy of the artist and Matt's Gallery, London. **p. 176** Cibachrome on aluminum, 48 x 72 in. Edition of three. Courtesy of the artist and Alexander and Bonin, New York. **p. 178** Black-and-white photograph, 48 5/16 x 71 11/16 in. Courtesy of the artist.

pp. 185–188 Chris Marker, *Dial M for Memory*. One "processed" image from each of four films by Chris Marker, with corresponding quotes from these films' narrations. All images and text courtesy of the artist.

p. 216–222 Cildo Meireles, *Memory of the Senses*. Titles and dates appear with images. **p. 216** Mixed media installation (tent; 6,000 bills of American countries; 3 tons of bones; 70,000 candles; charcoal; audio tapes), 129 7/8 x 242 1/8 x 242 1/8 in. Photograph by Rômulo Fialdini, courtesy of Galeria Louisa Strina, São Paulo. **p. 217** Mixed media installation (wood; ash; candle; smell of gas) 118 1/8 x 157 1/2 x 590 1/2 in. Installation at Galerie Lelong, New York, 1995. Photograph by Wit McKay, courtesy of Galerie Lelong, New York. **p. 218** Mixed media installation (*Eureka*, 1970–71; two pieces of wood, each measuring 12 x 3 x 3 in.; a cross formed by two pieces of wood identical to the first two; antique scale. *Blindhotland*, 1970–75: nylon netting; felt; 200 rubber balls between 100 and 1,500 grams in weight; audio tapes), dimensions variable. Installation at Galerie Lelong, New York, 1997. Photograph by Wit McKay, courtesy of Galerie Lelong, New York. **p. 219** Mixed media installation (books printed with images of water, wooden pier construction, audio tapes). Installation at the 1997 Johannesburg Biennale. Photograph by Werner Maschmann. **p. 220** Mixed media installation, 590 x 590 in. Installed at the Kanaal Art Foundation, Kortrijk, Belgium. Photograph courtesy of Galerie Lelong, New York. **p. 221** Print on Coca-Cola bottles. Photograph by Pedro Oswaldo Cruz, courtesy of Galerie Lelong, New York. **p. 222 (left)** Print on paper currency. Photograph by Pedro Oswaldo Cruz, courtesy of the artist. **p. 222 (right)** Print on paper currency. Photograph by Wilton Montenegro, courtesy of the artist. All images courtesy of the artist, Galeria Luisa Strina, São Paulo, and Galerie Lelong, New York.

RAIN TAXI

review of books

reviews • interviews • essays

DJUNA BARNES • RIKKI DUCORNET • STEPHEN DIXON • ARNO SCHMIDT •
• MINA LOY • PAUL BOWLES • AMIRI BARAKA • JANE MILLER • ATLAS PRESS
SAMUEL R. DELANY • ANTONIN ARTAUD • LESLIE SCALAPINO • IVAN KLIMA •
• ROSARIO CASTELLANOS • ROBERT WALSER • DAVID FOSTER WALLACE
CAROLE MASO • MIROSLAV HOLUB • JOHN WIENERS • PAUL METCALF •
• PETER HANDKE • RUSSELL EDSON • CHARLES FORT • BURNING DECK

One Year Subscription (4 issues) $10, International Rate $20
Send Check Or Money Order: RAIN TAXI, PO Box 3840, Mpls MN 55403

tongues
contemporary world literature

art essays fiction interviews
poetry & translation

featuring:
John Ashbery
Mempo Giardinelli
Santoka
Robert Kelly
Bradford Morrow
Gregory Orr
William Weaver

plus works from:
Argentina China France
India Indonesia Italy
Japan Russia & the United
States of America

to **subscribe** for
$8.95 for 1 year, 2 issues
send check or money order to:

Tongues
1300 Wertland Street #C2
Charlottesville VA 22902

GRAND STREET
BACK ISSUES

36 *Edward W. Said on Jean Genet; Terry Southern & Dennis Hopper on Larry Flynt* STORIES: Elizabeth Bishop, William T. Vollmann; PORTFOLIOS: William Eggleston, Saul Steinberg; POEMS: John Ashbery, Bei Dao.

37 *William S. Burroughs on guns; John Kenneth Galbraith on JFK's election* STORIES: Pierrette Fleutiaux, Eduardo Galeano; PORTFOLIOS: *Blackboard Equations*, John McIntosh; POEMS: Clark Coolidge, Suzanne Gardinier.

38 *Kazuo Ishiguro & Kenzaburo Oe on Japanese literature; Julio Cortázar's HOPSCOTCH: A Lost Chapter* STORIES: Fernando Pessoa, Ben Sonnenberg; PORTFOLIOS: Linda Connor, Robert Rauschenberg; POEMS: Jimmy Santiago Baca, Charles Wright.

39 *Nadine Gordimer: SAFE HOUSES; James Miller on Michel Foucault* STORIES: Hervé Guibert, Dubravka Ugrešić; PORTFOLIOS: *Homicide: Bugsy Siegel*, Mark di Suvero; POEMS: Amiri Baraka, Michael Palmer.

40 *Gary Giddins on Dizzy Gillespie; Toni Morrison on race and literature* STORIES: Yehudit Katzir, Marcel Proust; PORTFOLIOS: Gretchen Bender, Brice Marden; POEMS: Arkadii Dragomoshchenko, Tom Paulin.

41 *Nina Berberova on the Turgenev Library; Mary-Claire King on tracing "the disappeared"* STORIES: Ben Okri, Kurt Schwitters; PORTFOLIOS: Louise Bourgeois, Jean Tinguely; POEMS: Rae Armantrout, Eugenio Montale.

42 *David Foster Wallace: THREE PROTRUSIONS; Henry Green: an unfinished novel* STORIES: Félix de Azúa, Eduardo Galeano; PORTFOLIOS: Sherrie Levine, Ariane Mnouchkine & Ingmar Bergman—two productions of Euripides; POEMS: Jorie Graham, Gary Snyder.

43 *Jamaica Kincaid on the biography of a dress; Stephen Trombley on designing death machines* STORIES: Victor Erofeyev, Christa Wolf; PORTFOLIOS: Joseph Cornell, Sue Williams; POEMS: Robert Creeley, Kabir.

44 *Martin Duberman on Stonewall; Andrew Kopkind: SLACKING TOWARD BETHLEHEM* STORIES: Georges Perec, Edmund White; PORTFOLIOS: Fred Wilson, William Christenberry, POEMS: Lyn Hejinian, Sharon Olds.

45 *John Cage's correspondence; Roberto Lovato: DOWN AND OUT IN CENTRAL L.A.* STORIES: David Gates, Duong Thu Huong; PORTFOLIOS: Ecke Bonk, Gerhard Richter; POEMS: A. R. Ammons, C. H. Sisson.

46 *William T. Vollmann on the Navajo-Hopi Land Dispute; Ice-T, Easy-E: L.A. rappers get open with Brian Cross* STORIES: David Foster Wallace, Italo Calvino; PORTFOLIOS: Nancy Rubins, Dennis Balk; POEMS: Michael Palmer, Martial.

ORDER
WHILE THEY LAST

47 *Louis Althusser's ZONES OF DARKNESS; Edward W. Said on intellectual exile* STORIES: Jean Genet, Junichiro Tanizaki; PORTFOLIOS: Barbara Bloom, Julio Galán; POEMS: John Ashbery, Ovid.

48 *OBLIVION* *William T. Vollmann: UNDER THE GRASS; Kip S. Thorne on black holes* STORIES: Heinrich Böll, Charles Palliser; PORTFOLIOS: Saul Steinberg, Lawrence Weiner; POEMS: Mahmoud Darwish, Antonin Artaud.

49 *HOLLYWOOD* *Dennis Hopper interviews Quentin Tarantino; Terry Southern on the making of DR. STRANGELOVE* STORIES: Paul Auster, Peter Handke; PORTFOLIOS: Edward Ruscha, William Eggleston; POEMS: John Ashbery, James Laughlin.

50 *MODELS* *Alexander Cockburn & Noam Chomsky on models in nature; Graham Greene's dream diary* STORIES: Rosario Castellanos, Cees Nooteboom; PORTFOLIOS: Katharina Sieverding, Paul McCarthy; POEMS: Robert Kelly, Nicholas Christopher.

51 *NEW YORK* *Terry Williams on life in the tunnels under NYC; William S. Burroughs: MY EDUCATION* STORIES: William T. Vollmann, Orhan Pamuk; PORTFOLIOS: Richard Prince, David Hammons; POEMS: Hilda Morley, Charles Simic.

GAMES
David Mamet: THE ROOM; Paul Virilio on cybersex and virtual reality
STORIES: Brooks Hansen, Walter Benjamin;
PORTFOLIOS: Robert Williams, Chris Burden;
POEMS: Miroslav Holub, Fanny Howe.
52

FETISHES
John Waters exposes his film fetishes; Samuel Beckett's ELEUTHÉRIA
STORIES: Georges Bataille, Colum McCann;
PORTFOLIOS: Helmut Newton, Yayoi Kusama;
POEMS: Taslima Nasrin, Simon Armitage.
53

SPACE
BORN IN PRISON: an inmate survives the box; Jasper Johns's GALAXY WORKS
STORIES: Vladimir Nabokov, Irvine Welsh;
PORTFOLIOS: Vito Acconci, James Turrell;
POEMS: W. S. Merwin, John Ashbery.
54

EGOS
Julian Schnabel: THE CONVERSION OF ST. PAOLO MALFI; Suzan-Lori Parks on Josephine Baker
STORIES: Kenzaburo Oe, David Foster Wallace;
PORTFOLIOS: Dennis Hopper, Brigid Berlin's Cock Book;
POEMS: Amiri Baraka, Susie Mee.
55

DREAMS
Edward Ruscha: HOLLYWOOD BOULEVARD; TERRY SOUTHERN AND OTHER TASTES
STORIES: William T. Vollmann, Lydia Davis;
PORTFOLIOS: Jim Shaw, ADOBE LA;
POEMS: Bernadette Mayer, Saúl Yurkievich.
56

DIRT
John Waters & Mike Kelley: THE DIRTY BOYS; Rem Koolhaas on 42nd Street
STORIES: Mohammed Dib, Sandra Cisneros;
PORTFOLIOS: Langdon Clay, Alexis Rockman;
POEMS: Robert Creeley, Thomas Sayers Ellis.
57

DISGUISES
Anjelica Huston on life behind the camera; D. Carleton Gajdusek: THE NEW GUINEA FIELD JOURNALS
STORIES: Victor Pelevin, Arno Schmidt;
PORTFOLIOS: Hannah Höch, Kara Walker;
POEMS: Vittorio Sereni, Marjorie Welish.
58

TIME
Mike Davis on the destruction of L.A.; John Szarkowski: LOOKING AT PICTURES
STORIES: Naguib Mahfouz, Nina Berberova;
PORTFOLIOS: Spain, Charles Ray;
POEMS: James Tate, Adonis.
59

PARANOIA
Fiona Shaw on life in the theater; Salvador Dalí on the paranoid image
STORIES: David Foster Wallace, Nora Okja Keller;
PORTFOLIOS: Tom Sachs, David Cronenberg;
POEMS: Fanny Howe, Lawrence Ferlinghetti.
60

ALL-AMERICAN
William T. Vollmann tracks the Queen of the Whores; Peter Sellars: THE DIRECTOR'S PERSPECTIVE
STORIES: Reinaldo Arenas, Guillermo Cabrera Infante;
PORTFOLIOS: Rubén Ortiz-Torres, Doris Salcedo;
POEMS: Octavio Paz, Aimé Césaire.
61

IDENTITY
Edward W. Said on Mozart's dark side; actor Marcello Mastroianni explores his past
STORIES: Can Xue, Marcel Beyer;
PORTFOLIOS: Mona Hatoum, Robert Rauschenberg;
POEMS: Christopher Middleton, Robin Robertson.
62

CALL
1-800-807-6548

Please send name, address, issue number(s), and quantity.
American Express, Mastercard, and Visa accepted; please send credit-card number and expiration date. Back issues are $15 each ($18 overseas and Canada), including postage and handling, payable in U.S. dollars. Address orders to GRAND STREET, Back Issues, 131 Varick Street, Suite 906, New York, NY 10013.

CROSSING THE LINE
John Waters interviews "drag king" Mo B. Dick; Elias Canetti's aphorisms and adages
STORIES: Franz Kafka, Patrick Chamoiseau;
PORTFOLIOS: Lygia Clark, Justen Ladda;
POEMS: Guillaume Apollinaire, Hilda Morley.
63

Some of the bookstores where you can find
GRAND STREET

Magpie Magazine Gallery, Vancouver, CANADA

Newsstand, Bellingham, WA
Bailey Coy Books, Seattle, WA
Hideki Ohmori, Seattle, WA

Looking Glass Bookstore, Portland, OR
Powell's Books, Portland, OR
Reading Frenzy, Portland, OR

...On Sundays, Tokyo, JAPAN

ASUC Bookstore, Berkeley, CA
Black Oak Books, Berkeley, CA
Cody's Books, Berkeley, CA
Bookstore Fiona, Carson, CA
Huntley Bookstore, Claremont, CA
Book Soup, Hollywood, CA
University Bookstore, Irvine, CA
Museum of Contemporary Art, La Jolla, CA
UCSD Bookstore, La Jolla, CA
A.R.T. Press, Los Angeles, CA
Museum of Contemporary Art, Los Angeles, CA
Occidental College Bookstore, Los Angeles, CA
Sun & Moon Press Bookstore, Los Angeles, CA
UCLA/Armand Hammer Museum, Los Angeles, CA
Stanford Bookstore, Newark, CA
Diesel, A Bookstore, Oakland, CA
Blue Door Bookstore, San Diego, CA
Museum of Contemporary Art, San Diego, CA
The Booksmith, San Francisco, CA
City Lights, San Francisco, CA
Green Apple Books, San Francisco, CA
Modern Times Bookstore, San Francisco, CA
MuseumBooks–SF MOMA, San Francisco, CA
San Francisco Camerawork, San Francisco, CA
Logos, Santa Cruz, CA
Arcana, Santa Monica, CA
Midnight Special Bookstore, Santa Monica, CA
Reader's Books, Sonoma, CA
Small World Books, Venice, CA
Ventura Bookstore, Ventura, CA

Honolulu Book Shop, Honolulu, HI

Page One, SINGAPORE

Baxter's Books, Minneapolis, MN
Minnesota Book Center, Minneapolis, MN
University of Minnesota Bookstore, Minneapolis, MN
Walker Art Center Bookshop, Minneapolis, MN
Hungry Mind Bookstore, St. Paul, MN
Odegard Books, St. Paul, MN

Chinook Bookshop, Colorado Springs, CO
The Bookies, Denver, CO
Newsstand Cafe, Denver, CO
Tattered Cover Bookstore, Denver, CO
Stone Lion Bookstore, Fort Collins, CO

Asun Bookstore, Reno, NV

Nebraska Bookstore, Lincoln, NE

Sam Weller's Zion Bookstore, Salt Lake City, UT

Kansas Union Bookstore, Lawrence, KS
Terra Nova Bookstore, Lawrence, KS

Bookman's, Tucson, AZ

Bookworks, Albuquerque, NM
Page One Bookstore, Albuquerque, NM
Salt of the Earth, Albuquerque, NM
Cafe Allegro, Los Alamos, NM
Collected Works, Santa Fe, NM

Book People, Austin, TX
Bookstop, Austin, TX
University Co-op Society, Austin, TX
McKinney Avenue Contemporary Gift Shop, Dallas, TX
Bookstop, Houston, TX
Brazos Bookstore, Houston, TX
Contemporary Arts Museum Shop, Houston, TX
Diversebooks, Houston, TX
Menil Collection Bookstore, Houston, TX
Museum of Fine Arts, Houston, TX
Texas Gallery, Houston, TX
Bookstop, Plano, TX

Bookland of Brunswick, Brunswick, ME
University of Maine Bookstore, Orono, ME
Books Etc., Portland, ME
Raffles Cafe Bookstore, Portland, ME

Pages, Toronto, CANADA

Dartmouth Bookstore, Hanover, NH
Toadstool Bookshop, Peterborough, NH

Northshire Books, Manchester, VT

Wootton's Books, Amherst, MA
Boston University Bookstore, Boston, MA
Harvard Book Store, Cambridge, MA
M.I.T. Press Bookstore, Cambridge, MA
Cisco Harland Books, Marlborough, MA
Broadside Bookshop, Northampton, MA
Provincetown Bookshop, Provincetown, MA
Water Street Books, Williamstown, MA

Main Street News, Ann Arbor, MI
Shaman Drum Bookshop, Ann Arbor, MI
Cranbrook Art Museum Books, Bloomfield Hills, MI
Book Beat, Oak Park, MI

Afterwords, Milwaukee, WI

Farley's Bookshop, New Hope, PA
Faber Books, Philadelphia, PA
Waterstone's Booksellers, Philadelphia, PA
Andy Warhol Museum, Pittsburgh, PA
Encore Books, Mechanicsburg, PA
Encore Books, State College, PA

Accident or Design, Providence, RI
Brown University Bookstore, Providence, RI
College Hill Store, Providence, RI

Yale Cooperative, New Haven, CT
UConn Co-op, Storrs, CT

Rosetta News, Carbondale, IL
Pages for All Ages, Champaign, IL
Mayuba Bookstore, Chicago, IL
Museum of Contemporary Art, Chicago, IL
Seminary Co-op Bookstore, Chicago, IL

Indiana University Bookstore,
Bloomington, IN

UC Bookstore, Cincinnati, OH
Bank News, Cleveland, OH
Ohio State University Bookstore, Columbus, OH
Student Book Exchange, Columbus, OH
Books & Co., Dayton, OH
Kenyon College Bookstore, Gambier, OH
Oberlin Consumers Cooperative, Oberlin, OH

Encore Books, Princeton, NJ
Micawber Books, Princeton, NJ

Community Bookstore, Brooklyn, NY
Talking Leaves, Buffalo, NY
Colgate University Bookstore, Hamilton, NY
Book Revue, Huntington, NY
The Bookery, Ithaca, NY
A Different Light, New York, NY
Art Market, New York, NY
B. Dalton, New York, NY
Coliseum Books, New York, NY
Collegiate Booksellers, New York, NY
Doubleday Bookshops, New York, NY
Exit Art/First World Store, New York, NY
Gold Kiosk, New York, NY
Gotham Book Mart, New York, NY
Museum of Modern Art Bookstore, New York, NY
New York University Book Center, New York, NY
Posman Books, New York, NY
Rizzoli Bookstores, New York, NY
St. Mark's Bookshop, New York, NY
Shakespeare & Co., New York, NY
Spring Street Books, New York, NY
Wendell's Books, New York, NY
Whitney Museum of Modern Art, New York, NY
Syracuse University Bookstore, Syracuse, NY

Iowa Book & Supply, Iowa City, IA
Prairie Lights, Iowa City, IA
University Bookstore, Iowa City, IA

Box of Rocks, Bowling Green, KY
Carmichael's, Louisville, KY

Louie's Bookstore Cafe, Baltimore, MD

Xanadu Bookstore, Memphis, TN

Bridge Street Books, Washington, DC
Chapters, Washington, DC
Franz Bader Bookstore, Washington, DC
Olsson's, Washington, DC
Politics & Prose, Washington, DC

Library Ltd., Clayton, MO
Whistler's Books, Kansas City, MO
Left Bank Books, St. Louis, MO

Daedalus Used Bookshop, Charlottesville, VA
Studio Art Shop, Charlottesville, VA
Williams Corner, Charlottesville, VA

Paper Skyscraper, Charlotte, NC
Regulator Bookshop, Durham, NC

Chapter Two Bookstore, Charleston, SC
Intermezzo, Columbia, SC
Open Book, Greenville, SC

Square Books, Oxford, MS

Books & Books, Coral Gables, FL
Goerings Book Center, Gainesville, FL
Bookstop, Miami, FL
Rex Art, Miami, FL
Inkwood Books, Tampa, FL

Lenny's News, New Orleans, LA

And at selected Barnes & Noble and Bookstar bookstores nationwide.

Green Mountains Review

10th Anniversary Double Issue

American Poetry at the End of the Millennium

– featuring –

Marvin Bell
Robert Bly
Mark Doty
Stephen Dunn
Lynn Emanuel
Alice Fulton
Albert Goldbarth
Paul Hoover
Joy Harjo

Yusef Komunyakaa
Maxine Kumin
Ann Lauterbach
William Matthews
Heather McHugh
David Mura
Carol Muske
Naomi Shihab Nye
Mary Oliver

Molly Peacock
Robert Pinsky
Stanley Plumly
Gary Soto
Elizabeth Spires
David St. John
James Tate
Chase Twichell
Charles Wright

Send check or money order for $10 to:
Green Mountains Review, Johnson State College,
Johnson, VT 05656

David Scher, crater, 1997

Jack Tilton Gallery

David Scher   April 15 – May 9 1998

Rebecca Purdum   May 12 – June 13 1998

Artists Represented by Jack Tilton Gallery

Francis Alÿs	Fabrice Hybert
Herbert Brandl	Alan Johnston
Leo Copers	Minuro Kawabata
Huang Yong Ping	Matvey Levenstein
Marlene Dumas	Joep Van Lieshout
Nicole Eisenman	Eva Lundsager
Jan Fabre	Rebecca Purdum
Michelle Fiero	David Scher
David Hammons	Nancy Spero
Lyle Ashton Harris	Fred Tomaselli
Jocelyn Hobbie	The estate of Ruth Vollmer

49 Greene St   New York NY 10013   T. 212 941.1775   F. 212 941.1812

◆ *Boston Review is pleased to announce its* ◆

FIRST ANNUAL

POETRY

CONTEST

Judged by Jane Miller

$1,000 First Prize ◆ *Deadline: June 15, 1998*

Complete guidelines: The winning poet will receive $1,000 and have his or her work published in the October/November 1998 issue of *Boston Review*. Submit up to five unpublished poems, no more than 10 pages total. A $10 entry fee, payable to *Boston Review* in the form of a check or money order, must accompany all submissions. Entries must be postmarked no later than June 15, 1998. Simultaneous submissions are allowed if the *Review* is notified of acceptance elsewhere. Manuscripts must be submitted in duplicate, with a cover note listing the author's name, address, and phone number; names should not be on the poems themselves. Manuscripts will not be returned; enclose a SASE for notification of winner. All entrants will receive a one-year subscription to the *Review* beginning with the October/November 1998 issue. Send all submissions to: Poetry Contest, *Boston Review*, E53-407 MIT, Cambridge MA 02139.